Spirits
of the
ordinary

Spirits
of the
ordinary

A Tale of Casas Grandes

KATHLEEN ALCALÁ

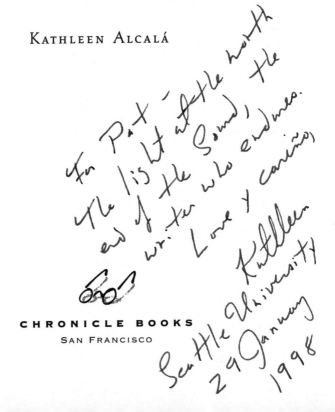

CHRONICLE BOOKS

SAN FRANCISCO

For Pat — little worth the light at the [Sound], the end of the [Sound], writer who endures. Love y cariños

Kathleen
Seattle University
29 January 1998

The author would like to thank the Institute for Texas Cultures,
The Cottages at Hedgebrook for time and a place to write,
and Artist Trust for funding.

JACKET: Painting copyright © 1993 by Claire B. Cotts. "The Orange Tree," oil on
canvas, 48" x 60", Private collection. Background by Andrew Faulkner Illustration.

All characters in this novel are fictitious, with the exception of Governor
Luis de Carvajal.

Excerpts from this novel appeared in slightly different form in *The Writer's Journal*
and under the title "Indago Felix" in *The American Voice*, No. 32, 1994.

Library of Congress Cataloging-in-Publication Data:
Alcalá, Kathleen. 1954–
    Spirits of the ordinary : a tale of Casas Grandes / Kathleen Alcalá.
    256 p.   14 x 20.3 cm.
    ISBN 0-8118-1447-5
    1. Family—Mexican American Border Region—History—Fiction. 2. Mexican
American Border Region—History—Fiction.   3. Mexican Americans—Texas—
History—Fiction. 4. Mexican American families—Texas—Fiction.   I. Title.
    PS3551.L287S65   1997
    813'.54—dc20   96-15665
                                                                            CIP

Printed in the United States of America
Designed by Laura Lovett
Composition by On Line Typography

Distributed in Canada by Raincoast Books
8680 Cambie Street, Vancouver, B.C. V6P 6M9

10 9 8 7 6 5 4 3 2 1

CHRONICLE BOOKS
85 Second Street, San Francisco, CA 94105

Web Site: www.chronbooks.com

This novel is dedicated to my family.

In love is found the secret of Divine unity.
It is love that unites the higher
and the lower stages of existence,
that raises the lower to the level of the higher—
where all become fused into one.

The Zohar

Esmeralda

Straightening the ruffles on the curtains, she could not forget it. Stirring the soup in the kitchen while Josefina bit her lips and waited for her to leave, she could not forget it. Sewing the torn lace back onto the hem of one of her daughters' petticoats, she could almost forget it, but Estela cringed every time she remembered the hurt, closed look on Zacarías' face as she tried to talk to him.

"Papá would love for you to join him in the business," she had begun. "With two daughters and the twins so far away, he has no one to help him, no one to accompany him on his travels. You could travel," she had added, thinking this might appeal to Zacarías' perverse sense of adventure. "Every year, he goes from Piedras Negras to Tampico, taking orders for thread and cotton cloth."

Zacarías' silence had persisted as he continued to pack his saddle bags. Estela felt awkward, out of place standing in the supply shed next to the stables, still wearing her indoor shoes. Zacarías was not yet dressed in his travel clothes, so she felt that she had time.

"I do not want to sell dry goods," he had said, finally, as he measured oats from a large sack into one of two bags that would hang on either side of the horse.

"Why can't you be like other men?" Estela had finally exclaimed, then run back to the main house; but not before seeing that look on his face, a mixture of hurt and stubbornness that seemed more and more to characterize their entire marriage.

A few minutes later, she heard the gate to the street open and the horse clattering away, and thought he had gone out for more supplies.

But upon looking in his bedroom, she had seen Zacarías' town clothes abandoned on the floor, and knew that he was gone.

That was yesterday, and she had slept badly. Rising early to make sure the servant began to boil water for laundry that day, Estela saw dark shadows smudging the fair skin under her eyes.

"A widow," she thought as she pinned up her reddish-brown hair in the mirror. "I feel like a war widow, except that just when I'm used to his being gone, he comes back."

She tucked a perfumed handkerchief into her sleeve and left her quarters. A wonderful miniature carriage stood by the house in the breezeway, awaiting a second son.

She could see her two daughters in the garden, one with curly black hair, one with straight, reddish hair like her own, bent and giggling over something she could not see. The day was warming up, and she felt weary already. She stood with her hand pressed to the side of her face, watching them. The perfume from her handkerchief filled her head.

From the darkened kitchen doorway, Josefina watched and saw the woman's mother in her tired eyes.

"Señora," she called. "There's good coffee here for you."

Estela swept the hair out of her eyes as she helped hang the sheets to dry and saw a vee of cranes crossing the brilliant blue sky.

They were heading northeast, towards the Gulf and fishing in abundance. She stabbed a clothespin onto the line, nearly tearing the sheet in the process. The laundry maid, who came once a week, would rather have done without her help, and Estela knew this, but she had to keep busy or she felt that she would go mad.

Gabriel, her eldest child, returned from his classes at the Ateneo Fuente. He came out to the courtyard to greet her with a kiss.

"My papá has left?"

Estela sighed. "Yes."

She watched her son out of the corner of her eye. He had accompanied his father before on his adventures, and she worried that someday she would lose them both.

But Gabriel just shrugged and removed his bookbag from his shoulder.

"I'll be at Chucho's until merienda."

Gabriel was good at school, and friends had been saying that the best thing for him would be to continue his studies at an American university, one that was far to the north and would allow him to pursue his studies in engineering.

She watched her tall, dark-haired boy as he walked back into the house swinging his books, and felt another pang in her heart.

Estela just had time to visit her sister Blanca before late afternoon merienda. She changed her dress and shoes, draped a shawl over her head and shoulders, and called Josefina to accompany her the two blocks to her sister's house.

Expecting a child in four more weeks, Blanca no longer went out. Instead, swathed in layers of pink silk and lace, she received friends on the cool, lemon-scented veranda, where the maid brought cold manzanilla tea and freshly baked pecan cookies.

"Estela!" exclaimed Blanca from behind a sandalwood fan, as though she had not expected to see her. "How nice of you to come!"

Estela pecked her on the cheek and sat down at the white, wrought iron table. The tea tasted good.

"You look wonderful," she said. This would be Blanca's eighth child. She would have to hire an additional woman to help care for the children.

"Thank you, Estela," said Blanca. "I would rather have cooler weather, but it won't be long now. Look what my mother-in-law gave me. Rosa?" she called, "bring me the little confection from my mother-in-law."

The maid returned with a tiny, lace-infested dress with an overskirt of tulle.

"How can you be so sure it's a girl?" asked Estela while admiring the dress.

"After seven children, I know," said Blanca emphatically. "She floats like a little angel, she's not heavy like the boys."

This made Estela laugh. Blanca always cheered her up. Still, she could not help but feel a little envious of her sister. Estela was thirty-four years old, and had not had a child in twelve years. She longed for the joy that a new baby would bring.

"Zacarías is gone again?" said Blanca more gently, laying her pudgy hand on her sister's thin one.

"Yes," said Estela. "I guess everybody knows."

"I can tell by your face," said Blanca. "You look so sad when he's gone."

"I want him to be happy," said Estela, "and he's so restless when he's home. Papá wants him to go into business with him. He likes Zacarías. But my husband just wants to spend money on prospecting."

Estela moved the little dress away from herself so that she would not pick at it.

"Have another cookie," said Blanca, and took another herself. "You can't worry about things you can't control. Men have to be men."

"Is that right?" said Estela. She could not hide the bitterness in her voice.

"Just think. He could have a mistress and a dozen children on the side. He could be a drunkard and roar down the streets of Saltillo at all hours. That would be an embarrassment."

"For all I know, he does have a mistress," said Estela, "but I don't really think so...."

"I don't either," said Blanca emphatically. "He's had eyes only for you since we were children. Even that scary father of ours couldn't keep Zacarías from courting you."

Estela smiled briefly at the memory of Zacarías sitting nervously in her father's parlor while she made him wait.

"Papá was afraid that he would want to observe Jewish ceremonies. But he promised that we would raise the children Catholic, and we have. I think it's mostly his parents who are that way.

"I just don't understand why he has to be gone so much."

"Don't worry," said Blanca. "Men go through these phases." She laughed. "If I asked Gustavo everything that he does, he would be insulted. We all have our little secrets."

Here she imitated her portly husband with her elbows out to her sides: "It's not women's business what I do. Go! Tend to your children. Don't I give you everything you ask for?"

Estela's eyes widened and she laughed out loud. The imitation had the ring of a real conversation, something she had not suspected between Blanca and Gustavo.

"Still," said Estela, "it seems to be getting worse instead of better."

She wanted to tell Blanca about all the money he took each time, but thought better of it. Saltillo was not a big city, and everyone knew everybody's business anyway.

Estela sipped her tea and stared moodily at the canary in its painted cage as it sang and sang and filled the fragrant garden with sound.

· · ·

Estela and Josefina hurried across the main square to attend early Mass. With her head partially down and wrapped in a rebozo, Estela had not seen the large, black shape bearing down on her until it was too late.

"Good morning, Estela," Doña Carmela sang out as she blocked Estela's path.

"Good morning, Doña," answered Estela. She knew what was next.

"We haven't seen Zacarías around lately." Doña Carmela's eyes searched Estela's face for a reaction.

"No, he is out of town," answered Estela.

"Again?" said Doña Carmela, feigning surprise. "I certainly hope he finds what he's looking for."

"Thank you," said Estela, and hurried into the church.

She was grateful for the flickering shadows that would hide the humiliation burning on her face. Everyone knew about Zacarías. Her marriage, once her greatest joy, was now the subject of common gossip.

Watching the numerous votive candles burning before the Virgin, Estela could not decide whether or not to light one herself. Her thoughts whirled about as she tried to pray.

"What shall I do, Holy Mother?" she found herself asking over and over. "What shall I do?"

The impassive porcelain face gave no hint. Estela realized that she could not make up her mind if she wished Zacarías safe or wished him dead. The lights seemed to flare, intensifying the blue in the Blessed Mother's robe and illuminating the overwhelming amounts of gold in the church. Estela fled without receiving absolution.

Josefina, waiting at the back of the sanctuary, was startled by the sudden flight of her mistress. She crossed herself quickly before hurrying after.

. . .

Estela cut the string holding together a skein of heavy thread and spread the cotton over her daughter's outstretched hands, shaking it gently to loosen the strands from each other. Then she began to wind the pure white cotton into a smooth, fat ball.

"For Christmas," she said, "For Christmas we will crochet new napkins to go with the tablecloth. I'll have Lupita starch them until they're so stiff that they just lie there on the oak table, straight as a board, until you pick them up. Then they'll unfold like angels' wings."

María giggled and held her hands up without effort as her mother wound quickly.

"Will I get a new dress?" she asked.

"Of course, mijita," answered Estela. "Don't you always?"

María hummed to herself happily, imagining herself at midnight Mass, the whole town turned out to see her in a new, sky blue velvet dress with a white lace collar. Her older sister, Victoria, would wear a dress very much like it, only a different color. María imagined the family, lined up in a row in church, then wondered suddenly if her father would be there.

"¿Qué piensas?" asked her mother. "What are you thinking? You look so serious."

María shook her head and smiled, concentrating on the growing ball of white in her mother's hands, dipping and raising her own hands in a rhythm to smooth the passage of thread.

Zacarías woke with smoke in his eyes and a weight like stone in his heart, his bones fighting the rocky ground. The campfire had burned out at least an hour earlier, and the remnants of burning ironwood sent a low, greasy smoke creeping along the beaten ground to where he lay tossing under a tattered wool sarape.

Coughing and rubbing his eyes, Zacarías sat up in the chilly dawn and looked across sparse hills to where the cerras hunched like sleeping animals on the horizon. His mare, lightly hobbled, snorted at his stirring as she grazed on the desert weeds. He would not reach his destination for another two days.

In the intervening miles lay several promising streams, where Zacarías would sample gravel beds and stream cuts with his prospecting equipment.

"Ah, the magnificent outdoors!" said Zacarías without much enthusiasm as he stood and stretched in his long johns. It was deadly still except for the soft snuffling of the horse and pack mule. Twenty-four hours earlier, he had made a hasty retreat from his home in Saltillo, his wife's recriminations still echoing in his ears.

"How can you waste my father's money on this rubbish?" she had said, dismissing a miner's pick he had just purchased at Severino's shop. It had a fine, curved head, with a blunt back for cracking open ore samples.

"You have everything you could want right here, yet you insist on endangering yourself in the hills. Every day there are new reports of Texas Rangers and marauding indigenes. Papá needs help in the store. Why can't you be like other men?"

Like that sniveling brother-in-law of yours? he had thought.

Why can't you be like other men? he asked himself as he shaved by touch. Why can't you sell women's cotton goods and go to the symphony and give your wife yet another child? They had only three, and a man was not commonly considered macho until he had four, and at least one son. Fortunately their eldest was Gabriel.

Zacarías buttoned his shirt, hitched up his braces, and donned his coat. Whistling in low, short bursts to his animals, he flung the pack saddles over the wooden frame on his mule's back, tying them down securely. La Gata, as he called his horse for her pantherlike walking gait, stood calmly as he saddled up and mounted for the day's ride. Clamping his pipe between his teeth,

Zacarías swung about and headed across the sandy flatlands, west towards the Sierra Encantada.

Zacarías topped a rise and looked into the Indian camp. Three children and an old man stood and stared back at him. He recognized this family. He knew that there was an old woman and a young one as well, and sometimes one or two younger men who probably worked in the mines. They seemed to wander the same area as his own, eating God knows what that they found in the desert. The man, whom Zacarías knew as Matukami, wore a long, belted shirt and no trousers. Only young men or city dwellers affected the wearing of long pants that caught in bushes, collected dirt, and impeded a runner's progress. These people carried everything they owned on their backs and traveled many miles in a day. The children wore nothing at all. Zacarías dismounted and led his horse and mule at a leisurely pace down the steep hill.

Greeting Matukami in his own language, Lagunero, Zacarías seated himself by the fire, where he cut off a piece from his tobacco plug and passed it to the old man. They both sat and smoked in silence while the children resumed their game of kicking a small, black ball made of some gummy substance back and forth between them. The family's dogs had caught and killed something and growled over its small remains with pleasure.

This went on for close to three quarters of an hour before Zacarías pulled out his ore samples and began showing them to Matukami, asking him if he had seen any rocks like these, and if so, where. He handled them lovingly, the red dirt from some staining his hands and nails, and set them in a semicircle around his feet as he finished with each one.

Zacarías declined Matukami's offer to share their stewpot and led his horse and mule up the other side of the gully.

Just as he remounted, Zacarías could see the two women returning to camp, carrying heavy baskets of wet clothes balanced on their heads. They had been down at the stream, washing. One looked to be in her mid-twenties and the other could be her mother, but it was hard to tell. The nomadic life gave the Indians of northern Mexico a hard, wind-blown look, and one of their women could be twenty or fifty and still have a small child clinging to her skirts. As the children ran up to the women, Zacarías wondered how many of them belonged to the younger of the two.

Zacarías reached the base of the next line of low-lying mountains by nightfall.

Waking early the next morning, Zacarías took the time to brew a pot of coffee and open some tins of food.

"I'm getting soft," he complained to La Gata, "and so are you."

She was nuzzling his gear with soft, snuffling noises.

"Each time I return to the hills, my bones find more rocks in them. But never the right kind of rocks."

He slapped the canvas bag of samples that lay beside him. Matukami had pointed at a shiny black and gray rock and indicated that he had seen that before. It was Zacarías' most valuable ore sample, loaded with silver and a trace of gold.

"Maybe this time," he said, "maybe this time."

Zacarías relented and let the horse feed from one of the bags of oats he carried to supplement her diet of weeds and grass.

Zacarías spent most of the day crossing a high, flat plain with little relief from dust or sun. The horse sweated profusely. Zacarías wiped his face constantly with his bandana. He had learned long ago not to remove his hat in the hot sun. The air seemed to hum with intensity.

Just before dusk, he reached the village of El Socorro and was able to have a decent meal before bedding down for the night at the outskirts of town. He was very close now, and the stars in the high, clear air seemed to line up and point the way into the Sierra Encantada.

The next day he came to a fence and gate marking the road to a mine entrance, with a sign warning that trespassers would be shot. He skirted the fence to the east until he was able to get a clear view of the entrance. Armed guards lounged about against the bare rock. It must be producing, he thought. It must have something besides lead coming out of its bowels. This was the place the old man had talked about. It was called La Esmeralda.

Zacarías kicked his horse and continued up the flank of the mountain to the high ground that produced too little for the large companies to worry about, where mountain streams brought forth the treasures of Mother Earth. He thought of his ore samples and began to hum a little tune.

"Andale," he urged La Gata. "Let's find a nice little stream where you can rest all day and I can get covered with mud like a monkey."

They continued to climb upward as the air turned cooler and the desert landscape gave way to scrub pine and inviting pockets of meadow. The horse and mule tried to turn away and graze, but Zacarías continued up towards the rocky high ground, his head filled with a vision of black sand flecked with gold at the bottom of a crystal clear stream.

Zacarías remained on Sierra Encantada for seven days. During that time he hardly left the streambed, reaching into his gear for beef jerky and drinking directly from the running water. He sang out loud as he worked, folksongs and popular songs of the time, and delivered long speeches on the state of the economy and the moral deficiencies of modern man. La Gata took it all in with a grave air, never daring to interrupt her master.

"Ay, Gata," he said, "what is the world coming to? First the Norte Americanos invade us, then Spain and the English for debt owed. Haven't they taken enough from us already? And if it weren't for Benito Juarez, we would all be speaking French right now. All we need is a little peace and quiet so that our country

can have a chance to grow up.

"Then the Norte Americanos still want everything. You'd think this was the land flowing with milk and honey, rather than a desert with a few saguaros and a few poor Indians.

"If I were king," and here he straightened up and groaned at the eastern horizon, "if I were king, what would I do?"

He sighed and shook his head. "I'm glad I'm not king. Or presidente. I'll leave it to Díaz. I can't even handle the politics of my own household."

La Gata snorted and moved a little farther away, hopping on her hobbled front legs.

"Always a critic," said Zacarías. "I'll bet you couldn't handle things any better than I do." But he wasn't so sure.

Zacarías wished that he could have brought Gabriel on this trip, but school had already started. Gabriel studied too much, he thought, and needed to spend more time outdoors. Still, Zacarías was very proud of him—Gabriel was the scholar that he himself was not. Zacarías was afraid Estela had turned her only son into a mama's boy, and would probably turn him against his father as well.

At nightfall, when it became too dark to tell the iron from the gold, Zacarías would fling himself down on his bedroll, exhausted, and contemplate the fiery stars overhead. He often imagined holding Estela in his arms out here, showing her the Milky Way and the Three Sisters and the meek deer before Orion, the mighty warrior's arrow pointed at its heart.

But he knew that she would not enjoy it. She would be afraid of coyotes and Indians, and worst of all, of what the neighbors would think. Zacarías tried not to let these thoughts disturb him, but at night they came unbidden.

One night Zacarías dreamed that a fiery chariot came out of the sky, like the kind that came for the prophet Elisha. A man with a flaming beard held the reins, a man who looked like his father,

only bigger, fiercer. He pointed into the black, flowing waters and disappeared in a shimmer of light. The next day Zacarías found two large nuggets at the spot.

He woke each morning with the dew on his matted hair, his clothes soaked. Zacarías saw no other humans.

Towards the end of the seventh day, his supplies running low, Zacarías packed up his gear and descended the Sierra Encantada. He had filled two small rawhide bags with nuggets — one with silver, and one with gold. He planned to cross the burning plain during the early evening hours, but his head began to throb with fever.

Unable to remember the passage, Zacarías gave the mare her own lead as he struggled to remain upright. Although he drank all of his water, his canteen filled at the running stream before he had left, his mouth continued to feel dry and cottony. By late evening Zacarías passed a half-mile north of El Socorro without even seeing it. He wandered into the seemingly endless line of low hills beyond, vomiting and dismounting every few miles to relieve himself due to excruciating cramps. The last thing he remembered was seeing the smoldering fire in the valley before him and not knowing if it was that of friend or foe.

Ernesto Vargas, counselor at law, came to the house the next day promptly at ten. Estela had known him since she was a little girl, but his dark, severe appearance — he was always in an expensive suit, a high cravat strangling his narrow neck — never ceased to startle her. She remembered that he was a distant relative of Zacarías'. Nevertheless, he had handled her father's legal matters for many years and she trusted him implicitly.

Estela sent Josefina to get them coffee as Señor Vargas set his briefcase on the floor next to his perfectly shined shoes.

"Now," he said, clearing his throat. "Exactly what is it that I can do for you?"

Estela hesitated. This was going to be harder than she thought.

"I want to restrict access to our money," she said. She tried to control her hands from ringing her handkerchief nervously.

"I see. Access by ... your husband?" he asked discreetly.

The coffee arrived, and they each paused to take a cup and saucer, waiting until Josefina left the room before continuing.

"Yes," said Estela. "You see, Zacarías recently took twenty thousand pesos for a trip into the Sierra Encantada. He, as you may know, looks for gold. But this is the fifth time this year that he has done so. Each time, he takes a lot of money."

Señor Vargas raised his eyebrows over his coffee cup, but Estela plunged ahead.

"You see, it's not me I'm worried about," she said, "but the children. We would like to send Gabriel to college in the United States, but it is very expensive. I'm afraid all the money will be spent before he turns eighteen."

"I see," said Vargas. "This is a serious matter. But under the laws and customs of this country, you do have the right to do this. Especially since you brought most of the material wealth to this marriage."

Estela felt relieved. She had thought as much.

"Furthermore," said the lawyer, carefully setting his coffee on the low table between them, "you have just cause.

"Now this sort of thing normally comes up," here he paused delicately and wiped his lips, "when one partner, usually the husband, is spending money on another person who is a threat to the foundation of the marriage itself."

Estela looked at her hands and blushed.

"In that case, concrete proof is usually needed in order to bar access to the family's finances.

"However," here Vargas leaned over in a somewhat consoling posture, "conspicuous waste of the joint assets on a common vice, such as drinking or gambling, is also just cause. I think that having the gold fever probably qualifies under the second set of circumstances." The lawyer paused again, forcing Estela to look up and meet his gaze. "Is this what you want?" he asked.

"Yes," she said, "yes it is. I have considered all my options and prayed long and hard about it. I don't see what else I can do."

"Very well then," said Vargas, picking up his satchel and setting it across his knees, "I will have the proper documents drawn up."

"It's not for me," she said again, somewhat plaintively. "I care nothing for myself. Only let there be something left for the children."

Vargas paused in his notetaking and gazed at her over the top of the briefcase. "I feel," he said carefully, "that you are making a wise decision. If I did not know the persons involved, I might caution you to wait awhile. But in this case,"—he closed the satchel with a firm click—"it is a known fact that Zacarías may well ruin the family, if left unchecked."

Estela felt as though she might faint or cry. Instead she drained the last of her coffee in a somewhat unladylike manner.

Vargas rose to leave, and Estela stood with him.

"I will have the necessary documents drawn up and bring them by for you to sign. Once that is done, a copy will be left with your banker to assure that your wishes are followed."

"Thank you," said Estela.

"I am your faithful servant," said Vargas with a slight bow. "I will see myself out."

Her composure having reached its limit, Estela sat back down on the velvet couch and wept.

The first thing Zacarías was aware of was the stench of uncured hides. Opening his eyes he found himself in a smoky interior, too dim to make anything out. His eyes would not focus. His head whirled in confusion and he felt sick at his stomach. My God, thought Zacarías. I've died and gone to Hell.

He closed his eyes and dreamed strange dreams. He saw people from a world somewhat like his own, yet oddly different: a woman at a piano, a sailor, a tiny yellow bird, and an old woman dressed like a gypsy bending over a strange, shining road. Zacarías felt somehow that he was remembering the future, that he stood midway in a stream of time that parted and flowed on either side of him like running water. He felt that he was a sailor riding on a storm of possibilities, rocking back and forth, back and forth on a rough sea that threatened to toss him overboard if he did not cling to the deck as tightly as possible. He pressed his face to a surface that was at times smooth and hard as a piano, and was at other times harsh and prickly with cactus needles.

The next time he opened his eyes, Zacarías saw sunlight through chinks in the brush-covered structure. When the young Indian woman pulled a blanket back from a low doorway and came to stand over him, he realized the Lagunero family had somehow found and rescued him, and that he lay on a clean hide on firm ground. He closed his eyes in gratitude and rested until a cool tea was pressed to his lips.

Zacarías slept peacefully for the rest of that day, then pulled himself up and staggered outside at dusk. Matukami sat by the fire smoking, and regarded him with a calm eye.

"What happened?" asked Zacarías. "Where did you find me? I—I can't remember anything."

Matukami waved his pipe westward. "Bad water," he said. "You got the bad water sickness. We could smell you coming."

Zacarías remembered his state while crossing the desert plain and broke into a shaky grin. He brushed back his greasy hair and sat down opposite the old man.

"I owe you my life," he said.

Matukami waved his pipe again, dismissing it. Zacarías saw for the first time that the old Indian had a lizard tattooed on the back of his hand.

The next day Zacarías saddled his mare and tried again to thank Matukami. He knew better than to try to talk to the women, although he knew that they had tended him. They would only lower their eyes and back away from him, shaking their heads that they didn't understand, though he had been told that his Lagunero was very good.

Zacarías rode into Monclova, about two hours farther east. He stopped at a dry goods store and went inside, intending to buy a peace offering for his wife. When he spotted the roll of sky blue cotton calico, however, Zacarías realized that he wanted to give it to the family he had just left. He spent the last of his currency on the bolt of cloth and rode back into the hills. The camp was empty when he returned, but he laid the cloth just inside of the hut, careful not to disturb the crossed sticks that had been placed there to protect their belongings from evil spirits and superstitious marauders. Then he headed south and home again.

Estela was not prepared for the sight that greeted her when she went outside to see what all the commotion was about. His beautiful mare caked in dried mud, Zacarías looked like a scarecrow on top of the saddle. Gabriel helped his father off La Gata, and the horse was led away to be brushed and fed. Zacarías smelled, and Estela covered her nose and mouth in spite of the bad example it set for the children.

"Querida," whispered Zacarías as he brushed past, and the heart of stone that she had prepared for almost a month melted and drowned at the touch of his hand upon hers. The lawyer had prepared a document barring Zacarías from further access to their cash holdings, but Estela had kept it rather than signing it. Now she saw that he had been sick and that there had been a reason for his long delay. She would nurse him back to health, slowly, and he would courteously ask her father for indoor work, due to his frail constitution.

Zacarías' daughters met him at the door.

"Bonjour, Monsieur."

"Bonjour."

Both girls curtsied and giggled. They were wearing oddly low-cut blouses and high-waisted, dark skirts.

"What's wrong with them?" Zacarías asked his wife.

"It's only the fashion. The French language and dress are all the rage."

Zacarías whacked at his boots and chaps with his hat, raising a cloud of dust.

"People visit from Mexico City," said Estela in an apologetic tone, "and the local girls get all excited about the latest trend. They are infatuated with monarchies."

The girls stood giggling in the still-open doorway, talking to someone outside.

Zacarías ground his teeth. While he wasn't especially political, talk of monarchism, especially European monarchism, greatly irritated him.

"We shed the blood of brave men to get out from under Spain's thumb and that crazy Hapsburg so that we can imitate the French?" Estela said nothing. "Tell the girls to put on something decent," he said and made his way wearily down the open veranda.

The giggling stilled as Estela pressed her finger to her lips and drew the girls inside. "Go put on something else," she said, "something mas Mexicana. Your father says so."

"But Mama—"

"Right now, do as he says," she repeated more firmly.

The girls went off to their room, swishing their skirts around high-button shoes, wondering at the tension in their mother's voice.

Bathed and fed, Zacarías fell into a deep slumber. He dreamed of the stream bed, the rich red earth, and the salamanders he sometimes disturbed in the shallow waters. They said if you threw a salamander into a fire, two would emerge. Then he dreamed of the tattoo on Matukami's hand and realized that it, too, was a salamander.

Early the next morning, Zacarías awoke to the smell of leather and sweat and something worse. He opened his eyes and saw that he was in his own bedroom, dressed in a clean nightshirt. Rising and opening the window that faced onto the courtyard, he saw that the servants were tending a small fire. When one of them lifted a shirt with a stick and placed it in the fire, Zacarías realized that they were burning his clothes.

Zacarías felt renewed, reborn. For the first time in several days, he allowed himself to think of the bag of gold and the bag of silver in his possession. They rested on the desk below the window, probably placed there by his son. Zacarías drifted lightly down the passageway to where his wife slept. He sat by her side, admiring the flawless skin and the braided hair, like fire and gold, that rested upon her breast. Unable to restrain himself, he pulled back the covers and got in beside her. Half asleep, Estela pulled him to her with a small sigh.

A loud noise woke Zacarías the second time that morning.

"Who was she?" screamed Estela.

She sat bolt upright in the bed, twisting the blankets between her hands.

"How could you come here to my bed after lying with your, your fancy woman?"

Tears streamed down Estela's face as Zacarías tried to blink himself to consciousness. He must have been talking in his sleep.

"She saved my life," he said, thinking he must have talked of the woman who had nursed him. "Nothing happened. I was sick. She was just an Indian."

"No Indian is named Esmeralda!"

"Esmeralda?"

"Esmeralda! Esmeralda! Esmeralda!" screamed Estela as she

gained her knees and struck him rhythmically across the face.

"Go back and squander her money on your adventures."

"La Esmeralda!" exclaimed Zacarías, now fully awake and finally comprehending that he had been dreaming about the mine. He burst into helpless laughter and lay back on his wife's lace-embellished sheets.

Almost strangling with fury, Estela grabbed her robe and fled from the room. She had left the document on the small writing desk in the study. Her hair in disarray and her robe barely concealing her nightdress, Estela sat at the desk and signed the document, Josefina clucking at a disturbance so early in the morning, and so soon after the master's return to his household.

"There!" said Estela, bursting back into her own bedroom. "I've signed it! What is mine is no longer yours! Now get out! Get out!"

With surprising strength, Estela dragged Zacarías from her bed and propelled him towards the door. Confused and a little insulted, Zacarías shook her off and left of his own accord. She slammed the door with a mighty crash, leaving Zacarías to make his way back to his own room to dress and have his first pipeful of the day. It was not until later that Zacarías understood the full meaning of her malediction.

Zacarías urged La Gata up the steep cobblestoned street leading to the bluff above town. Up, up they went through a twisting narrow way between high, secretive walls. On the right they passed the ruins of a dwelling, abandoned over two hundred years earlier, all but the foundation carted away. Morning glories twined around the weathered stones in rampant growth.

The narrow lane opened into an ancient growth of cedars at the top of the bluff, and the streets leveled out to parallel the cliff edge.

Zacarías rode away from the cliff, behind the former site of a ruined building to his father's house.

The house, set low against a slight rise, nearly invisible in its lush surroundings of cedar, jacaranda, bottlebrush and wisteria, did not seem to have a front, only a backside it presented on all sides, as though it was self-effacing and wished to be forgotten. The pose must have worked, for the house had stood, or squatted, for over four hundred years.

Zacarías dismounted, dropped La Gata's reins on the ground, and took out a curiously shaped brass key he carried in his waistcoat. Unlocking a small wooden gate in the wall, he struggled to pull it outward against the unchecked growth.

Within the enclosure was a miniature garden almost gemlike in its perfection. Low boxwood hedges hugged the wall on two sides, filling the air with their pungent odor. A portico flanked the other two sides along the house. Alongside the portico grew blood red roses, almost funereal in their intensity of color.

Huge pots of fuschias hung from the protruding vigas, catching the sun and contrasting sharply with the deep shade against the house.

At the center of the garden, a fountain as squat as the house itself gurgled softly. The cold spring water spilled over its thick, green-stained lips and ran obediently along channels in the flagstone paving to form a shining ribbon that laced the garden in severe Moorish symmetry before disappearing under the hedges. The fountain had run steadily since the house was built, the springs within the earth seemingly inexhaustible.

Zacarías walked to a small door and knocked. This was his father's study, and only the old man had a key to this door. After a moment the door swung slowly inward, leaving Zacarías straining to see into the gloom of the interior before stooping to enter the doorway. His father was already reseated behind his massive desk, as though he had willed the door to open of its own volition.

With large unblinking eyes like those of some nocturnal creature, the small, sallow-skinned man sat regarding his son.

Zacarías always felt awkward in this study, large and clumsy among the fragile books and stacks of tissue-thin papers that would crumble to dust in a good gust of wind.

Here lay his father's treasure. Here were his books, the books accumulated one at a time, sometimes a few pages at a time, smuggled in saddle bags wrapped around preserved foods, or a trinket from overseas. It had taken thirteen generations to compile this library, thirteen generations since all things Jewish, all signs of learning and Hebraic study, had been burned by the townspeople of Saltillo, since Zacarías' forebearers had gained the lives of their wives and children by changing their names and agreeing to be rebaptized into the Holy Roman Catholic Church.

A special branch of the Inquisition had been imported directly from Spain, like any other luxury not afforded by the New World, for the purpose of eradicating an outbreak of heresy in this remote outpost. It was especially unbearable that several families of Semitic heritage held appointed posts within the provincial government, owned rich farmland, and had some of the finest homes to be seen. A group of merchants had written to the Papal Nuncio in Mexico City and demanded that these affronts to their faith and their pocketbooks be rectified. The Governor of the Province was roasted alive in a dry cauldron for admitting that he was a Jew.

Zacarías' father was named Julio Vargas Caraval. Zacarías was the first son in thirteen generations to bear an overtly Jewish name, a name whispered from generation to generation, written on a scrap of parchment and pressed furtively into the unsuspecting palm of a boy on the verge of adulthood, accompanied by the revelation: "I have something important to tell you, my son. You are a Jew."

Zacarías' full name had been written in the parish register, Zacarías Carabajal de la Cueva y Vargas, a Biblical name, a good name, but one which caused the priest to pause and look more carefully at Julio Caraval Vargas and Mariana Vargas Caraval before pursing his lips, blotting the excess ink from the page, and closing the sacred tome with heavy finality. It was done. Zacarías was named after the unhappy Governor Luis de Carabajal who had lost his skin, then his life, in 1596 after publicly declaring that were it not for the Inquisition, there would be fewer Christians in this kingdom than he could count on the fingers of his hands.

Zacarías stood too tall in this dark, crowded room, hemmed in by precariously balanced stacks of books, half-empty inkwells, broken quills, and glass vials of mysterious chemicals. His shoulders hunched under the weight of thirteen generations, under the name he bore, pinned against the six-inch-thick door at his back by his father's unblinking gaze. Zacarías had no love of books, of tradition, or of enclosed places. He had come to tell his father goodbye.

Julio Caraval had, of course, already heard of his son's situation. The old scholar regarded Zacarías through his shaggy eyebrows for a long while. "This gold business," he said finally, "it is an addiction, like whiskey or gambling. No one in my family has ever had an addiction before."

Zacarías looked around the crowded room and shrugged. "What do you call this?" he asked.

Julio was taken aback. "I call this the word of God."

"God lives in many places," said Zacarías, "not just in this room." He was astonished at his own outspokenness. He had never addressed his father in this manner before.

Julio regarded Zacarías for several more moments. "You have a beautiful wife," he finally said, "and beautiful children. Gabriel will be a scholar, even if you're not. Try not to lose them."

For this, Zacarías had no answer. Unable to meet his father's eyes again, he took his leave.

The old man sat in the dark room, lit only by small windows on either side of the door, and pondered this wild stranger who was his son. He recalled Moses' parting words to the People of Israel shortly before they entered the Promised Land. God had offered both a blessing and a curse: That the People would be led to a strange land, far beyond their knowledge, where they would worship gods of wood and of stone. The sky would be like copper and the ground below them like iron. That part had been meant as a curse, but Zacarías pursued the minerals in the hills as though they were the Holy Grail, the Seven Cities of Cíbola, the voice in the wilderness.

Julio shook his head and returned to his studies.

Zacarías stopped in the kitchen to say goodbye to his mother.

Tall and rangy like her son, Mariana had not spoken in almost forty years, since she was twelve years old. She had fallen into a trance for thirty days, neither alive nor dead, and had lain still and waxen upon the bed. During all those days, she had spoken only one word, from the edge of death, but said it clearly and distinctly. "Angeles," she had exclaimed, as though a presence filled the room before her half-opened eyes. Three days later color had returned to her cheeks, and she gradually got well, but never spoke again.

The family said that Mariana had seen angels in her trance, and though her life was spared, she had paid for the privilege with her tongue.

Zacarías found her making bread, kneading and turning the dough at the big kitchen table.

"Mamá," he said coming up behind her and kissing her offered cheek. "You know that I am leaving for awhile."

She nodded and turned her sad, glistening brown eyes on Zacarías as he stood next to her. Mariana wiped her floury hands on a cloth and pushed his hair out of his face. She was very fond of her son and knew that her husband sometimes blamed her fierce, silent love of him for Zacarías' lack of interest in learning. Julio thought her indulgence had made his son undisciplined and intellectually lazy.

"I don't know how long I'll be gone," said Zacarías. "I'll probably go to Monclova, where I've been offered a partnership in a business."

Mariana looked at him questioningly. She knew that he had consistently rejected offers from his father-in-law.

"This is something I can do for myself, without people doing me special favors or making me part of an existing business. It's new," said Zacarías, as though he needed to justify it. He had told no one else in Saltillo about his plan. "You know that Estela has cut me off financially?"

Mariana nodded yes.

"Well, perhaps she's right. Maybe it's time I did things for myself. About time your son became a man." Zacarías smiled fondly at his mother.

She signed to him in the language they had invented between them when he was a child. "You will always be my little boy," she said.

Zacarías laughed and hugged her before he left, and she pressed her fingertips to her lips and held them out as he left through the kitchen door of the house.

Mariana had not been especially pretty and was at least a foot taller than Zacarías' father, but that had not been important to Julio when he chose a wife. She was also his cousin. Her mother had been Jewish, and that is what had mattered, that Julio Caraval's children would be Jewish on their mother's side as well as on his own. That was the Law. The Law was also to choose life whenever possible, and Julio had learned to be a careful man, a thorough man, in order to do just that. He could not understand Zacarías' constant flirtations with death, and Zacarías had long ago stopped trying to explain.

A bag of silver and a bag of gold. Zacarías touched his saddle-bags where the precious metal was carefully stored. This time he also carried a petaca, a leather trunk behind his saddle, with a few of his worldly possessions. He stopped on the low rise north of Saltillo, where he could catch a last glimpse of the spacious streets, the generous houses, and the spreading branches of the well-tended gardens. Home. Or was it his home anymore? He was too confused to know. Perhaps that's what the salamander meant, he mused. One man, two worlds.

Behind him stretched the wilderness, ragged hills running north to the Texas border, outlaws and cold nights and shining bits of metal reflected in limpid water. The image of shining water continued to fill his head, water rushing swiftly, wearing away the black soil and rock accumulated over generations to reveal the heart of gold beneath.

With a series of low, short whistles, Zacarías spurred his mare and turned her towards the setting sun.

"Go!" he said. "La Esmeralda is waiting for us."

A sudden flight of birds or movement of wind made Estela stop and gaze out the window. She could not say why, but she felt a lightness she had not felt in many years. She should feel terrible, she thought. Left alone to cope with the household by herself; her surly father, the prying neighbors; an abandoned woman. Estela tried to feel sorry for herself, something she had done often enough before, but today she could not.

The last flowers of the season were still blooming. Her daughters played in the courtyard, their embroidery in a careless heap on a table. Gabriel read in a corner of the patio, his feet up, sweet tea at hand. My little man, she thought.

Zacarías was gone again, but this time she had done something about it. Perhaps that was the difference.

Leaving the kitchen, Estela wiped her hands on her apron and pulled it off over her head. She walked into the parlor and opened the wide windows onto the sunny yard. Reserved for guests, the room stood unused most of the time. Estela picked a book of verse from a shelf, sat down in the most comfortable chair near the window, and decided to read until it got too dark.

Somewhere, a cock crowed, a horse whinnied, a cry of elote, elote, roasted corn, floated on the evening breeze. She smelled sewage for a moment, followed by orange blossoms.

"Oh wretched moment of my birth," said the first verse she read,

When I opened eyes that one day would gaze upon you,
That one day would see the hand that never would be mine
Eyes that would see you speak the name of another,
See your lips tremble on that name

Normally, Estela would find her heart beating rapidly when she read such things, but today the words were full of air. A pleasant light came in from the west-facing window, bathing her in its golden glow. Soon it would be too cool to enjoy the evenings like this. A soft wind lifted the leaves of the trees, the wind from the mountains that blew everything clean, that cleansed the air of the town of the eternal dust of the desert.

2

Noche Lluviosa

Zacarías watched the storm advance towards him across the desert for nearly two hours. The heavy gray curtain enclosed one mountain range, then another, before the temperature began to drop and the wind, laden with the smell of sage, picked up. Zacarías stopped and unfurled his poncho. Both he and the horse instinctively turned their backs to the storm as it hit and swept over them. The poncho shed water down his back, protecting the petate and packs on either side of La Gata, flowing water down over the animal's rump.

The sky darkened immediately, though it was only four in the afternoon.

Zacarías pulled his hat low over his eyes, wrapping the wet reins securely in his left hand. "Ay Dios, que no me olvides," he thought, for the land itself looked forgotten, drowned in the downpour that seemed to reflect his own gloomy cast of mind.

All that went before shall pass away, shall be washed away, and I shall become a new man.

The mare's hooves sucked mud as they crossed the barren landscape towards La Fontina. The pick and shovel clanked on one side, while the supply bags dragged and thudded on the other.

Zacarías remembered his son's face as he left—carefully unreadable. Zacarías took this as a bad sign, since his wife had not been present at the time, and Gabriel did not have to hide his emotions from her.

Zacarías still felt twinges in his guts as he rode, a peculiar hollowness, and soreness of his anus from his recent illness. Clean water, he thought, an admonition from Matukami. Next time, make sure the water is clean.

But he quickly forgot about his pains as his eyes began to automatically scan the streambeds they crossed, searching for that bit of metal that might be dislodged from further upstream by the downpour. They were fifty miles outside of Monclova, in regions that had been heavily prospected, Zacarías knew, but there was always the chance that some small vein had been overlooked.

It began to grow dark early, catching Zacarías miles from any town. He lifted his eyes from the ground and began to search ahead for shelter. Rather than passing on, the downpour had intensified, chilling Zacarías and causing even the patient La Gata to begin balking and tossing her head.

Zacarías could make out some low cliffs ahead, with dark shadows that might be caves or mineshafts. Urging La Gata up the crumbling shale slope, Zacarías found some relief in the lee of the cliff. Walking precariously along a narrow shelf, he dismounted and peered in the low, dark entrances. They appeared dry and smelled free of fresh animal droppings that would signify occupation.

Pulling off the saddlebags and saddle, Zacarías slapped La Gata on the rump so that she would seek shelter on her own. There was a bit of an overhang just up ahead, and the resourceful mare soon found a spot that was mostly out of the rain. After stuffing the saddle and supplies into one of the openings, Zacarías followed on his hands and knees.

Zacarías pulled a candle stub from his pack, lit it, and dripped a little wax onto a rocky outcrop before fixing the candle. He was in an abandoned mine shaft, common in these parts, with hand-carved walls and crude wooden braces. Pulling at a handful of jerky with his teeth, Zacarías made a mental note to see if it was marked on any of his maps. Almost simultaneous with his last, dry swallow, Zacarías fell asleep against his saddle.

As dusk approached, Mariana hung heavy cloth over the windows that faced the street. She knew that they were not the only ones who did this, but everyone was discrete. Certain families were simply not seen on Friday evening, no matter how balmy the weather, how sweet the blossoms, or how dewy the air. She then draped a dark mantilla over her head.

Julio stood at one end of the table, a yarmulke folded in his hands. He did not place it on his head until Mariana began to light the candles. Julio watched his wife carefully as her mouth shaped the unspoken words of the Hebrew prayers. "Amen," he said. "Amen."

They had performed this ritual in near silence for so many years that he no longer knew if even he could say the prayers aloud. They had had no daughter to learn the woman's part of the Shabbos, only Zacarías. Against his will, Julio glanced to the place where their son used to stand. They always celebrated Shabbos standing up. It was easier to snuff the candles and put away the yarmulke and prayer shawl if someone appeared at the door with a sudden knock.

Mariana motioned three times over the candles, her still-beautiful face lit by the wavering light, her silent lips repeating the ancient ritual in the glowing light between them.

It is not dead, thought Julio. No matter what they say, our religion is not dead. Each Shabbos he felt it recreated, re-formed in the simple, beautiful prayers that united God to home, home to family, and family to God. Julio blessed the bread and wine before he removed his yarmulke and prayer shawl and they took their chairs.

With the windows covered, Julio and Mariana had not seen the suddenness with which dusk descended on Saltillo. Distant thunder now rolled towards them from the west, followed quickly by sheets of rain that drummed upon the roof and caused the gutters to flow and gurgle like many voices.

They ate their meal in silence. Then Mariana carefully wrapped the white Shabbos candles in blue cloth and removed the hangings from the windows, one by one.

Lamentation

In silence we wait. In prayerfulness we wait. With long patience and suffering we wait. How long, oh Lord? How long will you leave your children alone, how long must the flock be without a shepherd, the maiden without a husband, the lioness in the desert without a mate? We wait like the turtledove, like the fish in the sea, like a rock in a river. We wait, oh Lord, for Thee.

Julio took a fresh sheet of paper and carefully printed out the letters at the top. He spent the next two hours laboriously rearranging them, searching for the correct combination to give him the key to the next passage of text. His candle burned low and guttered for several minutes, casting wild shadows around the room before he impatiently lit another and replaced it.

After three fruitless hours and sixty-seven nonsensical combinations, Julio wrote the words out in Spanish, counted the numerical value of the letters, and added them up. It fit perfectly.

Splendid one, holy giver of knowledge. For now we see dimly, but with the passage of time, all things shall come to fruition.

Julio dipped the plume of an eagle in a small receptacle of

stone. He spelled out the words in mercury across the surface of a sheet of lead that had been carefully pounded out by hand. The letters shimmered briefly, then seemed to shrink in on themselves. The acrid smell of burnt quill filled the silent room.

The letters began to grow large, bulbous, and shiny. The plate emitted a slight glow as it grew soft and malleable. Julio leaned forward eagerly.

Suddenly it expanded and shattered. Julio fell back, covering his face against the brilliant explosion of blue heat and light. He cried out before falling into a deep, unconscious state.

Mariana heard her husband's cry and dropped her crocheting. Running out of the kitchen, she knocked once on the door of the study she was forbidden to enter without permission. All was quiet within. She pounded on the door, then tried the handle, but the latch would not lift, try as she might.

Mariana pressed her face against the rough wood and wept silently, the storm drenching her, afraid to seek help lest her husband's terrible secret be revealed.

Over breakfast the next morning, Mariana dared to ask why. She gestured angrily: Why? Her hands cut the air in dangerous arcs.

Julio shrugged his shoulders. "Something went wrong." He knew he shouldn't have tried to write in Spanish with Arabic letters, but he couldn't help it. He knew better now. And he also knew that he really shouldn't be writing on the Shabbos, but he was so busy the rest of the week.

Julio dabbed at his face gently with his napkin. He had suffered burns on his hands and lower face, but his eyes, fortunately, seemed unharmed.

There was no sign of the storm this morning. The birds sang sweetly, and the fountain in the courtyard was the loudest noise. Occasionally a horse and cart or a carriage could be heard thumping across the bridge below.

Mariana refused to meet his eyes. He knew that she was angry with him.

"It's for our own good," he said, as a way of placating her.

"But why?" she turned and gestured. "Why all this birlibirloque? You might harm yourself. What would happen to me?"

"Ah, querida," said Julio, drawing her to him and holding her hands. "The birds of the garden would care for you. They would bring you the fattest worms, and the choicest caterpillars. The flowers would give up their nectar for you."

Mariana pulled away, with a wry smile, not placated.

"I hasten the Messiah's coming," sighed Julio, sitting back, "by contemplation of his holy name. My father did it before me, and his father before him."

Mariana moved about the kitchen like a ghost, her expressive hands wiping and placing dishes, straightening towels, moving candlesticks.

"Since you do not read Hebrew, I cannot share with you the wonders of his words."

She turned to him. "I can read the human heart," she gestured, "and I know that you seek something else."

Julio looked away. He felt caught out. How could she know? "I seek only to know God's will," he answered. "God's will for our son."

Outside, a small piece of mortar slipped from between two stones of the garden wall. The upper rock was left unsupported but did not fall.

"Must be some damage from the storm," said Julio, then turned back absently to his breakfast.

Only because the sugar had completely run out and Josefina had the day off and the girls were bathing did Estela venture out by herself that day.

If it hadn't rained so hard the night before, she would have taken Calle Santa Ana directly to the market, but the arroyo was flooding, covering the small bridge, so Estela went down another street that took her south of the Plaza de San Francisco, by the government building, and into the warm brown gaze of Captain José Luís Carranza.

Even here the streets were inundated, so pedestrians and riders alike were forced to one side or the other to avoid standing water over a foot deep.

Skirting a boy driving two goats ahead of him and a viejita loaded down with kindling, Estela stepped directly into the path of a tall palomino on which Captain Carranza, medical doctor to the Eleventh Battalion, was riding. Pulling the palomino abruptly to the side, the Captain succeeded in blocking both the goats and the lovely but preoccupied woman who carried her shopping basket as though it were something she had never seen before in her life.

Startled, Estela looked up to see if the rider would trample her. She lost her footing on the cobblestones and turned her ankle, falling into the muddy street.

Instantly Captain Carranza was off his horse and lifting her to the side of the street.

"Bring me a chair, quick!" he demanded of a merchant.

Estela was seated on a crate before she even knew what had happened and why this stranger in uniform was holding her hand.

"I'm a doctor," he said. "I'm so sorry to cause you distress. I'm Dr. José Luís Carranza de Sandoval, a su servicio."

Estela knew she was supposed to say something polite at this point, but was too confused to do so.

"Does anything hurt? Are you all right?"

"I'm—fine," she stammered. "Thank you for your help."

"On the contrary, I caused your fall. My deepest apologies."

Estela tried to stand, but cried out when she put weight on her left foot.

"It's probably turned," said Carranza. "I doubt that you could have broken it, but it's possible."

"It's these cobblestones," said Estela. "They're so uneven that under the best conditions, it's difficult to walk."

"I'll take you home," said Carranza.

"No, no, my son will come and get me," she replied.

"It would be my pleasure," replied Carranza. "It's the very least I can do after causing you so much distress."

Blushing and dazed at the sudden attention, Estela agreed. Carranza lifted her side-saddle onto his horse and proceeded to lead it up the steep streets, following Estela's directions. She pulled her shawl close around her face and hoped no one would recognize her in this predicament.

On gaining Calle Santa Ana, Carranza knocked on the door before helping Estela down from his horse.

"Abre la puerta," called Estela. "It's me, your mother."

Her eldest, Victoria, hair still wet, opened the door and stared wide-eyed at her mother and the Captain.

"Help me," she said to Victoria, who rushed out to support her mother on one side, as the Captain held her elbow on the other.

Seated in the parlor, Estela removed her shawl while the Captain drew up another chair. Victoria stared in fascination at his mustache and uniform.

"If you would permit me, please," he asked, "to examine your ankle for breaks before I go."

"I'm sure I'm fine, Doctor," Estela answered. "I'll just rest it for a bit."

The Captain stood and moved the chair closer.

"Then please elevate it and place a wet rag around it," he said, gently lifting her foot and placing it on the chair. "I could tell it hurt you very much to place weight on it."

"Would you please bring me a wet rag?" said Estela to her daughter.

Victoria ran to the kitchen while María, her younger sister, came in to take her place staring at the officer.

"Here is my card," said Carranza, bowing to Estela. "Please send for me if your ankle is not better in two or three days."

"Thank you," said Estela. "I appreciate your kindness, but it's not important."

"I understand," said the Captain. "Again, I'm so sorry to cause you discomfort. Please forgive me this interruption of your life."

"That's all right," said Estela. "It could not possibly be helped."

"María, would you please see the Doctor to the door?" Estela placed his card on the table next to her.

Victoria returned with a wrung-out rag and handed it to her mother with barely a glance. Both she and María stood at the open door as the Captain mounted his palomino, tipped his hat, and was gone in a clatter of hooves.

"Close the door, please," called Estela. "And remember to bolt it." She realized that, thanks to her daughters, everyone would soon know of her embarrassment.

"Mamá," said Victoria, hurrying back into the room, "I thought you told us never to talk to soldiers."

"You shouldn't," said Estela wearily, removing her shoe and stocking and wrapping the rag around her tender foot. It had begun to swell. "I fell in front of his horse. He stopped to help before I could do anything."

"He is so handsome," said María, and both girls squealed with glee.

"I'm glad you're so concerned about your poor old mother," said Estela, "because you have to do all my work for the next few days. You can start by emptying your bathwater into the garden."

While her daughters went out chattering, Estela lay back in the chair and glanced idly at the calling card. He had been handsome, she had to admit. Probably from some landed family in Mexico City. Estela wished for a cup of tea. And there still wasn't any sugar.

3

Indago felix

Horacio thumped an arroba of raw sugar on the counter, then another, for a total of five sacks. He rubbed his shoulder as he regarded the sacks; he was no longer a young man.

Horacio Quintanilla Navarro normally did not deal in perishables or foodstuffs—because of rats—but a client had been unable to pay in currency, or what passed for currency these days, so Horacio had accepted the sugar.

Horacio turned and surveyed the stacks of goods behind him—undyed muslin, boxes of spooled cotton thread, paper, wool, needles and thimbles, a few fancy dress goods. In spite of these, he seemed to be dealing less and less in actual things, and more and more in ideas. Currency, Horacio had come to understand, was merely an idea, an agreement, that these papers or coins could be exchanged for those goods or services. As governments changed, and the Spanish, the French, and the Americans came and went, so did agreements, and so did currency.

It was a nasty business, surviving in the world, thought

Horacio. The early coyote got snakebit.

Gustavo, his son-in-law, let himself in the front door.

"The wife let you sleep in a little?" asked Horacio.

"Are you joking?" answered Gustavo. "That baby has had us all up since 4:00."

"How is my little granddaughter, my little hummingbird?"

"Healthy," said Gustavo, taking off his jacket and filling a pipe. "Just like her mother."

"Good, good," said Horacio. "I'm going over to see Ahmed, that old Arab, to see if he'll take this sugar in exchange for some tea. I don't want to haul this stuff all over creation. Too heavy, and no one's going to kill us for tea."

"Fine. I'll finish the books from last week," answered Gustavo, taking a pair of spectacles out of his pocket and putting them on his nose.

Horacio put on his coat and hat and let himself out of the shop. The bell clanged behind him as he shut the door firmly. Already the streets were filling with people — cooks buying food for the day, firewood vendors, bankers, traveling businessmen. His grandsons would be in school, and their sisters helping their mothers with household chores. Early Mass was over, and the black-shawled widows cast shadows in the early morning sun.

Horacio made his way to the narrower streets of the Arab quarter and turned in at a shop with the word "Babilonia" written in white script over the door. An unfortunate name, thought Horacio, in a Christian country. But then, Ahmed would be too stubborn to admit that, since it was the city of his birth.

"¿Qué tál?" Horacio hailed the old merchant as he entered the shop. The place smelled of cinnamon, cardamom, curry, and spices that Horacio could not identify. Every last corner was filled with rice or some kind of legume.

Ahmed parted the beads that curtained off the rear of the

store, also his living quarters. "There you are, old man!" shouted Ahmed and clasped Horacio's hand warmly with one hand while clapping him on the shoulder with the other.

Horacio winced.

"Winter's coming on, eh? I've got some herbs that will help you feel better."

"That's what I've come to talk about, only not for my own health," said Horacio. "It's about a little trade."

"Then I'm just the man," said Ahmed, clearing a squat stool for Horacio and taking another for himself. They set them out front, the better to smoke and see the sights.

"I'd like to trade you for some tea," said Horacio around his pipe as he lit it.

"Well, let's see," said Ahmed. "I've got rubea tea from Ceylon. Also alwazah. I have the highest quality jasmine and darjeeling, alwadi kalmi, very pungent, and cinnamon from Brazil. There's Gulabi and Barooti Gulabi. Good for the digestion. The best black is from the Antilles, the West Indies, but nobody knows that. I prefer green tea myself, Chinese. Very beneficial to the health."

"Black tea is the best for my purposes," said Horacio. "I plan to take it up north for trade. The niceties of green tea would be lost on them. They like things strong."

"Perfectly understandable. It takes strength to live there, so far from Allah."

Horacio let the remark pass and they smoked in silence for a moment. "Besides, they use the tea to dye fabric. Makes a light brown color," added Horacio.

"Are you offering gold?" asked Ahmed. "If so, I can give it to you very reasonably."

Horacio snorted. "If I had gold to bargain, would I be in this business?"

"Ah, credit, then," said Ahmed, disappointed.

"No, no, I've got payment," said Horacio quickly. "Good, in

fact. Almost as good as gold. I've got Cuban sugar. Five arrobas of it from a client in Tampico."

"That is almost as good as gold up north," said Ahmed, raising his eyebrows. "Why trade it here?"

"Because a man can get killed for sugar out there," said Horacio. "You've got it plush here in town, with attractive ladies coming to you for this little thing and that. I've got to drive hundreds of miles between towns. That's why I limit myself to dry goods and fabrics—valuable, but you don't usually get shot for a new pair of trousers."

Ahmed nodded.

"Besides," added Horacio, "I know that you sell it in half-libra sacks, like gold dust, and can turn quite a profit that way."

Ahmed grinned. "How much do you have?"

"Five arrobas in five sacks. I'll keep one for my family, so, un quintal."

Ahmed considered. "I can give you five hundred libras of Ceylonese for that."

"So little?"

"That's—" Ahmed squinted his eyes up and to the left—"about fifty sacks the size of a lamb. You have room to store more?"

Horacio had to admit that he did not. He either had to build or rent more storage if he was to deal in a larger inventory. Bah!

They shook hands and Horacio prepared to go.

"I'll send a cart around with the sugar, and pick up the tea," Horacio said.

"By the way," said Ahmed. "Speaking of pretty ladies, your daughter Doña Estela was in our street the other day."

"Eh? some little thing she couldn't live without?"

"Hard to say. Seems she met a soldier, an officer, and rode home on his horse. Hurt her ankle or something."

Horacio did not know what to say. Everyone knew that Zacarías was gone.

"She was by herself?"

Ahmed nodded. "At least, when she arrived. I'm sure it was nothing," he added upon seeing his friend's discomfiture. "I don't think she was badly hurt."

"That's not what I'm worried about," said Horacio. "But thank you for the information. I'll send a boy around tomorrow with the sugar."

Ahmed bowed, his hand to his heart, as Horacio jammed his hat on and hurried back out onto the street.

He would never understand his daughter, thought Horacio. Her bed still warm from that crazy husband of hers and she's already chasing soldiers in the street like a common whore. For someone who read so much, Estela didn't know the first thing about life. Horacio was sorry that Altagracia, his wife, had died so young, but at least she had been spared these humiliations.

Horacio stomped up the street, oblivious to the lingering rain puddles that lay before him, splashing people to his left and right without noticing.

"If it weren't for the indigenes, we would all be so inbred we would quack like ducks."

This was the pronouncement made by the doctor nineteen years earlier at the birth of the enigmatic twins that had taken their mother, Altagracia, from this earth.

They had been christened with decent Christian names, but since anyone could remember, they had been called Membrillo and Manzana, for if you knew the difference, you could tell them apart.

When the twins were born, Membrillo was delivered first. A boy, bald, with hazel eyes. The midwife cooed and comforted the wide-eyed child. It was a boy, although his private parts were minuscule. He was Don Horacio's first son, after two daughters, and she knew that he would be pleased.

As Altagracia cried out again, the midwife carefully swaddled the baby, set him in a basket, turned, and took the pink, bloody placenta in a towel and began to bundle it up for disposal when it seemed to move. Opening the towel, she found another tiny baby, blue-lipped and squirming. Cutting and tying the cord, she set it in the warm, bloody water in which she had just bathed the other infant and cleared its mouth with her finger. The baby gasped and cried weakly. It was a tiny girl, also bald and hazel-eyed.

In a daze, unable to believe that she had not foreseen this outcome after thirty years of delivering babies, the midwife swaddled the second infant and carried both out to their sisters and father.

Altagracia bled and bled, expelling the true placenta on her life's blood, which slipped off the bed and towards the door, where the midwife found it when she returned. The midwife stooped and examined it carefully to make sure it was not a third child before she realized what had happened. A river of blood flowed from the womb of the unfortunate Altagracia, who lay pale and spent upon the ruined sheets. Her cries had gone unheeded and she had died alone.

The twins were strange from the very beginning. A wet nurse, Ana, was found to suckle them, a sturdy Tlaxcalan whose ancestors had been brought from the south to work the looms in Saltillo.

Ana tried to nurse each child in turn, but they cried inconsolably if separated even for a moment and refused to suckle. So she held one at each breast, a fountain of life, and still had milk for her own two year old.

Estela and Blanca, bereft of their mother at the ages of ten and twelve, turned their leftover love onto the infant twins. They lavished affection on them, outfitting the two in identical dresses of the finest cotton and lace, with woolly sweaters and booties and hats to match. Horacio, stunned at the sudden loss of his wife, allowed the girls to distract themselves with the twins, glad that they could submerge their grief in the care of the doll-like babies.

Horacio threw himself into his trade with a renewed fury, determined to provide security, if not affection, for his four motherless children. He could barely bring himself to look at the twins, much less love them, for he could only see in them Altagracia's dead and pale face. Her photo, framed in silver, sat on the family altar ever after that, votive candles burning in perpetuity before it.

The twins were nearly identical except that one was slightly male and one slightly female. Their behavior never changed into that of boy and girl as they grew older, however, and Membrillo's testicles did not descend.

"They're all mixed up," said the doctor. "An aberration of nature, marica y marimacho. They must have gotten mixed together in the womb, with each taking parts of the other. Don't expect a very masculine son," was his final word to Horacio. "Educate him for something refined."

The twins, perfect in every other way, remained unperturbed by these predictions. They spoke a language all their own to each other, incomprehensible to anyone else, and spoke almost nothing at all to others. Estela, Blanca and Ana anticipated all their physical needs, and they took any other comfort and entertainment they needed from each other.

Horacio, heeding the doctor's advice, determined that Membrillo would learn to read and write, and tried to send him to El Ateneo Fuente, Saltillo's premiere school. It was for boys only, however, and he refused to be separated from his sister. A private tutor was finally brought in. Keeping his thoughts to himself, Horacio remembered his own experience at El Ateneo, the cruelty of small boys, and felt that Membrillo was safer at home, anyway.

As babies, the two were dressed identically, but as they grew to five years old, it was time for Membrillo to wear pantaloons and Manzana to wear dresses. Again, the twins cried inconsolably if dressed differently and immediately removed their clothing if left unattended for even a moment. It was finally decided to dress them both in knee breeches, stockings, and frilly shirts, in the manner of French dandies. This seemed to suit them fine.

Even Horacio had to admit that they were a charming pair, with pale hair and large, luminous eyes. One was left-handed and one right. And when they spoke, which was seldom, it was in a sweet, modulated tone, neither high nor low.

Membrillo and Manzana could be separated long enough to walk on either side of their father, hand-in-hand, and they always drew admiring glances and comments from passersby on the street. He would seat them on the counter in his merchant's office, eating identical sweets, and do his bookkeeping, for they were extremely well behaved.

Once, a man with a very large mustache came into the shop. He had either followed the unusual family or been told of them in town. An American, he said that his name was Mister Eustace Black, and that he represented a famous "purveyor of family entertainments" from the United States. After admiring the demure pair seated at their usual places on the worn shop counter, Mister Black took Don Horacio aside and spoke to him in low tones, all the while glancing nervously over at the twins as though they would evaporate from his sight should he cease to pay careful attention to them. When he had made clear his intent, Don Horacio's face turned a beet red.

"I will not have my children exhibited like animals in a cage," he spluttered upon regaining his powers of speech. "I will not have them turned into a sideshow!"

Don Horacio escorted Mr. Black from the premises under the identical hazel gaze of Membrillo and Manzana. Upon returning home, the twins asked their older sisters the meaning of the foreign word, sideshow, and the sisters were able to guess what had happened. Although never within their father's hearing, the older girls used the dreaded word as a threat when the twins failed to behave perfectly.

It was also in Don Horacio's shop that the twins met La Sirena and discovered, at the age of eight, their great talent.

La Sirena was a strange and notorious figure throughout the northern territories. Dressed in voluminous black rags, she rode a small burro everywhere, flapping and blowing across the desert like some great crow let loose upon the landscape.

La Sirena was no mere decorative mermaid, her ripe breasts drooping over ears of corn and bundles of squash and baskets of fish, but someone even better: La Sirena could discover water where nothing had previously grown, where cattle and men alike had died of dehydration.

La Sirena had entered Don Horacio's office one afternoon on the pretext of finding out the date of his next scheduled foray into the north country. Merchants and travelers often formed trains for crossing the wide wastelands and through the disputed territories of Apaches, Americans, displaced Irish immigrants, rurales, and various outlaws. La Sirena really didn't have anything to worry about, since everyone thought she was a powerful witch, so Don Horacio knew she had something else in mind.

Membrillo and Manzana were playing chess when La Sirena found them, silently taking turns at the game they had learned merely by observing the old men in the plaza. Each was dressed impeccably in full, beige shirts with ruffles at the cuffs, hunter green knee breeches, and identical embroidered vests provided by the St. James Women's Auxiliary, who felt it their duty to provide for the motherless children. Turning her wide and somewhat alarming gaze on one and then the other, La Sirena reached into the folds of her tattered skirt and pulled out a forked stick.

"Take this, my children," she said, placing one branch of the stick in a hand of each child, "and see where it leads you."

The children, puzzled, stood looking at the stick between them. Don Horacio paused at his calculations to watch.

At first, nothing happened, and Horacio was about to return to his books, thinking that La Sirena was just trying to amuse the children. Then the twins began to feel a slight vibration. It turned to a visible shaking, and then the stick began to wave up and down between them. The pens upon the counter began to dance, and the stacked rows of bolts of cloth on the shelves began to rattle and move about in such an alarming manner that their father thought an earthquake was occurring. The twins tried to drop the offending branch, but their hands refused to obey them. The stick led them forward, and La Sirena opened the door just before the children would have gone crashing through it.

"What have you done?" screamed Don Horacio as he vaulted the counter and pursued the children out the door. La Sirena followed silently, her piercing eyes intent upon the children stumbling helplessly down the street, slaves to the powerful limb between them. The group attracted a larger crowd as they went along, dodging between carts, horses, people and pigeons as the branch led them mercilessly down the narrow streets and alleys. By the time they reached the main plaza, twenty or thirty people had been acquired along the way to swell the always substantial population of drifters and dreamers at the center of town.

Membrillo and Manzana had no time to appreciate the spectacle. The forked appendage, as though possessed by a thirsty devil, led them wide-eyed and silent to the huge fountain and pulled the hapless children into the icy water. Only then did it release its pernicious hold on them.

Don Horacio and La Sirena pulled the spluttering children, soaking wet, from the chilly water.

"What is the meaning if this deviltry?" demanded Don Horacio. "What do you mean by doing these things to my children?"

La Sirena enfolded first one wet child, then the other, in her smoky embrace.

"What you have witnessed, Don Horacio," she croaked, "is the spirits choosing their masters. Your children are natural diviners. As long as they live, they will be blessed with a special affinity to water. If you will permit me, I will return for the children when they are older and will teach them everything I know—for I am not long for this earth, and someone must carry on my work. It is called *Indago Felix*, the fruitful search."

Don Horacio immediately grasped the significance of what she was saying. Ever since the visit of the circus man from the United States, he had worried about the fate of his beautiful twins. If La Sirena could teach them to waterwitch, he would never have to worry about their ending up as ignominious creatures of public ridicule.

Still, he had some doubts. Although not a superstitious man, Don Horacio was concerned that divining was a form of witchcraft that would lead the twins into darker and more demonic pursuits. Altagracia might not approve, and he found himself consulting the silver-framed photo of his wife for advice.

The answer seems to have been in the affirmative, for Don Horacio agreed that La Sirena could return to take the twins into apprenticeship when she felt that her time was growing short.

"Only promise me," he had asked her, "that you will never display my children as unnatural creatures."

"All God's creatures are natural," croaked the old bruja. "As long as they see themselves as natural, no one will have the power to take advantage of them. I promise."

This seemed to reassure the don, who had raised his children in as unaffected an atmosphere as possible. Membrillo and Manzana really did seem to see themselves as the most natural beings in the world, and viewed the rest of humanity with a curious detachment, as though the wide ocean of variable and questionable beings around them were slightly farther away from the peaceful center of the universe upon whose bosom they rested with perfect ease.

· · ·

As the twins approached the age at which most children enter the treacherous shoals of puberty, there was much speculation about what would become of Membrillo and Manzana. The twins had grown even more beautiful with each passing year, their eyes clear and green, their hair in identical waves, one with hair parted on the right, the other on the left. Their limbs had grown straight and graceful, and when seated on a matched set of palominos, they resembled nobility from some forgotten age of enlightenment.

The only thing awkward about them was their nicknames, but no one seemed able to recall their given names, even their father and older sisters. For some mysterious reason, even the church registry had identical waterstains upon it that blotted out their Christian names, and although many people were present at the christening, and all agreed that the twins were the most beautiful babies they had ever seen before the baptismal font, in their long embroidered dresses, no one could remember their names.

Much to Don Horacio's relief, the twins remained exemplary in their behavior, modest to the point of demureness, and totally oblivious to the growing interest elicited by their budding adolescence. One thing that did disturb him, however, was the increasing number of men who seemed to loiter around the house in the evenings. More than once, he had looked outside late in the evening to see young men smoking just up the street, throwing sidelong glances at the windows that they supposed (and supposed correctly) to belong to the twins. If he thought that these glances were meant just for Manzana, he would have been somewhat pleased. Her size and strength and the faint mustache on her upper lip were more than adequately balanced by her quiet nature and overall grace. Having raised and married off two older daughters, he felt well-acquainted with the negotiations that would ensure a proper marriage to gain his youngest daughter a position of respect in the community.

But Don Horacio knew very well that almost no one outside of the family could tell the twins apart and even he would probably find it difficult if he did not know that Membrillo was right-handed and Manzana left-handed, with the wave of their hair corresponding in direction. No, the glances and occasional loud sighs that floated up the cobbled street from the shadows were definitely meant for both twins, and Don Horacio wondered how long he could protect them from the depredations of these men, some of whom seemed a bit older and whose profiles even seemed a bit familiar to the don before they stepped back into the doorways and nearby alleys; Don Horacio was pretty sure that a few were married men with teenage children of their own.

Membrillo and Manzana ignored it all, discussing philosophy and mathematics with each other, pausing to scratch out a formula in the dirt to make a point. They measured the wind direction and speed, and the pressure of the air, sketched the clouds, and studied the stars at night with a huge telescope they had constructed with the assistance of their devoted tutor, Don José. The twins seemed to have accepted La Sirena's pronouncements about their future with equanimity and prepared themselves as much as possible with a scientific approach for a livelihood in the divining arts.

One evening, when the shadows hovering near the house seemed especially oppressive and the air seemed dense and thick, the family sat restlessly in the front room. Doña Blanca, her three children, and her husband Gustavo lingered for awhile after sharing dinner with Don Horacio and the twins. The twins sat on the floor, playing marbles with the little ones. Don Horacio paced and smoked before the cold fireplace.

Suddenly the wind picked up and sharp drops of rain splattered against the side of the house and flew between the wrought iron bars covering the open windows. The rain increased to the point where Blanca and Don Horacio hurried to close the shutters, then ceased as quickly as it had begun. Don Horacio glanced out the door and saw that the alley and street were now quite clear of lurking shadows, save for a lone figure on a burro that made its way slowly up the narrow street.

Don Horacio's heart sank, for he immediately recognized the crow-like figure in black rags. As much as he had resented Membrillo and Manzana when they were first born, leaving their care to Estela and Blanca and the nursemaid Ana, Horacio had come to love them for the very qualities they had banished forever from this world — namely, the gentility and refinement that had belonged to Altagracia—and that he now saw had been embodied all along in every breath they took. Don Horacio caught his own breath in a near sob, and Blanca stepped to the door just as La Sirena reined in her little donkey.

After helping La Sirena off her small steed, every inch of which seemed to be covered in mysterious bundles and baskets and items of tin of obscure purpose, Horacio and Blanca supported her elbows as she entered the house. They placed her gently in a chair by the fireplace, and Blanca went to fetch her fresh water. As far as Horacio could determine, La Sirena had to be at least one hundred years old, for she had been ancient when he was small, and he was now nearly fifty.

La Sirena waved the water away. She never drank the stuff herself.

"We must hurry," she said. "I have a job up north, in the Texas territories, and it will be their maiden divination."

Without a word the twins stood and went to their rooms to prepare to leave. Don Horacio drank the water down himself, then followed it with a brandy. He poured one for La Sirena as well, which she gladly accepted.

When Membrillo and Manzana appeared around the side of the house on their identical palominos, dressed in dark blue capes that covered them to their knees, Horacio could barely keep the tears from springing to his eyes as he embraced each of them in turn. Their sister Blanca, who had been like a little mother to them, did not try to hold back her emotions.

Horacio could not help but note the mixture of excitement and fear in their faces, and even the horses sensed their apprehension and danced a little on the rough cobblestones. Yet the twins maintained the external calm for which they were so well known. It was as though they had prepared for this moment all of their lives.

La Sirena, gathering up her black skirts, hoisted herself back onto the patient burro and turned it around.

"We will write to you soon," called Membrillo—or was it Manzana?—as the trio proceeded down the darkened street. A fine mist began to fall again, obscuring their passage and blotting out any sign of their having been there at all. The twins were not quite fourteen years of age, and Horacio wondered if he would ever see either of them again.

4

The Tree of Knowledge

Zacarías rode across a countryside just at the end of the harvest.
The last crop of summer corn was in, squash still lay in the fields,
and the mozos were moving cattle across the vast expanses of
open country down to the lower elevations. They saluted him as
he passed, sometimes stopping to share a cigarette rolled in a
corn husk. It was a bittersweet time of year, Dia de los muertos
having passed and the spirits having been propitiated and laid
to rest.

Julio had always dismissed this custom as pagan, but Zacarías
saw how it matched the landscape, prepared people for the more
interior life of the winter months by allowing them to offer the
best that they had to the past, the ancestors, and to the future, before turning back to their own concerns of having enough food
and fuel for the cold months of winter. He thought of it as more
particularly Mexican than any of the other religious customs that
were observed, and rather enjoyed going with Estela and Horacio
and Blanca and Gustavo and the children to Altagracia's grave,

which was decorated with flowers. It wasn't grief, exactly, that was expressed, as much as solidarity.

Bundled in a new Saltillo sarape, his hat pulled low against a cold wind, Zacarías noted how the landscape unfolded before him like a striped blanket: each small rise that he topped on his steady mare revealed a new landscape, a miniature kingdom of rock and field, cañon and cerro, dry places and wet. Great clouds of birds sometimes rose before him, blackening the skies with their wings as they sought roost for the night, or passed on their way south for the season.

Zacarías rode west and north, avoiding the settlements as much as possible, sleeping in the open or under a sheltering cliff or tree at night. He was in no particular hurry.

Zacarías tried to describe to Tomás what he had seen in the desert that day: thousands of tiny creatures swarming in the hollow of a boulder, prehistoric creatures such as he had never seen before, with long, jointed legs and antennae. The air boomed all around him, even the ground at his feet giving off a strange, repetitive noise. The desert, so familiar to him, had of a sudden become an alien place, as though inhabited by spirits that had remained silent all of this time, only to manifest themselves in a wild chorus.

"Oh, those are the camarones," said his companion. "They come out of the rocks if it rains steadily for three days. They're like shrimp. You could have eaten them. Very nice. Crunchy."

"And the noise?"

"The booming noise was from the toads. They also come out when it rains, to mate. In some places, it only rains every two or three years, but the animals stay asleep under the ground until then. They are very patient."

Zacarías and Tomás, a mixed blood trapper from the vicinity of Santa Teresa, sat and gazed out over the great, shallow basin that stretched before them, filled at places with a tall, coarse grass that rippled light green, then dark as the wind touched it. They sat with their backs to a limestone cliff; two hundred feet above them the mesa top was cool and wooded with cedar and scrub pine. The sky was a brilliant pale blue, and far off to the southeast was a slight disruption of the horizon where rainclouds marked another set of mountains.

"The old men say that this was once ocean, that's why it is full of sand," said the trapper, whose territory coincided with Zacarías' usual haunts.

Zacarías suddenly saw the desert in a clear aqua light, the rocks, cliffs, grey-green vegetation submerged in a rippling sea. He imagined huge leviathans drifting purposefully past the cliffs on the other side of the canyon, and silent, deadly shapes coming nearer. Schools of flashing fish turned and darted as one entity through the long grass. It sent a shudder through him, sitting there in the warm sunlight.

"Where are the fish?" he asked.

Tomás shrugged, then pointed to a large rock in the sun, but Zacarías saw nothing. The mestizo picked up a small rock and threw it, causing a grey lizard to dart forward. It flared the frill at the back of its neck, showing a bright yellow-green underneath, and Zacarías could almost imagine gills. He found something vaguely blasphemous about this idea but he wasn't sure what. Things should remain what they are, he could hear his father saying.

But what was his father? Outwardly Catholic, inwardly Jewish. Did he seek change or only a perpetuation of who he was, like some creature of the desert that has adapted from more bountiful times?

And what did he seek through the Cabala? With all his manipulation of words and chemicals and numbers? The manifestation of the divine through the mundane? A sign of God on the surface of a plate? A still pond in which to discern a reflection of the future? And what did any of it have to do with him, Zacarías?

There were many things that he did not understand.

The landscape wavered and swam before him for a moment, as though its reality was about to dissolve before his eyes.

Tomás suggested a game of taba, played by rolling the knuckle-bone of a deer, marked on each side, and soon Zacarías was absorbed in the business of small predictions.

Zacarías arrived in Monclova covered, as usual, with dust. He dismounted in front of La Panadería and led his horse around to the stables in back.

Unstrapping his leather trunk and other gear, Zacarías poured out water in the trough for the thirsty animal, then poured an additional bucket over his own head. Thus refreshed, he felt ready to face la Magdalena Hinojosa O'Connell.

Magdalena was up to her elbows in dough, showing an Indian woman how she wanted it kneaded. As soon as Magdalena's back was turned, the woman would go back to preparing the dough her own way. This produced a chewier bread, more substantial, but not to the liking of Magdalena's town customers. Magdalena sighed a mock sigh and smiled when she saw Zacarías, wiped her hands and greeted him with a small kiss.

"¿Qué tal? Why such a long face?"

"It's an even longer story."

Zacarías spread both hands on the counter between them and looked her straight in the eyes. He had a long, fine nose between heavy dark brows.

"I've come to talk to you about your business proposal," he said.

She looked at his hands. They were not the hands of a gentleman. Rather, each pore, each line was etched with dirt, the fine red clay of riverbanks, the harsh, dry dirt of the llanos, the backs scoured and worn by the desert sands. They were hands not used to fine linens and drawing rooms, but more accustomed to holding leather reins and wooden handles. They were the hands of an adventurer.

And Magdalena knew right then although he did not, that soon he would be in her bed. She smiled and put her own strong hands on the counter inches from his.

"Fine," she said. "I'm glad you reconsidered. You have good hands for a baker."

Zacarías, absorbed in his own miseries, looked startled.

"I have customers who come all the way from Musquiz for bread. There are enough to open a bakery there. Why don't you do it for me?"

Zacarías did not know what to say.

"I've never baked anything in my life," he said.

"It doesn't matter. I can teach you. Just like I taught this donkey," she said, not quite softly enough so that the woman did not hear. "Not that you're so slow. We could be partners. You open and run a bakery in Músquiz and keep half the profits. I'll teach you my secret recipes for bread. And other things."

Zacarías blushed and stepped back. He had heard of such women but never encountered one before.

The other woman kept kneading, her head down as if deaf.

" ¡Ya basta!" said Magdalena to her. "You'll kill the yeast. Now cover it and set it over there to rise."

"Well, then," she said to Zacarías, "come have some supper with me. We're so behind on orders from the north. What do people do with their bread? Build houses? Feed it to their animals? I'll have to charge more."

Magdalena chatted easily as she moved from the bakery to her parlor, a soothing stream of words calculated, Zacarías knew, to put men at ease. It worked. So unlike Estela, he couldn't help thinking as he followed her swishing skirts into the expensively appointed room.

Although a widow, Magdalena usually dressed in emerald

green, a color that set off her wavy black hair and dark eyes. Magdalena was, for all practical purposes, without family. She had been sold to Frank O'Connell at the age of fifteen by her parents, who disappeared back into the interior with their other, darker-skinned children. Having inherited a small fortune from the late and only slightly lamented Mr. O'Connell, Magdalena had decided that, given her age and circumstances, she could do anything she pleased.

Magdalena sat in a chintz-covered chair. She had a dab of flour at one temple, or was it a little gray? It was not unbecoming. Zacarías folded his long frame into another chair.

Magdalena had sold off all but a few breeding stock from her husband's ranches, and these she put out to stud at exorbitant prices, guaranteed, however, to produce strong, drought-resistant offspring. There was always a waiting list.

The resulting profits had been put into properties, and now this business. Magdalena liked things she could keep her eye on, difficult with cattle spread out over hundreds of miles of desert.

"Café, por favor," she called into the other room, and a steaming cup of coffee soon comforted Zacarías as night settled over the town. A confused rooster gave out with a last crow.

"I didn't expect you back so soon," said Magdalena.

"Nor did I," answered Zacarías, clearing his throat. He was unable to go on.

"Your family?" Magdalena hazarded.

Zacarías nodded, his gaze concentrated deep within his cup.

"It's serious this time, isn't it?"

"Yes." He waited a little longer. "My ... wife has cut me off financially."

Magdalena did not press him further, and a late supper was soon served in the dining room.

Zacarías' hunger was such that he could barely restrain himself from setting down his utensils and picking up the potatoes and beef with his hands. Instead of tortillas, there were steaming fresh bolillos—rolls that were light inside, hard and crusty outside. Zacarías slathered them with butter and took great bites, finishing each roll in about four swallows. Magdalena's maid brought more.

"You have known that you could work for me," said Magdalena. "I've told you that often enough."

"What would I do in a bakery," he asked between bites. "I'm clumsy. I hate shops."

"I don't want you waiting on customers. What a disaster!" she laughed. She got her business look. "I need a reliable man in Nueva Rosita." She held up her hand to silence him until she finished.

"I just need him to supervise construction, make sure those people don't steal all the building materials, and get the place ready to open. A nice facade, paint, that sort of thing. I already have a woman there who bakes bread to my specifications. She's doing it out of her house, but she needs a bigger oven. I can pay you expenses, plus a little more, then you're free to go off into the blessed mountains and break your neck."

Zacarías laughed. With a little food, life didn't look so bad.

He retired to the loft in the barn, a place where Magdalena often let Zacarías sleep between forays into the desert. He amused her with his stories of society life in Saltillo and his adventures as a gold prospector, and it saved him a night's payment at a boarding house. The gente decente in Monclova had long ago given up on la Señora Magdalena, as she was usually called, and people were used to seeing strangers at her door.

Saturday dawned sunny and dusty from a west wind, and the bakery closed at noon. The bakers would tend to their own affairs until late Sunday evening, when the whole operation started up again for Monday. Magdalena, in an unusual inclination to spend time in the country, proposed a picnic.

The place was a few miles out of town. Riding their horses at a leisurely pace, they soon gained a little altitude, and the air immediately smelled fresher, if cooler. They entered the mouth of a box canyon out of which flowed a small but lively stream.

Magdalena removed her ankle boots and held up her dress as she waded across the water. Her foot slipped on a stone and she threw out a hand to balance herself, dropping the hem of her skirt into the stream. Laughing, she gained the other side and beckoned for Zacarías to follow. Trees lined the rushing water, and the horses, turned loose, had long since found the coolest spot and the sweetest grass on which to graze.

Mesmerized by the swirl of water around her ankles and bare feet, Zacarías roused himself and crossed the stream in three large bounds, getting his boots just about as wet as if he had waded across. Magdalena shrieked as water sprayed across her, then sat on the grassy bank to shake out her skirts. Her hair was coming out of its pins. Zacarías sat beside her and freed her hair so that it cascaded around her shoulders in a fiery black mass.

Magdalena put her hands around the back of his neck and pulled him towards her in a kiss.

Zacarías had never had a woman initiate a kiss with him, but hesitated only a moment before surrendering to his clamoring feelings. He put his hands to her warm sides and raised them up to cradle her shoulders, then the sides of her breasts. He felt his crotch swell as she leaned into him.

During the five years that he had known her, Zacarías and Magdalena had never been intimate, or even broached the subject. In truth, for all his wandering ways, Zacarías had never been unfaithful to his wife of seventeen years. The land had been his mistress, the earth and water and star-filled sky that served as a canopy to his bedroll and campfire.

Zacarías felt no resistance from Magdalena and knew that she wanted him to proceed. The most that Zacarías had ever expected of his wife was that she sometimes leave her bedroom door unlocked, so this uncloaked display of passion was new to him.

Awkwardly pushing up her layers of petticoats, Zacarías found the top of her bloomers and gently tugged. Magdalena obliged by leaning back and lifting her hips. Zacarías removed his jacket and struggled out of his braces. He unbuttoned his trousers, all the while staring at her exposed sex in the bright sunlight. This was so unbelievable he dared not think.

Magdalena's pubic hair was stiff and black and resisted his exploring fingers, but her sex was open and inviting just beneath. It was so red, like waiting lips, that he bent low over it with his mouth before suddenly raising up and thrusting himself inside.

Magdalena took her breath in sharply and stiffened around him, but he continued to thrust again and again, oblivious to her cries of pain, until he released himself with a shudder and collapsed on top of her.

After a moment, Magdalena rolled him to one side and sat up. Zacarías lay panting, hands to his forehead, his eyes shut tight. Magdalena gathered herself together, a bit shaken, and gazed on the man beside her, who appeared to be suffering from pangs of guilt. Smoothing back his hair, she finally said, "I can see you have a few things to learn about love."

Zacarías' head was pounding with such intensity that he barely heard her. A great noise like that of a smelting furnace filled his head. The inside of his eyelids were black with a pinpoint of fiery red, and Magdalena's voice seemed to reach him from a great distance. This happened whenever he bedded his wife as well.

Gradually the pain receded and Zacarías found himself on a grassy bank that appeared unscathed by the roaring inferno in his head. Rising up on his elbows, he saw that Magdalena had dressed and moved down the stream a little, where she pinned her hair back into its usual constraints.

His heart lifted in joy. Had this really happened? Since his pants were still unbuttoned, he assumed that it had. Zacarías began to dress, his gaze resting tenderly on the woman a few yards away, a woman who had just given him more than he had any right to expect.

What was it that she had said about love?

Zacarías rose and went to Magdalena, planting a kiss on the back of her neck. She looked at him a bit warily but smiled and did not resist when he took her hand and began to stroll back to where the horses carried a packed lunch.

Zacarías felt better—surer and more self-confident—than he had in a long time. While he pulled oranges, empanadas and a straw-wrapped bottle of wine from the saddlebag, the dozing horses swished at flies with their long tails. With a sharp crack Magdalena flicked her wrists and spread an embroidered cloth on the grassy ground. She did not look like a woman who had just had passionate, illicit sex outdoors, except for the fact that she was still barefoot.

Wetting his lips with the wine bottle, Zacarías wondered if he would have to sleep in the barn that night.

Tapping upon the window. Tapping against the pane of glass, insistently, relentlessly, until Zacarías turned over and opened his eyes. There, knocking at the window, was a tiny figure, hovering in the air. It looked like a tiny person, a fairy or an angel. He looked at it closely. It had his mother's face, and its mouth was open in a horrible, silent howl.

Zacarías awoke in a sweat, turned to look at the window. It was just beginning to lighten, still dark in the room. Magdalena stirred beside him, her cool, white shoulder bare in the pre-dawn light.

If he could only finish before the sun got too hot, thought Zacarías. Magdalena wanted him to paint the sides also, but damned if he was going to waste good paint on something people were only going to piss on. Paint cost money, and she'd told him to watch costs so he would.

Zacarías finished painting the facade of the store and stood back to admire his handiwork. It was now a shocking white, rather than the comfortable adobe color of the surrounding houses and businesses. He balanced the thick paintbrush across the edges of the bucket, careful not to get any more paint on himself than he had to.

This was the second panadería that Zacarías had constructed for Magdalena. She insisted that the bakeries be painted, that customers wanted a "clean, new-looking place" from which to buy their bread and tortillas. Zacarías had been forced to order paint from San Antonio, since no one in any of the intervening towns bothered to paint the sturdy, if humble, adobe finishes of their dwellings.

In order to bring the project in at the cost Magdalena had specified, Zacarías had also been forced to perform much of the work himself, once the building had been framed and the oven constructed. He flexed his hands and rubbed his shoulder, which was sore from holding the heavy, unwieldy brush above shoulder level with one hand, while balancing the bucket on a rickety ladder with the other.

"Are you planning to paint the inside of the oven, too?" asked Bruno, his construction jefe, sarcastically. Although he found him gruff, Zacarías had come to like the man very much. He got the work done with a minimum of fuss, and didn't abuse his workers.

"I've ordered a special hue of dove-gray for that," answered Zacarías, "guaranteed not to disturb the sensibilities of the loaves while they are rising."

Magdalena had also wanted to limit the output of the bakeries to bread, but the customers had insisted, the women who baked the bread insisted, and even Zacarías had insisted that they also carry the humble corn tortilla, food of the people, foundation

of the meal—napkin, starch and silverware all rolled into one—
humble table upon which all manner of thing might be served. A
crusty loaf of bread didn't quite serve the same purpose.

Both men stood and watched the paint evaporate in the dry
air. They knew that it would be adobe-colored within weeks, if
not days, from the constant dust kicked up by the horses, mules,
people, and carts that trafficked along this road. It was a good location, Zacarías had to admit. Magdalena knew what she was up
to. The first bakery, in Nueva Rosita, was doing a booming business. Still, he hated to see his artistry soiled so quickly.

Then Zacarías had an idea.

"Are you going to start work on the floor today?" he asked
Bruno.

"If it doesn't disturb your fine artistry," answered Bruno. "Will
you be painting inside?"

"No, at least, I don't think so. Not today. I want to check on
something else. Could you put this paint away for me?"

"But of course," answered Bruno, continuing his mock
courtliness.

Zacarías walked down the street to the single storefront with
any color on it. The heavy door to Pedro Zaragoza's place of business was painted a bright turquoise color. Inside the door, which
stood open, Don Pedro was setting out eight matched chairs he
had just crafted.

"Don Pedrito," called Zacarías, using the nickname everyone
applied to the gnomelike man, "what beautiful chairs!"

"Thank you," said Don Pedro, adjusting his spectacles and
rolling down his sleeves. "They are for the rectory in Nuevo Laredo. Someone is supposed to fetch them later this week."

"Are you going to paint them?"

"No, I think just stain. They will probably be upholstered
once they arrive, and I don't know what color of material they
will use."

"I was wondering if I could borrow a little paint from you, something colorful."

"If you mean to paint the whole outside of a building again, like a cathedral, no," answered Don Pedro. "Paint is expensive."

"Don't I know it," answered Zacarías. "I just want to put a little decoration on the outside of the store, high up, where it will catch people's attention."

Don Pedro thought about that. "I have some blue paint you could use," he answered. "It would look nice against the white. And a little red from the santitos."

Don Pedro was also known for his retablos of saints, especially Saint Sebastian, stuck full of arrows. People seemed to identify with him in a country full of uncertainties.

"I knew that you could help me out," said Zacarías.

Don Pedro rummaged about at the back of his shop for a moment before returning with two small containers of paint. Through a half-opened doorway Zacarías could see an Indian boy without a shirt, about twelve years old, sitting quietly on the hard-packed, earthen floor. Don Pedrito liked his assistants very young, and always male.

"Now, I won't lend you a brush," said Pedro, looking up at Zacarías over the tops of his lenses. "Because they are very hard to come by, and I need to keep them very clean for my detailed work."

"I understand," said Zacarías, "and I thank you for your kindness. I will make sure that the bakery owner treats you with the respect you deserve."

Again, Pedro peered at Zacarías over the tops of his glasses, but rather than answer he merely squeezed out a small smile.

The coarse clump of horsehair that Zacarías had used to paint the entire wall would never do for his purposes. After casting about for the better part of an hour, Zacarías finally settled on a length of cord he used to bind shut his petate, the small leather trunk in which he carried his few personal belongings. It was made of a slightly finer grade of hair than the usual homemade rope.

Zacarías measured off a length equal to half his forearm and cut it with a knife. Unbraiding a few inches of it, Zacarías combed out the end with his fingers and began to shape it to a point with the knife. It was slow going. When Zacarías was satisfied with the results, he bound the other end of it around and around with twine to provide a comfortable grip, then left it while he went to get some lunch.

When Zacarías returned, the workers were pouring water over sections of the dirt floor and pounding it flat. This would go on for several days until the floor was as smooth and level as a baked surface. It would be sprinkled with water and swept every day to keep its pristine appearance.

Zacarías dipped the homemade paintbrush into the blue paint and began painting letters on the newly whited wall. Not bad, he thought, not bad. Bright, pretty. He hoped that he had enough to spell out P-A-N in big letters. That much, he figured, most people could figure out, even if they didn't read.

He was starting to wonder about Magdalena and her ideas. She had just returned from a trip to England and Ireland. To settle her husband's estate, she claimed, to protect it from dozens of his relatives who thought her incapable of managing her husband's new world empire.

I showed them, she had said, with that laugh and toss of her head that meant she had left scorched earth in her path. The only thing that superseded Magdalena's interest in sex was her interest in business. She would pay him for his work on both bakeries, she had said, only after the second, this one, was completed.

In the meantime, he could stay with her, where he would have no expenses. Zacarías felt that this didn't leave him much choice, although he was learning things in Magdalena's bed that probably couldn't be purchased for any amount of gold.

Zacarías realized that, if he painted all the blue first, he could clean the brush, or cut off a new section, and do all the red at the same time as well. He finished the outline of P-A-N, moving his tongue to help shape the letters without realizing it.

Zacarías wondered if Don Francisco O'Connell had had any idea that his widow would one day be telling his accountants what to do and how to do it. Zacarías knew that Magdalena had married Frank O'Connell at an early age, and that she had come from a poor family in the mountains. What he could not know was that she had been sold to him for two mules and a sack of gold.

The girl was kicking and scratching like a wild animal when O'Connell first saw her. He had been told she was beautiful and that her parents were anxious to be rid of her. Too spirited for the Mexican men or even the Indian, he had been told.

Magdalena, as she was named, was the fourth daughter of poor peasants from the mountains. Her parents looked Indian, but Magdalena's fair coloring betrayed Spanish blood, and they figured they could get a fair price for her in order to support their other children.

The family met him at a crossroads outside of Piedras Negras at dawn one July morning. Even as he approached the meeting place, O'Connell could hear her screaming epithets in Spanish and Indian at her parents. Just as they came into view, he saw her father cuff her soundly on the side of the head.

Magdalena staggered back, clutching her ear, before letting out an ear-piercing wail. She was clad only in an old flour sack, tied loosely at the waist, but even this humble costume did not hide her precocious beauty. He judged her to be about fourteen, straight-limbed, about five two, with waist-length, wavy black hair.

Frank O'Connell had tired of the whorehouses of Eagle Rock and Laredo and decided that he wanted a girl to live with him.

After certain inquiries among the traders and travelers, he learned of this family and their impossible daughter.

It was difficult to bargain with the father, whose Spanish was limited. It was also difficult to hear over the racket that Magdalena continued to send into the indifferent air. The mother and two small children hung back from the main crossroads, all of them with silent, hooded eyes. O'Connell had planned to offer one of his mules in exchange for the girl if she was pretty, but the father insisted that she was a virgin, that no man had touched her, and O'Connell could see that this was entirely possible.

The girl's beauty and agitation excited Frank in a way that he had not been aroused in many years, and they finally settled on two mules and a small sack of gold dust. When the girl understood that a bargain had been struck, she broke and ran to the mother, clinging and swearing obedience if they would just keep her. The mother pushed her away and finally kicked her viciously as the father was given possession of both mules held by O'Connell. The family hurried away up the trail back to their home in the mountains, having gained as much material wealth in one encounter as the father could possibly have earned by the sweat of his brow in over a year's time.

Using a small whip that he kept on his horse, O'Connell lashed the girl about the ankles until she fell. He did not want to mark her face if he could help it. Straddling her like a yearling, he tied her hands securely behind her, then tied a lead rope to his saddle horn. He resisted the urge to rape her right there, deciding to draw out the delicious anticipation until he had her in a more private setting. Afraid to put her on the horse with him, O'Connell led her into town on foot like a criminal.

Back at his hacienda, Don Francisco, as he was called, turned the girl over to his housekeeper, Rosa, with instructions to bathe and feed the girl, but not to let the ranch hands at her, as she was to be his alone. Don Francisco then returned to work, the piercing shrieks of the girl filling the yard as her dress was taken from her and she was doused in water.

The girl refused to eat for three days and tried to bolt whenever she saw an opportunity. Don Francisco had her kept naked in a bedroom, and when he figured she was weak enough, he entered and raped her to his great fulfillment and satisfaction. When the girl seemed properly subdued, he had her given clothes and brought to his dinner table for meals.

Magdalena had suspected that something unspeakably bad would happen to her when her parents got her up well before dawn that day. She had heard them whispering for several days, looking at her the way they had when they plotted to marry her off to a priest. That time she had gotten away and hid in the mountains for several days, until the padre had tired of waiting and moved on. She knew she shouldn't have returned, but her village was all she had known.

The big man with dead blue eyes her parents left her with had whipped her like an animal. He had seemed to enjoy it, and when he finally went in to her at the hacienda, she learned the extent of his cruelty. Besides the bleeding that the maid Rosa said was natural, there was pus and a painful discharge for several weeks after the don started having relations with her. Rosa said that was a sickness that the men carried, and gave her herb teas to bring down her fever and dull the pain. Finally, her womb scarred and sealed itself up against these assaults, and Magdalena was left barren.

Once the fevers abated and she was able to think clearly, Magdalena determined to learn all that she could about these barbarous people in the lowlands. She appeared at the dinner table quietly, listening until she learned enough Spanish to respond to Don Francisco's taunts. She figured out that he liked her to fight with him just a little bit, to behave insolently so that he could later punish her in his bedroom.

After submitting to him, when the don was spent and languid

on his pillow, Magdalena could extract promises from him, and so began to build her store of belongings. In this manner, she first acquired fine clothes from him, then her own horse, and finally a legal marriage, much to the consternation of his family and especially of his fiancée in Ireland.

Magdalena learned to dress like a lady, swear like a teamster, and ride a horse both side saddle and like a ranch hand. She never learned to read or write but could do sums in her head, and by watching the don run his business, knew which men were trustworthy and which were not.

When Don Francisco succumbed to poisoning from bad meat at the age of forty-three, he left his considerable land and cattle holdings to Magdalena, who was at that time twenty years of age.

Magdalena still kept a ragged doll in her bedroom, its body made of soft cloth and its head of porcelain, with real glass eyes and human hair. Zacarías had seen the doll sitting on her dresser amid the perfume bottles and brushes, dismissing it as a childhood memento. He could not know that it was the first gift which Magdalena had extracted from her husband in exchange for his cruelty. Every night that her bed was not also occupied by a man, Magdalena still slept with it in her arms, a constant promise to herself that things would get better one day.

But that younger brother of his in Ireland, Magdalena had said, with a backward glance at Zacarías. Not too bad. Not bad.

Zacarías humphed and applied more paint to the wall. He moved the bucket and began painting a new section of wall. It was a good thing these bakeries were not too big, so they really didn't take that long to complete. They would soon build almost identical structures in Villa Frontera and Músquiz, where local women were being trained in Magdalena's secret recipe for European-style bread.

Zacarías wiped the paint off his brush with a rag as best as he could and moved back up the ladder with the tin of red paint. He was starting to get the feel of this operation. Zacarías outlined the letters, already painted in blue, with red paint now, along the right edge. P-A-N. He could just reach the design to the right, now, where he had already painted stems and leaves in the dark blue paint. Zacarías began to paint rose petals, leaving white space between each one, imitating stenciled designs he had seen on furniture and signs in Saltillo.

Not bad, he thought, leaning back to survey his work. Not bad, for a man who couldn't be like other men. His wife's words came back to him without bidding, and the sudden memory of her stung him. With an involuntary jerk of his hand, Zacarías left several drops of red below the rose he had just completed, making it appear that the rose was bleeding, or had wept tears of blood down the beautiful white facade of the bakery.

Zacarías returned to Monclova that evening, exhausted and frustrated. Everything had gone wrong that day — traffic from the north had been interrupted by bandits, his perfectly tuned construction schedule had been delayed by over a week because building materials had been held up, and his foreman, Bruno, had returned to his home village for family business. There had been some disturbance in the road outside of town that Zacarías, ever wary of getting involved in a dangerous altercation, had avoided by following a small footpath that ran beside the river.

The day had been bitter cold, the smoke from a thousand houses hanging heavy and listless over the town after several days of still air. When Zacarías saw the priest's horse outside Magdalena's house, he resolved not to stay for dinner.

Father Newman was well over six feet tall and could sing a ballad as lustily as a pirate. With his red hair and green eyes like some exotic bird, no one could mistake him for a native. He left Ireland under cloudy circumstances, and it was only natural that the priest should become friends with la Señora Magdalena, who had become wealthy under equally nebulous weather.

Father Newman traveled a circuitous route through the hill towns of northern Mexico and South Texas, hurrying through lower elevations, as the heat didn't agree with him. He ministered primarily to the Irish settlers, performed weddings, christenings, and funerals as needed, extreme unction just in case, and left in his wake a succession of red-headed children.

Their mothers, simple women of the countryside, swore that the children resembled him by force of his personality alone, that once they were in the dark of the confessional and under that piercing green gaze, his spiritual presence was so powerful that they couldn't help but bear red-headed children, God and the holy Virgin preserve us all. Besides, didn't Tío Chui have reddish hair?

Only the married men were unhappy to see him coming, and even then, the women were so happy for months afterwards to have the burden of their sins removed from their consciences that it was almost worth it.

Every Monday night that he was in the region, Father Newman came to supper at Magdalena's house. After the first of these dinners when Zacarías was present, he managed to be absent on those evenings, for he could see that this was a private and necessary ritual. For Magdalena and Father Newman were the rarest of commodities, friends who could discuss everything from the price of wheat to the consequences of immortality.

Zacarías and Magdalena, on the other hand, found that they discussed less and less, and often Zacarías, returning late from the town where he was building one of her bakeries, simply slept against his saddle in the loft of the barn. After so much time spent sleeping in the open on rocky ground, he was just as comfortable there as in a feather bed.

Magdalena had prepared the dinner with her own hands: potatoes, squash, beef, tomatoes, chile, and of course, bolillos of white bread, fresh from the bakery. She handed Father Newman a steaming cup of coffee as they retired to the comfortable green recesses of her parlor to take their accustomed seats.

"I came across a man today, Padre," said Magdalena, "beating his black in the road. With a whip. Everyone let him be. No one stopped him."

"Did this trouble you?"

"Indeed it did, Padre. I felt those lashes as keenly as though they were on my own skin."

"I'm sure he had a reason for it," said the priest. "Often situations are not merely what they seem when we happen upon them."

"Nevertheless, the man was unarmed and could not defend himself. I could not help but feel that circumstances would have been different if he had been given a fair chance." Here, Magdalena hesitated and sipped her coffee. "The owner was an Irish settler, and a small man. He was hurling epithets the likes of which I had not heard since, well since—"

"Since the passing of Don Francisco?"

She nodded, her eyes focused on the middle distance, her pupils wide.

"He kept slaves, you know," said the priest.

"And well I know it," she snapped.

"I'm sorry. I did not mean to imply—"

"But you should, because that's all I was. Of course I freed the others when I could. How could I not?"

"Very easily. They were your property. As mistress of the hacienda, you could have offered to sell them their freedom."

"I could have, but I didn't. Who can put a value on a human life?"

"Many people have."

"It's barbaric. Besides, it's always been illegal in Mexico."

"Always?"

"Well, in modern times. Since our freedom from Spain."

"Although working the Indians to death is not illegal."

Magdalena shrugged. "Everybody works. We're born, we work, we die. I haven't worked anyone to death."

The priest smiled slightly and crossed his legs. Magdalena was in a dark mood, clearly troubled by the scene in the road. Father Newman decided not to press his point.

"I just can't see it leading to any good," Magdalena continued. "There's plenty of labor available. I never have trouble finding workers."

"Everyone is free to work for whom they choose, now," said Father Newman. "The war is over. The Confederates lost, and Texas is part of the United States."

"But many of the blacks are still treated as slaves. They have no place to go. They work to keep themselves in debt to the white settlers."

"The settlers can't afford more. Many of the Irish came with little more than the clothes on their backs."

"Who invited them?"

"The Mexican government. To act as a buffer with the Americans. Many are now in the second or even third generation of settlers."

Magdalena looked up at him. She was aware that Don Francisco had come to Mexico under the sponsorship of an empresario, an Irish speculator who had received land grants from the Mexican government, but she had never given much thought to the government's role in the whole process—or its motivations.

"Most of them are decent, hard-working Catholics. It's difficult to grow cotton. No one wants to harvest it if they can find other work," the padre continued.

"For a decent wage they would."

"You can pay a decent wage because of your husband's wealth. He built that wealth, in part, on the backs of slaves."

Magdalena leaned back in her chair and looked at the priest.

"You make it sound so simple," she said. "Keeping people, even black people, in bondage to run a profitable business. I can't help but feel it bodes ill for the Mexicans, this northern practice. How did they determine if someone was dark enough to be owned as a slave? What about mixed bloods?"

"It's not so much a matter of hue," said Father Newman, "as of economic and social class."

"Even worse. Who determines class? Was that Irishman I saw today, using language not fit for the gutter, and who you just told me is too poor to pay a decent wage for labor, more upper class than the man he was beating?"

Father Newman set down his cup. "I don't claim to understand why things are the way they are. It is part of our fall from grace, when Eve offered the apple to Adam, destroying our innocence and exiling us forever from the Garden, and Esau sold his birthright for a mess of pottage. That was probably the beginning of slavery. I only know that there is a certain order, imperfect as it is, and that without that order, all civilization would be reduced to chaos.

"The blacks are child-like, wild. By virtue of our Christianity, they have been entrusted to us. Those who were brought as slaves are the luckier ones. We are obligated to care for them, having brought them so far from the heathen jungle to which they are native. They need to be controlled for their own good."

"I know that black who was being beaten," said Magdalena. "His name is Joshua. He can read and write, which is probably more than can be said for his owner."

"Control of the mental faculties is not the same as control over the spirit. I'm sure the Devil can read and write," replied Father Newman.

"I'm sure he can," said Magdalena, who could not. She shifted her seat away from the fire, rustling and resettling her full skirts. "Slavery is an instrument of chaos," she said, "of the Devil,

I'm sure of it. People use high-flown ideas to defend it, like the state of the soul and the economy, but a business based on the purchase and sale of such fragile creatures as human beings doesn't make sense. Even Don Franscisco understood that when he chose cattle over cotton. The longer it is tolerated in these regions, the worse it will go for all of us. We show our devilish nature by putting others in chains, no matter how wild, or how childish they may be. Do we chain children?"

Magdalena stopped short as soon as she had said that, and Father Newman could see the pain in her eyes. It was the first time he had noted a weakness in the armor of her character. Magdalena was a carefully constructed person, as were many people in the frontier territories, and there was much about her that Father Newman did not know. But he felt that he now knew a little more than before.

"Like it or not, there is a natural order to things of which we are a part. We are his creations. We were given dominion over the birds of the air and the beasts of the field. And so it follows naturally that some people are given dominion over others."

"Like white men over black men, or Indians," said Magdalena.

"Precisely," said Father Newman, feeling that he had finally made his point.

"What about mestizos, mixed race? Mulattos?"

"That's unnatural."

"All of Mexico and Texas are unnatural? Do we not have a right to exist?"

Father Newman could see that he wasn't going to get out of this easily.

"It's not a matter of rights. It's simply not according to God's plan. But God offers forgiveness to all. As he said to the woman at the well, 'Go, and sin no more.' Those of mixed race should not repeat the sin. They should abstain from reproducing."

Magdalena burst out laughing. "Only a priest would reach

that conclusion and come up with that solution." She was sorely tempted to mention the red-headed children that populated the towns along Father Newman's habitual wanderings, but knew that he would not take kindly to it. She did not wish to lose his friendship, for she would miss these little talks. Most men, outside of courtship, were so dull.

As though reading her thoughts, he said, "We are all human, Magdalena, we are all weak in the flesh. I'm only telling you the ideal, not the reality, of the human condition."

The disagreement was not to be resolved that evening. Father Newman took his leave shortly thereafter and made his way to his lodgings at a nearby town.

5

Julio

Julio dreamed a pear tree. It started with a small, shiny, dark brown seed cast on the ground by a sparrow. The seed burrowed its sharp end into the earth and sprouted and took root in the fertile, if rocky, soil, sending twisting shoots into the air until a small sapling stood upon the uneven ground.

Unrelenting sun beat down upon it, shriveling the sparse grass that had protected the seed. This was followed by torrents of rain that washed away the rich nurturing soil, the mindless fumbling insects, the microscopic roots that the dead grass had left behind. Still the sapling thrived, although no one came to examine it, to acknowledge its existence, to praise its tenacity.

After the tree was three years old, someone came and pruned its branches, cutting away those turned inward, leaving only those turned out. The tree was now enclosed on one side by a low rock wall, and as it grew, its branches leaned out over the wall and seemed to see the countryside beyond. The land was beautiful, low rolling hills, cattle and sheep grazing near gentle orchards. The sky was vast and deep in hue, and although the pear tree was not the sort to reach beyond its own capabilities, it spread itself out in a way that seemed to mimic the sky above, especially on days when flat-bottomed *clouds scudded in from the west, like ships sailing upon an invisible sea.*

The pear tree, pyrus communis, *its leaves dark and glossy, gave forth delicious pale blossoms, pollinated by wild bees, and then it bore fruit.*

Julio, a young man and still vigorous, stepped up to the sturdy tree, now about seven feet tall, and took one of the fruits.

Grasping the pear firmly, he took a bite: the flavor was indescribable, for each pear contained the essence of Mariana. As he looked back up at the tree, he could see that each pear was a miniature of her, folded about herself, waiting patiently to be discovered. Each bite was redolent of the aroma, the scent, the taste of Mariana, and filled Julio with such a terrible longing that he desired to eat each and every fruit of the tree. Yet he despaired of ever completing the job, for each bite contained such a wealth of information about Mariana, the melancholy look she had in the late afternoon, the texture of the skin over the back of her right thumb, the way she rolled her arms in a rhythm to knead the dough for bread, the scent of lavender that followed her after a bath, a coil of dark hair. . . .

And her thoughts! The pear contained, at last, a way to understand Mariana's thoughts. Julio was dumbstruck at the things in her mind: the percentage of sunlight that permeated the kitchen on a given day of the year; the number of birds that flocked to the fountain; the exact hue of green that was her favorite among the foliage of the garden, a green found only on the underside of the dagger-shaped leaf of a certain lily; the feel of the cobblestones under her shoes as she walked into town. . . .

Julio realized, having taken that one bite of that one pear, that if he continued to eat the pears, even this pear, he might find what she really thought of him, and of their son, and he longed for this and dreaded it at the same time. For who truly desires to know another's thoughts, even one so close and dear? What if the truth were ever so slightly different from the perception, yet different enough to cause despair and devastation of the heart?

He stood beside the sturdy little pear tree, its bark dark and smooth where the young goats had come to rub against it in the spring. He noted its proximity to the stone wall, and wondered if its roots would undermine the wall and cause it to crumble.

Just at that moment, Julio awoke and heard very distinctly in the courtyard outside another bit of stone work itself loose and fall from the wall. Mariana slumbered beside him, wrapped in sleep and white cotton, her thin dark hands upon the blanket, her eyelids fluttering slightly as she dreamed of being a pear tree in a rough yet loving land.

Julio made the coins dance across the plate one last time before he grew bored with the trick. A minor miracle. Hardly worthy of an heir to the teachings of Maimonedes.

He sighed and turned to the small, barred window that opened onto the courtyard. A lone bird was singing outside. Ever since Zacarías had left Saltillo, Julio had not had the heart to pursue his lifelong study of the Cabala. No one had heard from Zacarías for three months.

Julio remembered him as a little boy. He had been their only child, always restless, always vocal, as though to produce enough noise for himself and his silent mother. Mariana indulged him, of course, always making his favorite foods and taking him with her to the mercado. Those two had a special bond, thought Julio, something he had never managed to attain with his son. When Zacarías was born, Julio feared Mariana's silence would hinder the use of his tongue. As it was, Julio was sure that Zacarías' closeness to his mother, as an only child, had somehow rendered him unfit for responsible manhood.

The bird stopped singing abruptly. Julio got up and opened the heavy door to his study and looked out. The cat, Melchorio, crouched low on the ground and twitched his tail, but the prey was gone. The cat gave Julio a blank look and feigned total indifference.

Mariana came along the breezeway with Julio's afternoon coffee, which he took alone in his study. She looks sadder and more beautiful than ever, thought Julio. My fallen angel, condemned to earth for a lifetime.

. . .

Mariana was the youngest in her large family, a last blessing to her parents in their old age. Thin and long-limbed, she was quick to play and quick to learn.

The Morelos family, neighbors, had moved recently from Monterrey and looked down on them. Judios, they said. We know your name from those Christ-killers in Monterrey.

Let them go, said her father. God will take care of them in his own good time. The Morelos children heard this.

La Señora Morelos gave birth to twins. They were frail and small, and the slightest touch marked them with a bruise, like overripe pears. They lingered for two months before dying.

Mariana lagged behind her sisters walking home from school one day, examining insects. She loved to sketch them. Suddenly, she heard voices behind her.

Hey, Christ-killer!

She turned to see four or five of the Morelos. Her sisters were nowhere in sight.

You're father cursed our family, and now the babies are dead.

Mariana tried to run, but more children came and surrounded her.

One of the boys began to poke at her skirt with a stick, trying to lift the edge of the hem. My father says your father cast the evil eye on my mother when she carried the twins.

That's not true! screamed Mariana. My father's a good man!

Each time she tried to get away, one of them cut her off, like a pack of dogs. Christ-killer! they began shouting, then chanting in unison. Christ-killer!

A pebble was tossed, then a rock. See what it feels like to suffer like our Lord Jesus!

Mariana screamed. More rocks were thrown. She raised her arms to protect her face and tried to shelter against the stone wall behind her. ¡Quítense! was the last word that Mariana heard. It was the voice of her father, and she knew that she would be saved.

Mariana was breathing, but unconscious when her father carried her home in his arms. The doctor said that she was in a trance state and should be moved as little as possible. There was nothing he could do, he said, except visit each day. He advised bathing her in cool water and dripping a little mint water down her throat.

For five days and nights Mariana's family kept vigil, taking turns at her bedside. Her father, overcome with grief, refused to sleep or eat and stayed by her almost constantly.

On the sixth day Mariana's countenance changed. Her bruised face relaxed into a beatific smile, and the fever that had plagued her relinquished its hold. Mariana's father agreed to take nourishment and slept for a full day and night.

Mariana's hair, which had grown increasingly brittle with the fever, began to fall out in handfuls. Her sisters brushed it away until the smooth, shining skin of the skull was exposed.

Mariana's skin began to glow, and the many cuts and bruises to disappear. Her whole body began to give off a sweet smell like autumn roses. Mariana began to resemble an Egyptian statue, serene and immobile, a golden glow surrounding her.

Her mother, who had seemed to be in shock all this time, began to pray and cry, for she thought her daughter was surely dying. But Mariana seemed to repose in sweet dreams, although she never opened her eyes and seldom stirred.

Finally, on the evening of the ninth day, her hands began to twitch where they lay on the covers. Her father stood and touched them, but she reached out past him, opened her eyes and said

"Angeles."

Then Mariana seemed to wake from a dream, looked at her father, and hugged him. But she never spoke again.

Mariana seldom left the house after that, refusing to let her mother out of sight for many months. She did not return to school, although one of the nuns came to the house to ask that she be allowed to continue her studies. She had been the best student at the school for girls and was only two years short of a certificate. Someone would even take her to and from school, said the nun, to guarantee her safety from "certain rough elements."

But Mariana refused to go. She sat for long hours by the kitchen stove, a faraway look in her eyes, the same beatific smile on her face. When her hair grew back it was heavy and straight, while before it had been wispy and curly.

At the age of twenty-four she consented to marry Julio, an assistant apothecary to her father and a frequent visitor to their household. Her parents were so relieved that she had married that they gave their own home on the hillside above town as her dowry, the one with the beautiful, ancient fountain of sweet water, and moved in with one of Mariana's older sisters. They died shortly afterward, as though their duty to their children had been fulfilled.

Mariana continued to dream by the fire, and Julio, content to have a pious spouse, performed many of the duties normally expected of a wife.

Julio had heard the stories of her attack and recovery, and having seen the girl himself in golden repose, was convinced that Mariana had been blessed with a sacred vision. He longed to experience such a vision himself and spent long hours submerged in studies of the Cabala or chanting prayers in hopes of attaining a state of religious ecstasy.

When Julio's wife went outside, animals seemed to come to her. The beautiful courtyard, which might have been peaceful and empty all morning, would suddenly fill with doves, cooing and strutting. They would even land on her outstretched hand. Julio had watched her offer her silent lips for an affectionate peck.

Squirrels came to her, and dogs dropped their fierce demeanor. All nature seemed in accord with her, as though in opposition or apology for the terrible treatment she had received at the hands of humanity as an innocent child. Mariana took all of this as her due, remaining calm and demure, casting her eyes down when on her husband's arm in public. Only when she was alone did she seem to bloom, enclosing all of nature in her generous embrace.

Mariana used a sign language with Julio that she and her father had devised and shared through her adolescence. Her face and hands were so expressive that she seldom had to resort to pen and paper to convey her thoughts.

Julio was still a child, and stood at a gate to the Garden of Eden. Come in, beckoned an angel with blue wings. Go away, commanded another with fiery pink wings and a sword protruding from his mouth.

Julio was afraid. He did not know which angel to obey. Suddenly a book appeared on the ground before him. It opened and words begin to appear in flame. As each word appeared, it began to consume the page, so that Julio could not read what it said, though he knew it was very important, and that he would understand a great many things if he could read those words.

Santa sangre sagrada. Santo nombre de Dios.

The forty-seven names of his divine mercy, and in one of them lies my son's future.

I do not disbelieve, said Julio later to his wife. I only do not understand.

Understanding does not come through the mind, said Mariana, but through the heart. To return through the heart.

Julio concentrated on the scriptures in his hands. He closed his eyes and began to recite, slowly, eighteen of the Psalms of David. As the last words passed his lips, he gradually opened his eyes to see a blister of light rising before him. He stared into it intently, until a face came into view. This startled Julio greatly, for the face appeared to be peering back at him, an equally confused look on its face.

The face was that of an elderly woman, garishly dressed with paint on her eyelids and a bright scarf around her head.

"Gitana," whispered Julio.

He could see nothing but sky behind her, but then she rose into a standing position and walked away. It seemed she had been looking at a particular spot on the ground. Julio's view rose with her and he was able to follow her figure as she trudged across a desolate yard to a small house of curious design.

It was turquoise in color, with rounded corners, and seemed to be constructed of a thin material resembling metal. She climbed some precariously placed loose mortar steps and opened and shut a flimsy metal door behind her. Julio could see vast open spaces behind the house and a line of purple mountains on the horizon but he did not recognize the place. As he watched, the image faded, the bubble of light diminishing to a pinpoint, then vanishing.

He did not know what this meant. Julio suspected that the woman lived in a different *shemitah*, a future aeon, in which the laws of the Torah could be interpreted in an entirely different light.

Julio had come to think of Zacarías as resembling an ocotillo, that rangy, cactus-like tree, *fouqueria splendens*, reaching for the sky, never satisfied with what it can draw from the parched ground.

Julio could never understand how something so alien to him, so much a part of the new world landscape, could have issued from his loins. For although Julio had been born in Mexico, as had his father and grandfather, going back for twelve generations, he had the heart of an old world man, a Jew who still turned to his wife each Passover and said, "Next year in Jerusalem."

And although he had never been there, had hardly ventured from his corner of Mexico—once with his father on an expedition to Mexico City—Julio knew the dimensions of the Holy City as though they had been burned into his soul. He knew the designs in gold on the walls of Solomon's temple, the true measure of a cubit, and had calculated how much oil would have been needed to keep the eternal light burning for eight days had a miracle not occurred.

He imagined the landscape to be much like that around Saltillo, high ground surrounded by desert, rugged mountains pointing away to the north. The city itself must be of crumbling stone buildings — though of ancient design, rather than Spanish colonial. He had often thought of himself walking those holy streets, munching on a handful of dried figs until he came to the wailing wall, where he could worship as his ancestors had worshipped, crying for the dead, praying for the living, trying not to fear for the future.

Next year.

And yet here was his son, turned away from the holy scriptures. Julio should have intervened when Zacarías wanted to marry a non-Jew. But who could really tell anymore? Half of the families, although they would not admit it, had Jewish blood. The other half, although they would not admit it, dark as they were, had Indian blood. It was only a matter of time, Julio thought, before some had both.

The community of Jews, carried on in secret all these years, was still there, but the edges had become more and more blurred with that of the general population. There were people lighting candles on Friday night who hadn't the faintest idea why they were doing it. Only blind tradition maintained the tenuous thread.

Still, Estela had seemed a decent enough young woman. Her father was well respected and a regular customer who paid his bills. What more could one ask? Except that they weren't Jews.

Mariana had counseled Julio to let Zacarías follow his heart. Julio had, and Zacarías had followed his heart right out onto the pagan desert. Like the ocotillo, he twisted this way and that, never satisfied with his present condition, always seeking out the unknown, the high country, the streams and crevices where only a goat could be happy. The Indians used the plant to cure fright in children, but Zacarías caused Julio the greatest fear of all, fear of the unknown and the future.

And now this business with the widow.

Oh yes, people had seen him. At first, it was just that his son was doing work for her. That was fine. At least he was doing honest work for a living, although it was outdoor labor.

My son the builder, Julio had thought, trying out the sound of it. My son builds bakeries. He tried to be satisfied with that.

But then, people kept seeing him in her company, at all hours, and it seemed that he stayed with her.

A hired hand, thought Julio. What of it? She puts him up with the other hired hands. But Zacarías was seen with the widow on his arm, was known to have had dinner with that foul priest who occasionally came through Saltillo. Julio had overheard conversation, people implying that Zacarías was very close to the widow. "Like this," as they say, holding up two fingers together, and looking the way people look when they say things like that.

My son the adulterer. Julio tried that out for the sound of it, too, and didn't like it. Zacarías had taken Estela in legal matrimony, had children with her, Julio's grandchildren, and he should be faithful to her, non-Jew that she was.

Julio would have had a lot to say at the wailing wall these days, a lot of bitter tears to shed. My son, he thought. My only son.

What would next year bring for all of them?

Julio closed his eyes and concentrated on the future. His breathing became calm and regular and he seemed, to all appearances, to have fallen asleep. Only his lips moved slightly, as though reading scriptures or answering an occasional question from an unseen interlocutor.

When he opened his eyes again, they had a faraway cast in them, as if the eyes of a sleepwalker.

Again Julio saw the bubble of light rise before him, off of one of the metal plates he kept in his study, and again a desert landscape resolved itself within the bubble. But this time he saw what he had been searching for, across time and distance: he saw Zacarías.

Zacarías struggled up a steep cliff on foot, holding the reins of his mare and urging her upward. A burro struggled behind, laden with prospecting equipment and protesting loudly at this indignity. The land fell off steeply behind them, and Julio could see swallows darting through the thin air that surrounded the precarious trail to which Zacarías clung with his free hand.

Julio gasped and his eyes filled with tears. Surely Zacarías would not survive this climb. God did not make humans to live like animals, to struggle alone without a community.

Julio leaned forward and grasped the edge of the table, for he found himself suffering an attack of vertigo at the frightful sight.

At the same moment, Zacarías paused and passed his hand before his eyes, shaking his head as though to clear it. Just at that moment, two children appeared on the trail above him, calling out a name that Julio did not understand in their strange, alien tongue.

To Julio's surprise, Zacarías responded in kind, and the children, who looked as nonchalant as though out on a Sunday picnic, relieved Zacarías of his pack and took the horse by the reins, dancing ahead as though they climbed this trail in the sky everyday.

The vision faded, and Julio, dizzy with vertigo, stood shakily and flung open the door to his study. There, as ever, lay his peaceful garden, level and unmoving, his wife looking up questioningly from the lily to which she appeared to have bent her attention moments before. Julio leaned back against the cool stone wall and breathed deeply, not knowing whether to share this vision with Mariana, who did not altogether approve of his explorations in the supernatural.

Ever since his dream about Mariana as a pear tree and his meditation on Zacarías as an ocotillo, Julio had felt it was only fair that he subject himself to the same scrutiny, the same metaphor of the plant in the eternal garden of God's will.

If he was any plant, he sighed, it was a jade plant, *crassula argentea*—sturdy, demanding little, nearly eternal in its longevity. The many branched, many-leafed succulent was often grown in huge jarones in courtyards, where it provided its dusty green hues as a background for more spectacular plants, never complaining if it was left outside, never asking for more than an occasional drenching to rehydrate its many fleshy leaves.

The jade plant is tenacious and able to grow in a confined space. It is intricate in formation and pattern, gnarled, perhaps even repulsive to the eye accustomed to appreciate more ethereal beauties, but simpatico in its own way. As the plant must be cultivated over a long period of time, so perhaps must its appreciation be cultivated.

The jade is a plant that was discovered in the new world, then transported back to grace the gardens of the Medicis and other noble families who took it upon themselves to propagate the herbaceous riches of the new empires. It is adaptable to extreme conditions and straddles the two continents. It stands as a reminder, saying, there is continuity. There is a tradition. All is well. All is well.

Although Julio had been born in Mexico, as had many generations before him, he was a spiritual product of the old world, never quite at ease in this wild, open space, where the races intermingled freely and a man could outrun his reputation, if he ran far enough. Julio was rooted to place, to order, to predictability.

Julio had a jade plant in his own garden, a massive creature that was so old no one knew who had originally planted it. It had come with the house when Julio moved into it upon his marriage to Mariana. For all he knew, it had been there since the house was built two hundred and fifty years earlier.

The jade had grown steadily larger until it occupied a huge

earthen pot in a secluded corner of the courtyard. This was Melchorio's favorite retreat, and he could often be found lying in the shade at the base of the pot, stretched full-length to distribute his own body heat onto the cool flagstones beneath him.

Julio had never been good at articulating his thoughts, did not have the gift of the tongue like other members of his family, and lacked the refined looks that distinguished Mariana and her relatives. Julio had a mind for details, however, and could mix up a medicinal draught while barely consulting the pharmaceutical texts. In fact, the work at the pharmacy was so easy for Julio, who almost always worked at the back counter, and let his more loquacious nephews talk to the customers, that he hardly gave it a thought.

Julio worked from six A.M. to noon every day filling orders and reordering supplies, including the papers and chemicals needed for his own explorations of the metaphysical, the seventy meanings of each verse of the seventy faces of the Torah. In the afternoons, while most people took a siesta, Julio retreated to his dark and mysterious study, there to pray and plan his activities for the evening, when he could meditate without distraction.

Mariana watched all of this with understanding and forbearance. She saw that Julio labored so hard to understand everything that he missed the most obvious: the gentle breeze of the night air as it flowed smoothly into the city each evening, the delicate stems by which miniature orchids hung from their stalks. She knew that he loved her and loved Zacarías, but she was not sure he knew that it was Zacarías' love and fear of him that had probably driven their son away.

Mariana counted her stitches and resumed work on her lacework as Julio retreated to his study for the afternoon. From beneath her skilled fingers, sensitive enough to tell every grade of cotton and silk thread by touch, emerged an open-work piece of a spider's web. The oval orb held two exquisite praying mantises in its deadly embrace, and Mariana pondered the design of the spider for a few moments before setting down her work and going outside to find a living model to scrutinize.

In the afternoons, Julio tended his gardens, both actual and metaphysical, giving himself over to God's wisdom both through his creations and through the mystical teachings of the Cabala. He sought symmetry, order, divine balance in all that he said and did.

But the landscape of Zacarías' existence troubled Julio's mind. His thoughts were disturbed by the rough country of Esaiah's reported adventures — that he lived in a cave eating roots and wild game while hunting for gold; that he lived in a whorehouse and cleaned the rooms for a living; that he had a mistress and was prospering. Julio closed his eyes and saw sage and rocks and rabbit bush, briars and thistles, unclean lizards and animals with cloven hooves dancing on the sides of unnaturally steep cliffs.

Julio mused on the nature of the garden, and the nature of man. The garden, he thought, is used in literature for a good reason. The garden is symbolic of our control over the natural world, albeit in a limited way: the assertion of our will over a defined bit of nature.

And not just our will, for the garden can be an analogue for God's relationship to the world, and us in it. As Adam was given charge of the original garden, of the birds of the sky and the beasts of the field, so we have been charged with the conservation of the natural world. The garden even illustrates God's relationship to our existence, thought Julio, for as God created us in His image and demanded that we worship and obey him, so he has charged us with shaping the natural world to obey our wishes, to reflect our needs and hence, to be a further emanation of God's existence.

The more Julio thought about it, the more the idea appealed to him. It might be possible to affect the world around him by controlling his garden. If the minor exercises, *kavvanot*, and experiments that he had conducted in his study could provide him a glimpse into the future, then perhaps by approaching his garden with the same attitude of prayer and meditation Julio could influence the forces in his life that continued to defy his wish for wholeness in the world—namely, his son.

Like the world recreated in a book, or a meditative exercise, with its many levels of existence beginning with the thought of God and endlessly reflected in His holy names, perhaps the garden, containing a bit of the earth and landscape of Mexico, could be considered a miniaturization of Mexico. As such, by moving a plant here, by adding water there—and with the force of his meditations—perhaps Julio could manipulate events in such a way that Zacarías would quit his wandering and return home, would return to his rightful place in the world as a dutiful son and husband.

Julio attacked his garden with zeal. The garden, which had not received so much attention in many years, soon began to show a transformation.

At first Julio merely trimmed the existing plants so that they gave an overall appearance of order: the bushes were clipped into neat balls, the flowers were deprived of overreaching stems or long branches, the trees were cut back to their basic structures, and much of the undergrowth was exposed to the open sky for the first time in years.

But that was not enough for Julio. After further contemplation, Julio cut back or removed every plant that seemed slightly wild or reminded him too much of the desert landscape. He pruned and plucked and bridled the plantings to the extent that the courtyard soon became wan and severe. The roses looked strangled and the boxwood hedges hugged the ground in a defeated manner. The jacarandas and orange trees, their roots unprotected from the harsh sun, demanded more water, and the fountain gurgled more loudly without the muffling effect of undergrowth. The temperatures in the garden also became more extreme—chillier in the morning, and hotter in the afternoon—and Mariana had to wear a heavier rebozo when she first ventured out at the light of day. By afternoon the sun was merciless in its intensity, and even the plants that Julio had meant to protect, that he considered "civilized" for his new conception of a garden, began to suffer.

Mariana, seated at her usual place on the fountain's edge, looked small and unprotected amidst the austere openness created by Julio's innovative approach to his garden. It had become a place of intervention, of restriction, of strife, of a contest of wills between her husband and the natural inclinations of a group of plants and animals to create for themselves a climate of nurture and co-resplendence. For by forbidding the plants to have a free will in order to banish his thoughts of the wilderness, Julio had inadvertently created a desert region that reflected the desolation of his own heart.

Julio's books grew dusty with neglect, for they could not cure the despondence that hung over him the way the heavy smoke from many cookstoves lingered over the town on a winter morning.

6

Estela

Estela played the piece through once, and then again. She felt moody and irritable and light all at once. She stood, then promptly sat down again. Her ankle still pained her, three weeks after the sprain, but she was determined to attend the Feast of the Kings festivities with her children.

Estela had already been measured for a grey silk dress, the silk from her father's store. After all, she thought, it was her duty to see that they continued to have a normal life in the community, even if Zacarías was gone. Blanca always criticized her for dressing so conservatively, but Estela couldn't help herself. She was uncomfortable in bright clothes that brought attention to her person, and since her mother's passing when she was only twelve, she had taken to subdued colors and conservative styles.

In fact, she was very pleased with the dress, which was of a gorgeous watered silk that she would not have spent money on herself. Don Horacio had, of course, given it to her when she admired it.

"Take it," he had said, handing her the bolt and waving it away. "Have the dressmaker bring back what is left. You deserve something special."

His attitude, since Zacarías' last disappearance, had alternated between an anger that seemed directed as much at Estela as anyone else, and a fatherly solicitousness that manifested itself in gifts and confusing advice.

Although Estela had always run her own household, purchased supplies and paid the servants, Don Horacio was acknowledging it for the first time. He had been shocked and angered when Estela barred Zacarías from their joint assets but conceded that she had done the right thing when he saw the enormous sums Zacarías had taken for his adventures. It was the dowry money he had settled on Estela on her wedding day that was fueling Zacarías' expeditions. After he became aware of the situation, Horacio tried to share his cost-saving ideas with Estela, for which he was famous.

"You should buy wheat in quantity when it's cheap," he told her, "and store it."

"Where?" asked Estela. "The storage shed is full of Zacarías' ore samples. It looks like a volcano erupted in there."

"Then put it in the parlor. It'll be safe from the rats there."

Estela held her tongue. That was why her father could not keep a housekeeper, because he stored wheat in the parlor, sacks of tea in the kitchen, and bales of undyed cotton in the entryway. When Blanca and Estela married and moved out of the house, it had been left to Manzana and Membrillo to care for Don Horacio, until La Sirena took the twins away. Since then, a series of housekeepers had moved in and out of Don Horacio's home as quickly as they could find new situations.

The minute she entered the grand room, Estela felt Captain Carranza's eyes upon her. She greeted the neighbors, made sure that the girls had punch to drink, and saw that Gabriel immediately scooted off to join his friends from el Ateneo.

Estela felt the color rise to her cheeks as she slowly turned to scan the party, trying not to meet the gaze that she could feel fixed upon her slim figure in the modest grey dress. The glass cup and saucer she held, imported from Europe, shook slightly in her gloved hands.

When she finally saw him in full dress uniform, Estela nearly stopped breathing.

"Mamá, what's the matter?" asked Victoria, then stopped when she also spotted him.

Estela heard Victoria whispering to María, but did not care. It was the Feast of the Kings, January 6th, and they had spent Christmas without Zacarías. Estela figured there wasn't much more that could be said in Saltillo about their family that hadn't already been said.

"Good afternoon, Señora," said the Captain, at her side after excusing himself from his military friends. "I trust that you have kept yourself well?"

"Yes, Doctor, I have. You remember my daughters, Victoria and María?" said Estela. The girls curtsied, all lace and curls and blushes.

"Indeed I do," said the Captain in a booming voice. "How could I forget such lovely roses, such perfect examples of budding womanhood?"

The girls retreated under this compliment to leave Estela and the Captain face to face.

Estela began to examine the black piping at her wrist.

Carranza, who had enjoyed chasing the girls away, said to Estela more gently, a smile still in his voice, "and your ankle, Señora, has it healed properly?"

"Oh, yes, Doctor," and Estela used this form of address more for the people around them than for the Captain. "It was fine after a few days of having my children do the heavier work."

"And your husband, he did not help you also?"

"My husband is away on business," she answered, a bit haughtily. She hoped that he would not ask more, yet wondered how much he knew.

Five musicians in formal charro dress entered the room, took their places in a corner, and struck up a lively waltz. Women in sweeping dresses took to the floor with their escorts, several of them in the bright costume of the china poblana, a glorified peasant dress made up of dazzling colors. Much gold jewelry was in evidence. Next to them, Estela looked positively subdued, but her jet earrings shone brightly against her cheeks and her irrepressible hair was already beginning to creep out of its chignon.

"Madame?" said Captain Carranza, offering his arm.

"Oh, do you think I should?" asked Estela, a bit anxiously. "I mean, with my ankle?"

"If you tire, we will stop," said the Captain, smiling.

A rosy flush crept back up Estela's cheeks as she allowed herself to be led out onto the dance floor. She had been feeling awfully warm lately, and a bit light-headed in the morning. Too much "hot" food, her mother would have said, and would have prescribed strong draughts of herbal tea. She smiled at this, and the Captain, thinking the smile was directed at him, rewarded her with a dazzling smile of his own as he swept her into the swirling crowd that now clogged every inch of the dance floor.

When Estela heard the slow steps of a horse on the street later that night she wasn't surprised when they stopped below her window. It was late, after the children were asleep and the only people out were drunks and prostitutes, but she arose as though expecting it, though she told herself later, she really hadn't. There sat the doctor on his tall stallion, his mustache gilded with moonlight. He was humming to himself, a little distracted, perhaps a bit drunk. He was looking at the sky and humming, as though waiting for a star to fall upon him, or the moonlight to transport him to another world.

Not knowing exactly what to do, not having any practice in these matters, Estela redressed herself. She did not wish to imply anything improper if nothing improper was meant.

Estela stood and listened at the corridor for a moment. Satisfied that her children were asleep, she opened the door gingerly, peering around its edge like a frightened child.

Dr. Carranza's face broke into a broad smile and he dismounted. Walking slowly up to Estela he took her hands in his and sang very gently, very softly, the words to an old song, words full of yearning, holding his face close to hers.

Finally she drew him inside and shut the door.

Victoria did not know what made her get up that night. Perhaps it was too much punch and food at the party that made her step gingerly across the cold tiles to squat over her chamber pot. Perhaps it was the insomniac sinsonte, the mockingbird, that often broke the night silence with her lonely song.

In any case she was sure she heard low voices from the front of the house. Wrapped in a mist of sleep, Victoria followed the voices until they distinguished themselves into that of a man and woman exchanging low giggles and words. Victoria was mystified. Had her father returned at this hour?

Groggily looking from the dim passage that led from the dining room to the parlor, Victoria saw two people she did not recognize on the red velvet sofa. The man had his back turned to her, and the woman, her face obscured by the man's body, uttered low, cat-like noises. Victoria's eyes fell on a pair of grey kidskin shoes kicked carelessly aside and recognized them as her mother's.

Victoria was about to step forward, the word "Mamá" already on her lips, when she saw the uniform jacket folded carefully across a chair. She turned and stumbled down the passageway, biting her hand to stifle her cry. She lay wide-eyed in her bed as the noises continued without interruption. María, sleeping heavily in the bed next to hers, did not stir.

When morning came, as bright as any January morning, their mother did not arise early; not that she was expected to the morning after a party, but she usually got up early anyway, her nature being to try and oversee every day's activities.

Victoria opened the front door and looked out into the street, half expecting to find the tall white stallion. But the street was empty save for a servant desultorily sweeping the cobblestones a few houses away.

Perhaps it was a dream, thought Victoria. She had thought often enough of the men in uniform who were stationed in Saltillo on their way to this campaign or that. She had gone as far as to wonder what a kiss with one of them would be like, or the touch of one of their hands on her body.

She turned to look into the dark parlor, the sun just beginning to illuminate it. The furniture stood staidly in its place, the rich colors looking washed out in the morning light. If the room held any secrets of the previous night, it was not about to give them up to her.

Victoria scuffed her feet across the cool tiles as she walked to the kitchen, an old shawl trailing behind her. It was high time, she thought, that she had a soldier of her own.

Victoria's suspicions were confirmed when her mother finally arose and came out of her bedroom. Estela hummed softly to herself, seemingly oblivious to everyone and everything around her. She drew cold water from the pump and retreated to the laundry area to bathe in private. Why, thought Victoria, did her mother need a bath the day after a party?

As her mother came into the kitchen, toweling her wet hair,

Victoria searched her face for change, for explanation.

"What are you looking at?" asked Estela.

"Nothing," said Victoria, averting her eyes.

Estela continued to hum as she sipped her coffee and stroked the head of the gray cat that, sensing a receptive lap, insinuated itself between her arms.

As Lent approached, Estela's mood remained the same. Her thin face seemed to glow, and the neighbors began to compliment the girls on how beautiful their mother had become. They agreed, privately, that her separation from Zacarías seemed to have lifted a great burden from her heart.

Estela, for the first time in her life, let things take their course. She stopped haggling over every penny with the merchants and let Josefina do the housekeeping in her own good time and manner. Estela smiled at the neighbors, cooed at babies, watered the plants, and blessed the air she breathed everyday for her special secret, her prince on a palomino, her soldier from the capital who whispered compliments into her ears unlike any that she had ever heard before.

Estela had never really experienced romance. While European and Mexican poets declaimed its powers and declared all of them subject to its lurid red banner, the truth is that there was very little room for it in most of their lives. The fact that Estela and Zacarías had been allowed to marry each other was considered a triumph of romance over practicality, since there were no good financial or social reasons for the match.

Yet Zacarías, Estela had to admit, had not been a romantic sort of person. Though he had visited her father's home faithfully while they were courting, he had always been a bit timid with her. At the time, she had found his shyness touching and appealing. It seemed to set him apart from the soldiers and merchants who eyed every woman in the street, claiming for themselves what could be got for free. But even as a married man, he had seemed uncomfortable with physical intimacy and never displayed affection in front of others, not even the children, as though there were some evil in it. Their encounters in the bedroom were furtive and brief, always conducted under cover of darkness, silence, and secrecy.

Estela took this to be her due as a married woman but she wondered at her own hard-heartedness that she did not feel passion stirring in her heart after these encounters. The poetry she and her sister Blanca read claimed that it should be otherwise, that she should sing hymns to the heavens for the sake of mortal passion, that she should feel in tune with the music of the spheres. Instead she felt a vague dissatisfaction, as of opportunities missed in Zacarías' blind groping.

When she told him of her first pregnancy, she had expected a greater warmth between them. Instead Zacarías kissed her chastely on the forehead and didn't touch her for the duration of her confinement. The same was true for the other two, as though he welcomed the respite from his conjugal duties. Estela had felt like a brooding hen, an incubator, growing increasingly rounder as the months passed, her sole purpose in life the delivery of a child.

Zacarías loved and welcomed the children in his own reserved way, yet he was gone so much of the time that they had largely grown up without him. He always seemed to be off in the hills during the important sacraments in their lives — christenings, Christmas, Easter. He claimed that it was because he had to do his explorations during the dry season, when the roads were still passable, but Estela wondered if it wasn't his ties to his Jewish family. Zacarías said that it was not important to him, that all of that was part of a past that did not concern them, but Estela wasn't so sure.

With the doctor, on the other hand, she felt as giddy as a schoolgirl. Shorn of the trappings of decency, her relationship with him felt reckless and wonderful. He brought her flowers and candy and sang to her in a low, breathless voice as he drew his body increasingly closer and closer to hers, until she felt that the air between them might erupt in flame.

Carranza reveled in her body, praising the luster of her skin, the shape of her ankles—which he claimed were now shaped differently from each other—even the contours of her head. He displayed his own body to her, preening, insisting that she look and see how she made him rise. He made her blush and laugh and, in their increasing intimacy, made her feel a dazzling joy that she could not name.

Part of her knew that this was foolhardy, that it could not last, but in these days of uncertainty, of shifting boundaries and loyalties, of families picking up to move north or south or who knows where, of husbands run off to women of ill repute, nothing was predictable; and for once in her life, Estela would enjoy fresh fruit when it was offered to her.

Their time together was innocent enough, she thought. While they took great pains to keep their meetings secret, she did not share with the Captain the same intimacies she had offered her husband, and José Luís seemed content, even honored, with what she was willing to give. He covered the knuckles of her hands with fervent kisses and made her name sound like a caress.

For the first time, Estela began to see her body as a possible object of desire. Her belly and breasts seemed to swell with that acknowledgment, as though the recognition of their potential gave them more substance. Her step took on a firmer tone, and her voice, always modulated to stay within the parameters of lady-like behavior, often rang out in bright laughter.

Although Estela continued to confess her sins and attend early Mass, she did not admit to the priest the extent to which her thoughts had taken her. Father Arzuba, a mouse-like man who looked as though he would fade to nothingness if left out in the sun too long, was increasingly nervous with her, tending to cut her confessions short, as though he feared an actual revelation.

Estela smiled at the other women in their black rebozos who hurried in and out of the great church of St. James, hardly minding when they asked for her husband.

"Oh, he's away on business," she would answer, and had nearly come to believe it, this business of being gone. Doña Carmela now walked past her in the plaza acting as though Estela were completely invisible. For this Estela was truly grateful, for she had no idea that it might have anything to do with her own behavior.

Estela was content that the girls offered to give up sweets for Lent, and Gabriel, though not much of a believer, offered to chop extra kindling for the widows as his penance. Gabriel was spending more and more time with his cousins, and at times, Estela scarcely recognized the tall young man who had once been her baby. Victoria, bless her heart, offered some of her old clothes to give to the poor that season and took them to the poor box herself one afternoon, though she did take an inordinate amount of time doing so.

This buoyant mood continued until the early morning when she arose to start the woodstove and found Victoria fully dressed in the front corridor, a cape around her shoulders, shoes on her feet, her stockings bunched in her hand. It was clear that she had just returned.

"I don't know, I don't know, I don't know!" shouted Estela, throwing her head from side to side. "And you stay here!" she snapped at Victoria, pulling her back to her seat. "At least you stay where I can see you while we figure out what to do!"

"Ay, mamá!" wailed Victoria, the only thing she had said for the last hour, weeping copiously as Estela, her aunt Blanca, and her grandfather Horacio tried to unravel the events that had led to that unfortunate dawn.

"I don't know where my husband is, papá, or don't you think

I would like him to be here, too?" Estela said.

"In a house with no men, the women will get into trouble," pronounced Horacio from where he fumed by the hearth.

"In a house with no men, what do you think the men are out doing?" answered Estela.

"Santa Ana's leg!" said Horacio, turning to Blanca. "You see? She always wants to blame me. I've done everything for this family, and it's my fault."

"Déjala," said Blanca. "It's not you she's mad at."

"Then who's to blame? Who's been putting ideas in that girl's head about soldiers by running around with that—that doctor," he said, saying the word with venom.

"But I love him!" said Victoria plaintively.

"Of course you do," said Estela, distracted. She turned toward her father, "Papá, what are you talking about?"

"You think I don't know? You think the whole world doesn't know about you and this Captain?"

Estela caught her breath. "Our friendship is perfectly innocent," she managed to force out. "I've told you. I hurt my foot in the mercado, and he helped me. I couldn't walk. That's all."

Horacio snorted and refused to look at his daughter.

"You don't think there's anything, do you?" said Estela to Blanca. Since she hadn't even confided in Blanca, her sister and her best friend, she had been certain that her secret was safe.

Blanca shrugged. "I've never seen you look so happy in your whole life."

Estela, amazed, turned to Victoria. "*You* don't think there's anything between me and Dr. Carranza, do you?"

"They're in the same battalion," said Victoria, bursting into fresh tears. "Dr. Carranza is his superior officer."

Estela sat back in astonishment as Horacio and Blanca watched. "Well, I guess we'll just have to start straightening some of this out, even without your father," Estela finally said.

"He's not married, is he?" she asked Victoria.

"No," she said, shaking her head.

"Well, thank God for that," said Blanca.

"At least there's hope," added Estela, looking at her father as he leaned on the mantle, smoking.

He caught her look and thought for a moment before nodding. "I'll see what I can do," he said, and gathered up his coat and hat.

"There, there," said Blanca, kneeling next to Victoria. "Everything will work out. You'll only make your eyes all red if you cry so hard."

"If your husband doesn't come back soon," said Horacio at the door, "he'll be in worse trouble than that one." Then he went out.

Estela left her sister to comfort Victoria and went to look out the barred window after her father. She wondered what he might have heard about Zacarías to cause him to make that remark, or if it was a simple threat.

Estela stood there for some time, her hand to her face, as the shadows lengthened in the street below.

7

The Photographer

The photographer had left the last wagon train two days before, mesmerized by the fantastic play of light and shadow on the gaunt, soaring pinnacles before her. She had never seen anything like it, back in Kansas, or even in Denver, where she had learned her trade. Now out of food, she had decided to join the next party of travelers that passed on the road below, assuming they didn't look too rough. She had not revealed her sex to the party that brought her out here, and probably would not to the next. It was easier to present herself as an itinerant male photographer making his way across the Mexican frontier.

The idea of masquerading as a man had originated with her mentor, Mason Freewater, before she left Denver on her travels across the West. He liked to jokingly call himself a man of vision, but it was true. He had seen the hunger and interest of the young woman and allowed her to become his assistant, first setting up props for studio portraits, then cropping photographs, then developing the prints, and finally, exposing the plates herself.

"I'm teaching you the trade backwards," he used to say, "so that you'll remember that it's the final image that counts."

To say that she had a good eye was more than understatement. Corey had a burning vision that grabbed the viewer and said, in a cold, clear voice, "This is holy." It was this eye that Freewater recognized in her, an unwillingness to let something go at face value and the bulldog tenacity to stay with a difficult subject until she got it right.

At first, Corey had balked at the idea of venturing out dressed like a man. She knew that other travelers sometimes adopted this guise, but she had been taught by her mother in Kansas that if she acted like a lady, she would be treated like one. Now her mother was dead of the grippe, but Corey had sisters and brothers in Kansas and Colorado who expected no less of her.

"It's a different land out there," is all Freewater would say. "I think you'll regret it if you don't. Besides, as a lady in the West, you may be the most interesting spectacle, and it'll be hard to take photographs if everybody is looking at you."

In the end, he bought her some clothes, and his wife tailored them to fit her slender frame. Corey was tall, almost five foot seven, so that helped. Her sister Ida wept when she saw that they had cropped Corey's honey-blonde hair to just below her ears, but when Corey saw the portrait that Freewater took of her in masculine dress, she knew that he was right. The reserved but eager young man that looked back at her seemed the right person to venture out into the wild and capture the west before it became a thing of the past.

Corey purchased a wagon and a horse and practiced driving it around the dirt streets of Denver. Lacking a veil to keep dust out of her mouth, she learned to pull her neckerchief up like a thief. When they judged that the last snow had melted out of the pass going south, Corey loaded up and headed towards Pueblo.

She promised to write at least once a month, and Freewater told her he would wire money if she needed it.

She was primarily a landscape photographer, but increasingly, as she worked her way through the Mexican settlements of Colorado, New Mexico, and Texas, she was drawn to the landscape of humanity around her: faces fixed in the unself-conscious agony of poverty, the stomach never full, the body never clean or warm or cool. These were conditions not consciously considered because they had never been otherwise. Under such circumstances, it was difficult to distinguish the landscape of the soul from the landscape of the earth to which it is so precariously tied.

And the children.

Corey had first been approached one Sunday afternoon in a small town, where she wandered down the street, laden with her equipment, eyeing the haphazard shop windows and horses and the occasional colorful blanket draped across a shoulder.

The woman tugged gently at her arm, saying "Señor, Señor, por favor," and indicated that Corey should follow her.

The woman led her to the edge of town, to the section where the houses were built with one using the wall of the next to hold it up, with cooking sheds out back and chickens and children running through the corn that grew in every yard. The woman, clad in a grey rebozo that hid most of her features, led Corey to a house where a small crowd had gathered. People stood and talked in clusters but parted respectfully for Corey. The woman led her gently but determinedly into the only room, and Corey was struck with the overwhelming perfumes of many flowers. The single table had been elaborately decorated with cheap lace, paper cutouts, and flowers of every hue and description, all framing a tiny figure laid out in their midst. Corey caught her breath as she peered into the tiny face and beheld its elaborate costume, for the child had been dressed in a white robe, and tiny, real feather wings had somehow been tucked behind each shoulder. A paper halo lay across the child's brow, and a well-worn rosary was twined between its tiny fingers.

Corey judged the child, a girl, to be about four or five years of age. The half-open eyes were dark and dull. The woman who had led her to the house now pulled a young woman forward, the mother, and indicated that they wanted a photograph taken of the tableau.

Her hands shaking slightly, Corey proceeded to unpack her cumbersome equipment, which took up most of the space not occupied by the table and family before her.

She tried to calm herself and frame the composition before her. These are not grieving, stricken people doomed to a lifetime of poverty, she told herself; these are elements, like the wind and the rain. These are the elements that comprise a photograph — an upturned hand, the fringe of a shawl draped gracefully across the corner of the table, the white flowers framing the dark face of the child.

Corey tried to breathe deeply, but all the air seemed sucked out of the room by the fragrant flowers. The child held a rosary, but an additional crucifix made of pine boughs was laid upon her stomach. Corey wanted to know what it all meant as she fumbled with her clumsy equipment, but how do you ask such things, even if you speak the language?

If she didn't know better, thought Corey, as her eyes rested on the slight figure before her, dressed in fine clothes, beads woven between her lifeless fingers, the smell of ripe flowers filling the tiny house and nearly sending Corey into a swoon, she would say that this culture worshipped dead children.

Shutting her eyes to maintain the image before her, Corey set off the incandescence and exposed the plate.

Although she knew that they could not understand her, Corey motioned to the plate and promised to return with a photo just as soon as she could find a place to set up her chemicals.

Waving off the coins that a man tried to press upon her, Corey gathered up her equipment and escaped into the burning street, where she filled her lungs with the hot, dusty air of the living.

The saguaro—sentinels of life—pointed the way through the desert. Corey found herself drawn continually south and west—across the wasteland of the panhandle, deep into a corner of Texas where towns took on strange names and the landscape was even stranger. Here the cultures and even the races had been mixing for some time, and Corey found herself looking into dark faces with blue eyes, blond, green-eyed children speaking Spanish together with darker siblings, a pale, refined-looking woman holding a child Corey would have taken for pure Indian.

Here she saw types with which she was not familiar and decided it was due to the same mixing of bloods. There was a family with kinky red hair and pale, freckled skin, but negroid features. She was continually startled by types she expected to speak the King's English opening their mouths to use Indian and Spanish dialects, or some combination of all three that Corey came to think of as a sort of trade language, a lingua franca of the Southwest.

"Te voy a mandar unas tunas," she heard, "one dollar, un buen price."

By now Corey had taken on a hard-edged, shiny look, something she never liked in her photographs. Her skin had darkened and grown thicker from constant exposure to sun and dry air, and she had acquired a permanent squint from dealing with the extremes of sunlight and poorly lit darkrooms. More often than not, she developed the plates in the darkened bath or hallway of a rooming house, a dark cloth draped over her head and the bath as she worked.

The costume and mannerisms of a man had become second nature to her, and she worried that they seemed to have come so easily. All she really had to remember, Corey felt, was to walk as though she had something between her legs that she was proud of. She even emerged from her room in the morning with traces of lather deliberately left near her ears or under her jawline, as though she had been shaving.

Corey came to think of herself as the Outside Corey and the Inside Corey. At first the Inside Corey kept insisting on her due, that she deserved something better, like soft clothes and a little respect and pampering from other people. But the Outside Corey, who had developed muscles from lifting and carrying the photographic equipment by himself, who could reshoe a horse and push the loaded cart through a flooding stream, told her to wait, to bide her time, that the right moment, like the sunlight on a cheekbone, was just moments away. Each photograph was a singularity—a coming together of light and season, texture, mood, and those things which only absorb light, never giving it back.

Corey drove a horse and a small wagon with her precious plates heavily wrapped in layers of muslin. Even so, she had lost a few—the giant water jars stacked in a market, the old woman whose hands looked like a map of the badlands. These images would never again see light but would remain burned indelibly into her mind. Corey determined to ship most of her plates to Denver as soon as she found a reliable driver. There, Freewater would keep them for her until she returned.

One day Corey met a man from whose eyes no light escaped.

She had been warned away from such people by Freewater.

"They'll see through you," he had said. "Those Papists will see right through you because they'll see themselves in you. A man in a dress can spot a woman in trousers any day."

Corey, who had been raised a Methodist, couldn't understand what the fuss was all about.

"It's a religion based on finding fault," said Freewater, "and the more faults the priests can find with people, the stronger it makes them and their church. It's all about power."

"What's it to me?" she asked. "They haven't got any power over me."

"That's what you think," said Freewater, shifting his pipe.

"You get into those little Spanish towns further south, the priests run them. Lock, stock, and barrel. You get into one of those places, you keep your nose clean, if you know what I mean."

Since Freewater wasn't given to lecturing, Corey took his advice to heart. She figured if she spotted a town like that, she would just keep going.

But she hadn't counted on the funeral for the little angel, or the mercados, or the constant, unrelenting light that changed the way everything looked every two minutes and insisted that she stay and expose plate after plate.

Mayhem became home when Mrs. Moreno took Corey into her boarding house, and soon every family that could afford it and a few who couldn't were sitting for Corey's camera.

It soon became obvious that in spite of Mrs. Moreno's tolerance, her parlor wouldn't do for sittings. "I'm sorry, Mr. Findlay," she said. "But the other guests complain when the house is full of—families."

Corey knew that what she meant, what the boarders meant, were poor Mexicans, for they were the families that didn't want a sitting at home, and Corey couldn't really say that she blamed them. Crowded together into one-room adobe homes, a cooking shed on the side, there was hardly room to move in these places. Some families lived in jacales, hardly more than shacks built of unmilled wood and branches.

Life was lived outdoors, ranching or tilling the soil, selling in the market, weaving, fiestas, or working for the Anglo and Irish settlers. Home was for eating and sleeping.

So Corey went looking for a studio.

There were some fine private homes but that didn't do her any good. There was the dry goods store, the feed and tack, the land assayer, the judge's quarters, and the church. The mercado was assembled and disassembled on a daily basis, a floating ship of tables, awnings, boxes, umbrellas, fruit, chickens, goats, sarapes, tools, candlewax, horses, babies and blankets. That wouldn't do either.

So Corey went to the church, which was a pretty structure with a walled courtyard between the church and the rectory. She had noticed that there were some rooms across the back of the courtyard and couldn't imagine why a single priest, who was gone most of the time anyway, would have need of so much room.

The caretaker, an elderly woman who spoke little English, was dubious when presented with Corey's proposition. But when offered the opportunity to have her grandbabies photographed and to earn a little extra by bringing in her prize flowers from her garden to grace the sittings, she agreed to ask the priest the next time he was in town.

Father Newman readily agreed to the arrangement as he, too, had considered the rooms at the back of the church superfluous. The rent that Corey proposed to pay would mean that he could be gone for even lengthier periods of time, as he wouldn't be obliged to say as many Masses in town to cover his expenses. Father Newman preferred to stay on the move, seeking out the scattered communities of Irish immigrants and the chance encounter with a willing señora under the cover of the confessional.

Corey had set up her studio and been operating it for some time, and with some success, before she actually met Father Newman face to face. In that moment, she leaving the courtyard and he entering, Corey saw that he was the sort of priest Freewater had warned her about.

He was handsome, vain, with a curly head of bright red hair and a young boy behind him staggering under the weight of his trunk. Corey could see that he was used to being obeyed. He brusquely ordered the boy to take the trunk to his room before turning his attention to Corey, who introduced herself with as much Yankee swagger as she could muster.

"Much obliged for you renting this space to me, Padre," she said, using the local vernacular.

"I hope that it meets your needs," he replied coolly.

"Perfect," said Corey. "Quiet, dark, convenient."

"Good," said Father Newman. "Let's keep it that way."

Corey tipped her hat and bowed in passing before a chill ran down her back and into her boots. She didn't think that he had seen through her, but she couldn't be sure. Something in his bright gaze held the opposite of what Corey had followed into deep Texas, something cold and unreflecting and unyielding.

Corey resolved to avoid the priest in the future, if at all possible.

How the town of Mayhem had come to acquire its name was not yet clear to Corey, but she had found that each town, each cross-roads and railroad station, had a story of its own. If one was will-ing to take the time to find out about it, it gave one the slightest advantage in trying to understand the people of that area.

Corey found that Mayhem had a twin about fifteen miles away called Havoc. The reason for these strange and unsettling names was that nature had been disrupted in these parts. A com-pass needle would spin in circles and round objects would roll uphill. In fact, the main street of Mayhem was at a slant from south to north, but everyone knew that it was easier to trudge up-hill than down, and small boys could be seen blithely rolling bar-rel hoops up the incline with hardly a touch of the stick.

Some said the devil was responsible for these aberrations, but the towns were situated along a busy road, and many found it convenient to live there and do business. Also, each town had an abundance of water, though they did not when first founded. It seemed that some years earlier two mysterious people, a brother and sister, had come up from Old Mexico. The town fathers had asked them to find water but couldn't afford their fee. The two, who were identical twins, had asked instead that a home be built for each of them, one in each town, if they found the water. The town fathers, who felt they had nothing to lose since the land was worthless without more water, agreed. The two had found a gushing spring at each site, and the houses were built to their peculiar and eccentric specifications, each on properties encompassing the source of the water.

Each house was built on a slight rise above the town, with its back to the foothills that lumbered up and west from the road. Each house was built in the Spanish style, with adobe walls and tiled roofs, but every door and window frame was painted bright blue in the style of the pueblos. Each house had a flat-roofed cooking shed on the north side, and on this roof, on clear nights, the twins could be seen peering through mechanical telescopes at the heavenly bodies. Other instruments, of copper and brass and wood, cluttered the roofs and supposedly the insides of their houses, though no one could say for sure if anyone had ever been invited inside.

Next to each house stood a waterwheel, powered by the spring that originated on the property, that served as the main water source for the respective towns. But before descending to the other properties and the estanques that stored water for the local people and livestock, the powerful waters turned the wheel that supplied mysterious energies to the house of each twin. It was said that each house could be kept warm without wood or coal, and kept light without kerosene, but most people were too reasonable to believe this.

No one was sure what any of this meant. Doors were traditionally painted blue to keep the devils out, Corey had learned on her travels through New Mexico, but the use of telescopes and scientific equipment led her to think that these two were people of a sound and rational inclination.

The twins, whose names Corey could never remember, were the source of much gossip and speculation, as the most eccentric residents of the sparsely populated area. They were often gone for long stretches of time, riding off on their matching palominos to divine water for other towns and communities. Since they kept no livestock, no one was ever invited to watch their properties for them, though people often found excuses for wandering up and trying to peer into the dark interiors of the houses.

It was said that the twins could communicate through osmosis, or waves through the air, and so did not need to live too near to each other. Sometimes they could be seen meeting at the halfway point between the two towns, though no communication had been seen to have passed between them to arrange the meeting. The two would then turn and ride off on their matched horses, hardly a word spoken between them. Yet the twins were always civil to anyone who addressed them, gentle and mild-mannered, and were very pleasing to the eye.

Corey first laid eyes upon them coming down the main street of Mayhem, where she had set up shop for the season.

There seemed to be a stirring of the hot air, then a breath as of autumn wind. Corey looked up to see the horses stamping their hooves impatiently, the dogs suddenly silent and watchful. All activity came to a stop as the townspeople paused to watch the two figures ride slowly into town.

The twins were dressed in identical fawn-colored chaps and jackets of exceedingly fine leather. They had wide-brimmed hats pulled low over their eyes, and the silver on their saddles gleamed and jingled with every step. The horses seemed to know that their riders were the center of attention and stepped with a slow and ceremonious dignity.

Corey tried to discern which was male and which female but she could not. Each wore hair just above the shoulder, each seemed to have a fine line of mustache just above the perfectly shaped upper lip. As she peered into the face of the nearest as they passed, she was met by a startled, then bemused, look from one set of hazel eyes. The look seemed to say, "I *see* you," and Corey knew that her secret had been discovered. She almost laughed out loud.

Corey was, from that moment, determined to have them on glass.

8

The Kingdom of Xipa

Upon gaining open country, Zacarías and La Gata broke into a gallop of sheer joy. After so many months of city living both were sick of the uneven, cobbled streets, the bad air, the miasma of outhouses, and the constraints of living at someone else's pleasure brought on by their uneasy boarding arrangements with Magdalena.

All three bakeries had finally been completed to Magdalena's satisfaction and inaugurated with the initial firing of their ovens. All three were an immediate success, and in the light of her bright fortune, Magdalena had paid Zacarías in pure gold for his time and trouble.

Zacarías could not believe his luck. After so many months, he was certain that she would simply deduct his room and board from his fee, leaving him with a mere pittance for the purchase of mining supplies. Wishing it were otherwise, Zacarías realized that he had paid for her hospitality in other ways, for he had proved to be a willing and able student in her bed, soon overcoming his own natural shyness, overlaid with his strict and emotionally frugal upbringing, to become a generous and sensitive lover.

In the end, however, both had to admit that there was little between them besides a natural physical affinity and once that was exhausted, they had had little about which to converse. As accomplished a lover as Zacarías had become, he could not take a serious interest in the business world that fascinated Magdalena, in the political intrigues of international economics and politics, and he yearned for the simplicity of his stark mountains, for the open sky and the occasional companionship of fellow wanderers in the open country.

In addition, Zacarías had increasingly found himself feigning satisfaction and satiation after his bedroom interludes with Magdalena. In fact, his headaches had become increasingly worse as he had spent more time in romantic pursuits, reducing him to a near cripple with their severity, and it was with gratitude that he returned to the deprivations and hardships of a solitary bedroll spread upon the rocky ground.

He suspected that Magdalena, too, had grown bored with his company and probably welcomed the return to her former freedom. Increasingly, each had found reasons to spend less time together—purchasing construction supplies, a business meeting, the weather, the rough terrain—until they only dined together two or three times a week.

"Take care when you venture into the western territories," Magdalena had said to him that last night, "I am from those badlands and know just how cruel the people there can be."

Looking into her emerald eyes Zacarías couldn't help but wonder again at her mysterious past, something she had alluded to only in passing. "Give me the name of your people and I will look them up," he had said. "I will send your greetings for you."

"I have no people," had been Magdalena's reply, and her eyes had grown so cold, like the icy wall of a deep canyon, that

Zacarías had been unable to stifle a shiver that ran the length of his body.

So it had been a great relief to them both when Zacarías had mounted La Gata and bid Magdalena adieu. In fact, he had not bid her adieu in person, for she had left the previous evening without telling him, taking her carreta and a driver and setting out for towns farther north in order to seek out new franchisees for her booming bakery business. Zacarías had simply saddled up and ridden out of town through the heavy smoke of breakfast cookfires, another solitary figure in search of an indefinable Something Else.

It was now late March and the streams were running high. Even arroyos that were dry most of the year showed a fair amount of water, and Zacarías and La Gata had to navigate their rushing waters with great care, lest both horse and rider be swept downstream to a bruising death among the rocks and boulders. Having no wish to end up as supper for a pack of coyotes, Zacarías took his time. The mare, remembering the way, made a path to the high, mountainous region that lay to the west of Monclova, past the wide plains, past the low hills and endless open country that daunted both Indians and settlers unaccustomed to such a vast expanse of dirt and sky.

In spite of her additional girth from long afternoons spent at hitching posts, La Gata seemed as anxious to proceed as Zacarías. Towing the reluctant burro that carried their supplies, the mare needed almost no guidance as they made their way to the familiar backcountry of his most memorable mining expeditions.

Zacarías could remember the place that he sought perfectly—the small meadow surrounded by jagged mountain peaks, the glowing red earth where it sloughed away from the low banks, and the swiftly flowing stream that had revealed its treasure to him the morning following his mysterious dream. He longed to lay his pack and saddle in that meadow, free the mare and mule, to listen to the rushing water and the rustle of wildlife foraging in the brush, and plunge his hands into the icy waters of that sparkling stream—the one element to which he felt kinship, water removing minerals from the earth.

Within four days Zacarías had gained the high country and drew near the entrance to La Esmeralda, the mine that had been under heavy guard the last time he had entered these mountains.

Approaching the private road, Zacarías did not fail to note the lack of traffic to or from the mining works. He assumed that it was too early in the season, that perhaps the treacherous conditions brought on by winter had temporarily shut down operations. Yet upon closer inspection, Zacarías noted that the road had not even been cleared, and substantial amounts of mud and even snow still blocked all access to the mine.

Only upon gaining a low rise opposite the entrance could Zacarías see that the mine was not under operation at all.

At first Zacarías thought that the devastation was due to military action. He dropped his reins and approached warily on foot, unwilling to expose the mare and mule to gunfire should there still be soldiers or insurgents about. The fencing had been torn away and mining equipment, crushed bits of wagons, and iron tools and fittings were scattered across the slope. The TRESPASSERS WILL BE SHOT sign was nowhere to be seen.

After partially circling the former perimeter of the mining operations and stepping warily across the steep, muddy terrain, Zacarías realized that the mine had been hit by an avalanche. No human force was great enough to cause this kind of destruction, and the owners had been unwilling or unable to clear away the damage done to the mine entrance in order to continue extracting precious metals from the interior. The main entrance might be blocked, barring the use of wagons and mules, but chances were good that the interior tunnels and passageways were still clear and might be accessible to a lone miner on foot with a near suicidal urge for metallurgic adventure.

Returning to his animals and supplies, Zacarías resolved to have some lunch and consider the situation. He still had his old mining maps and had armed himself with the best lightweight equipment available in order to pursue his latest campaign.

After much chewing and consideration of his mining and topographical maps, Zacarías resolved to attempt to gain entrance to the mine. He moved the animals to a more sheltered spot at the base of a hill, with a small covering of scrub oak and plenty of grazing. Zacarías then armed himself with a lantern, a geologist's hammer, a sturdy sack, and plenty of hemp rope. He was dressed in a leather jacket with chaps over his calcones, long white pants, which would protect him from the cutting rock. He also took a canteen, though there was usually water in the mines, and some dried meat and fruits.

Zacarías left the animals unfettered, lest he fail to return.

After two hours of searching the ruined slopes Zacarías found an old entrance to the mine. It might have been the original entrance, judging from the age and condition of the supporting timbers, and led him to believe that the mine might have been worked before the arrival of the Spaniards. He didn't know how far north the Mexican empire had extended, but many tribes had made tribute to the rulers of Tenochititlan, paying in gold and slaves to be used for human sacrifice.

He eased himself carefully through the opening until he found secure footing, then stopped to light his lantern, for he was well aware how feeble any beams of natural light were once one ventured more than a few feet from the entrance. Casting his light down the rubble-strewn passage, Zacarías could see that it had not been used for many years. Loose rocks and dirt littered the floor, but the air was good, indicating an unrestrained flow to other open areas. He counted several smaller passages leading off the main shaft at angles that didn't seem to bear any relation to gravity or ease of passage. He knew that they either sought or followed the veins of ore, and that comfort was the last consideration.

Zacarías paused carefully before each small tunnel and finally entered the one through which he could feel the strongest movement of air. He crawled through the small opening, which led upwards for a few feet, then began to descend. The width of the tunnel was never more than three feet. After seventy yards or so the tunnel joined the main shaft and Zacarías could see what seemed like a fair amount of light.

Regaining his feet, Zacarías looked up and saw the main tunnel entrance to the south. It had probably been placed here in part because snowfall was lighter, but strong sunlight and warm temperatures early in the season could dislodge an avalanche such as the one that now blocked all but a few feet of the entrance, through which Zacarías could now observe swallows darting against the blue sky.

He immediately sat down and sketched out his route, checking his compass for directions. Zacarías then explored the main shaft as quickly as possible, searching out the passages that seemed to show recent activity, a sign that veins were still being worked in them. Many lay unused or blocked off, and he knew that he would have to descend deeper into the mountain to find new veins. A mine this old was all worked out close to the surface, and men had to enter as far as two or even five miles into the mine to extract the ores.

As Zacarías made his way north, away from the entrance and down the main shaft, he stepped reverently amongst the loose rock, dust, bird droppings, and bat guano that littered the mine floor. As he went farther in, the organic debris began to lessen and the dark of the mine, which had already seemed pitch black, grew even more profound.

Zacarías followed the wheel ruts made by the small carretas that were pulled by the unfortunate burros, which were worked to death in the mines on a regular basis. Indians, too, were often worked to death, carrying ore out of the mines in huge baskets on their backs secured by a strap to their foreheads.

When Zacarías judged that he had entered three-quarters of a mile into the mine, the tunnel veered to the left. Here the floor grew damp and water dripped slowly from the ceiling and covered the walls in a shiny second skin. The air became thick and moist, and he reached out to touch the wet wall, finding the water there quite warm.

Zacarías was drawn on and on, forgetting time or direction, drawn inexorably by the humid, close airs of the mine, which seemed to beckon him to its intimate depths. He thought of Xipa, who the Indians said was the god of the mines, and who would drive a man mad in order to protect his treasures.

The tunnel grew narrow, forcing him to stoop and finally to crawl on his hands and knees. The air was so thick with moisture that Zacarías breathed heavily through his mouth, and moisture ran down his face and neck into his bandanna. He set the lantern ahead of him, then advanced a few inches at a time behind it. Zacarías moved as though in a dream, intoxicated by the damp smell of earth within his nostrils, hypnotized by the repetitive movements of his hands and legs.

He nearly lost the lantern when he attempted to set it over a drop-off into empty air. Grabbing it and peering over the edge, Zacarías found that he had gained the entrance to a great chamber. The lantern light, strong in the small tunnels, now reflected back as a feeble flame from the distant walls and ceiling of the lozenge-shaped room.

Lowering himself over the edge, Zacarías scrambled down a steep slope that ended near the center of the chamber. Standing and holding out his light, he could see fantastic outcroppings of quartz formations — turrets and caverns of sparkling crystal. Interspersed among them, imbedded in porphyric rock, was the metallic glow of many impure ores, peacock ores as they were called, for the gaudy greens and blues that predominated in the iron-based mixtures. And there, far off in the most deeply carved recesses — for that was the reason that men had ventured so far from home and God — lay the glimmers of a vein of gold, the element of his desire. It spread its seductive fingers through the unyielding granite that served as both its cradle and its prison.

Zacarías was like a man possessed. Giving no heed to his own safety he clambered up the perilous rock wall to thrust himself deep between the upper and lower ledges that flanked the vein. He hammered mightily with his little hammer, again and again, until he was able to break off a fair-sized sample that, when held close to the light, showed a handsome amount of glittering, glorious gold.

Esmeralda gave up much ore to her only suitor that day, as Zacarías built a stack, then a mound, of gold-bearing granite. When he could no longer reach the vein that lay within that particular enclosure, Zacarías turned to the mound of rough rocks and proceeded to break them up further, for he had no intention of carrying out more of the host rock on his back than was absolutely necessary.

Scouring the perimeter of the chamber, Zacarías was able to find an abandoned head-basket, and this he proceeded to fill with his nuggets.

When he saw blood seeping through the worn fingertips of his leather gloves, Zacarías realized that he had worked for many hours. He drank some water and relieved himself in a far corner of the magnificent chamber, then decided that he should attempt to exit the mine with as much ore as he could carry, drag or push before him.

The egress took much longer than his initial exploration, for it was primarily uphill and he had with him over 120 pounds of gold and silver ore. Some he placed in the Indian head-basket, which he secured around his own forehead with a leather strap, and some he pushed before him in the sturdy canvas bag he had brought with him in the eventuality that he did, indeed, find something worth his trouble.

Upon gaining the main shaft, Zacarías realized that it would be much easier if he could haul his ore out of the main exit and down to his camp rather than pushing his burden back up the steep and narrow shaft by which he had initially entered the mine.

Zacarías set down the sack of ore and carefully lowered his headbasket. After some searching he found what he had hoped for. The wrapping did not seem brittle, the box was not damp, and he hoped that it had been brought in the previous season, just before the mine closed. Placing a stick of dynamite carefully near the pile of rock, snow, dirt, and rubble blocking the wide south entrance to the mine, Zacarías laid what he hoped was enough line to enable him to scramble to safety in a side tunnel.

The blast was deafening, and rocks and dirt rained upon him to the extent that he was certain he had just buried himself alive. But when the dust cleared and he had somewhat recovered his senses, Zacarías crawled back to the main tunnel, where he was greeted by glorious daylight.

Hauling and pushing his ores with the remainder of his strength, Zacarías was able to make his way over the remaining debris blocking the entrance. Once his eyes had adjusted to the exterior light, he was surprised to find it late twilight when he emerged from La Esmeralda, for neither day nor night make an impression on the kingdom of Xipa. Zacarías found that he could not stand with the head-basket in place, for his neck and back muscles were not used to such strenuous work, so he set it down, camouflaged it with juniper branches, and slung the equally heavy canvas bag over his back. Zacarías stumbled, almost senseless with elation and fatigue, back to where he had left the pack animals and his supplies. There he lay down his burden and slept the sleep of death, or of a sated lover.

Zacarías was awakened some hours later by shouts and whistling. Dazed and disoriented, he took a moment to remember where he was, drenched in chilly dew in a pocket of the mountain. People were approaching and they were not surreptitious in their demeanor. He quickly rose and began loading his horse and burro, which notwithstanding his long absence and the tremendous blast of the night before, had remained in the vicinity to serve their master, or at least receive a last meal of fresh oats, if possible.

As the party approached the mine, additional shouts of surprise went up, for they could see that the mine entrance had been cleared.

Just as Zacarías prepared to mount his already overloaded mare, he was spotted by one of the mining captains.

"There!" the man cried. "Ladrón! Get him!"

Zacarías swung into the saddle and headed straight north over the back of the mountain. Shots rang out behind him. Common sense took hold at the last minute and he cut loose one of the saddlebags loaded with ore, enabling his horse to scramble up an embankment, and Zacarías led his ragtag ore train safely out of range. He counted on the men to be too distracted by the mess at the mine entrance to continue their pursuit and guessed that the guards would also be slowed by the bag of refined ore he had left tumbling at their feet during his hasty departure. Zacarías dabbed blood from his face where a bullet had kicked splinters from the rock face near him. The animals appeared unharmed, protected by the heavy baggage on their flanks.

Zacarías rode and walked until noon to put plenty of distance between himself and La Esmeralda. He headed west, consciously or unconsciously seeking out the country of his friends the Laguneros.

• • •

Estela stood at the pump in the courtyard, dressed in a thin white blouse and a simple workingday skirt. Laughing, she took the dipper from his hands and put it to her lips. Her hair was insistent in its escape from the braids she had wound around her head, springing in small, reddish tendrils around her face.

She tilted her head back, closed her eyes, and drank as the water spread in small rivulets down her chin and forearms, dripping onto the hem of her skirt and staining the front of her blouse to make it, in places, almost transparent.

Zacarías woke with a strong yearning for Estela. He rolled onto his back to release his penis from its constrained position and relaxed to savor the fading image. It was late afternoon and Zacarías figured he could travel three or four more hours before making camp for the night.

The toils of the previous day were now becoming apparent. His hands and forearms ached, and were covered with innumerable scrapes and scratches that he knew would take a long time to heal. His face was nicked from the explosion and his ears were still ringing, though not as badly as the previous day. Every muscle was sore and he was sure he had torn something in his neck hauling the ore out of the mine. Pity, he thought, for the bag, equaling about a third of his labors, he had left behind. He could not yet calculate the worth of the remaining ore but he was sure that it more than equaled what he had borrowed from the family bank account over the last year and a half or so. Perhaps Estela would be mollified.

Then why, he thought to himself, opening his eyes, was he headed west instead of south and east? It struck him for the first time that what he had done was illegal. He had never before trespassed into a working mine. Oh, perhaps he had ventured onto the surrounding property, but the mine owners always claimed a swath much larger than the actual workings of their enterprise. This was primarily for timber and water rights.

But Zacarías had never walked directly into a shaft that was part of a mine in use. Individuals were seldom prosecuted, because they were either subjected to instant justice or because it was difficult to prove the exact source of their discoveries. Zacarías doubted that any of the men could recognize him again from the heat of his escape, and in any case, the mine owners should be grateful to him for reopening the main entrance.

Zacarías lingered on the ground, his head propped against his saddle, for a few more minutes. He still did not know where he was going, or why, but he knew that he wanted to see Matukami, who would perhaps have an explanation. Zacarías would have to find something to eat for supper, and so he loaded his small rifle in case he flushed a rabbit along the way.

At the end of the next day, Zacarías came across two Indian men crouched at the top of a small rise, waiting for game. They watched patiently as Zacarías made his way towards them, since most mestizos usually avoided them on their travels.

Asking for Matukami, he was told that he and his family were up at their winter home, another day's journey farther north and east. Looking towards the direction they pointed, Zacarías could just make out a ragged set of mountains that defined the horizon. He was now deep in the heart of the desert and the rainy season was about to begin. The cholla cacti were covered in buds, waiting for the moment to ripen and burst. Most other plants, like the Indians, waited in green and brown anonymity for the first rains.

Matukami was more than startled when Zacarías led his mare and donkey into what passed for a yard before his dwelling. Zacarías had heard of these villages but had never seen one before. His encounters with the Indians had always been on the open plains or desert where the families spent much of the year gathering plants and food, trading with town-dwellers, or traveling to the homes of relatives.

Matukami, who had been carving something, stood and

greeted him warmly. A pack of curious dogs surrounded Zacarías and his animals as Matukami helped him unload the tired beasts. Horses were rare in these villages, and even Zacarías had marveled at La Gata's sure-footed abilities in negotiating the narrow trail up the cliff. The burro had brayed and balked at one turn but eventually submitted to the sturdy rope that led her relentlessly forward and past the certain death that she sensed below.

The home was recessed into the side of the cliff, either a natural cave or, more probably, an indentation that had been deepened and widened to accommodate a family of six or eight. In front of it was a wall of loose rock piled up to protect the family from the elements. It permitted little light to enter, but Zacarías guessed that the cave was used primarily for sleeping and storage. Water was hauled from the stream far below and kept in large jars at the edge of the rocky clearing, which was little more than a wide spot above the deep canyon.

One of Matukami's daughters finally emerged from inside, the one who had nursed Zacarías, and he knew he was being watched by other family members. Spotting the sky blue material that was part of her costume, Zacarías said that he was glad she had liked the material. Again, as though his Lagunero was incomprehensible, Matukami repeated it, and for the first time Zacarías saw the woman cover her mouth, nod, and smile shyly. She held the skirt out from her side to show the brilliant blue that was worked in an elaborate pattern into the overall design before she scrambled down the trail and out of sight.

Zacarías lay in the yard and smoked and talked as Matukami carved. He was working on a violin, smaller than the ones Zacarías was accustomed to seeing the charros play in Saltillo. Eventually Zacarías helped haul some water up the steep trail, though the children made two trips in the time it took him to make one.

As night fell, the family reluctantly invited him inside to sleep, but Zacarías decided he would rather sleep under the stars.

"The lions might eat you," they said. Zacarías preferred to take his chances and protect his mare and burro.

That night Zacarías had vivid dreams, but he could not remember them in the morning.

The next day Zacarías met Matukami's son-in-law for the first time. Contrary to what Zacarías had expected, that he worked in the mines, Kasio farmed several milpas near the family home and usually stayed in the area to tend them when the rest of the family traveled.

Kasio and two teenaged sons came to the homestead each bearing a basketful of corn sprouts, the harvest of the winter crop. The women greeted them gleefully and proceeded to mash the greens, which were then strained through baskets into large earthen jars. They were tended very carefully, with a little water and other things being added little by little.

After two days of this, Zacarías realized from the smell that they were brewing a sort of liquor. Matukami finished carving the parts of his violin, glued them together with a viscous substance that he extracted from a lily bulb, bound it in leather strips, and set it to dry for a few hours. He then strung it up with the guts of some unfortunate animal and began to play. Kasio joined in on a drum, and the lively music carried far and wide down the echoing canyon.

By nightfall several other families had straggled out of the rocky embrace of the mountains to join the party, bringing more violins, a cane flute, and food. Zacarías saw bits and pieces of the sky-blue cloth worked into a skirt here, a shirt there, a baby carrier, a rebozo. He realized that the bolt of material had been traded, bartered, and shared with all.

A kid was set to roasting, and everyone down to about the age of twelve immediately began drinking large amounts of corn liquor. Not wishing to appear ungrateful, Zacarías joined in and soon discovered that the taste was not as unpleasant as he had expected. The scratchy music set everyone dancing, and the women swirled their graceful skirts in wide arcs around the men. The glances became more direct and the smiles less shielded. Even Zacarías, stumbling and unsure, was swept into the dance until the liquor set him to vomiting over the edge of the rocky precipice.

In fact, most of them eventually fell to vomiting, but it was not treated as a disgrace. The liquor was so low in alcohol content that large quantities had to be consumed to bring on inebriation, which seemed to be the point. Men and women vomited a ragged line of pale foam at the edge of the cliff, wiped their mouths, and joined back in again. A group of older men, well pickled, sat in a small group and intoned incomprehensible singings and mutterings to each other. One of them occasionally waved a cross made of evergreen branches at the sky.

"The matukami will make it rain," said Kasio.

Zacarías nodded in inebriated accordance. He then realized that Kasio had used the term "matukami" as a plural for all the old men, and that the name by which he had called his friend all these years was a more general term for elder, or teacher, or healer, and that he did not know the man's true name at all.

The children ate and chased each other and slept as the spirit moved them. Posoles bubbled on the fire and as dawn approached, the party showed no sign of abatement.

By the following nightfall Zacarías decided that the drinking ritual, called a tesguinado, was necessary in order to assure the procreation of the indigenes. Every so often, one couple or another stepped out into the sheltering brush, not necessarily with the same partner as before. Both men and women were as bold and forthcoming under the influence of the corn liquor as Zacarías had always assumed them to be shy and inhibited.

As the last of the corn liquor was consumed, a sprinkling of rain turned to a brief downpour, the first true rain of the season. The people turned their faces upward to the pale clouds and joined in the same song, an ancient melody accompanied by the thumping of the hand drums.

Zacarías, overcome with drink, fatigue, unexpressed sexual yearnings — though he couldn't be sure at this point — and the resultant sentimentality, broke down in tears that mingled with the rain on his face. He held out his hands and again, as when he had been consumed by fever in Matukami's desert encampment, he felt the flowing of time all around him, between his fingers, as though it were a tangible energy and he stood at the center of its rushing stream.

He saw a young woman seated before him, again as if from a different time and place. She trailed her hand in the waters of a stone fountain. When she stood and reached out her hand to him, Zacarías stepped forward to take it. Immediately he felt hands upon him and returned to his senses to find that he stood alone at the edge of the precipice and would have plunged to certain death if the Laguneros had not restrained him.

Zacarías could not say what this meant but he felt the gaze of all the matukamis upon him, as though he gave off a visible light, a reflection of that which he had seen only moments before.

Soon the families gathered their children and dogs, packed their food baskets, and set off to their respective homes and milpas, there to begin planting corn, squash, beans, and chiles to cultivate through the long summer season.

That night Zacarías was not eaten by coyotes, but a terrible screaming up the mountain set the mare and burro to dancing and snorting. A mountain lion, no doubt, and Zacarías took it as a sign that he should be moving on.

Matukami agreed. As before, he sat down in a clearing as Zacarías spread his ore samples before him and described each one in detail. But this time each was from La Esmeralda and held more than a trace of real gold. Zacarías asked Matukami to take what he wanted in return for his hospitality. After long consideration, Matukami asked if that was all Zacarías had.

As though found out like a naughty schoolboy, Zacarías had to admit that he had more. He produced from a small leather pouch five nuggets of pure gold, enough to fuel his wanderings for at least a year. He set them before his friend apprehensively, knowing that he owed this man his life, yet hoping that he would not take the cream of Zacarías' labors.

Matukami contemplated the nuggets at length, holding his hands over them and describing slow circles, as though warming himself over the heat of some invisible fire.

"You need to travel farther north," he said, almost as if speaking to himself. "I know a place that would take you in, a place that holds the thing you seek."

"Gold?" asked Zacarías.

"That, too. It is five, maybe six days' journey from here. Past the city of Chihuahua. If you go there, the people will take you in. Ask for my brother in Chihuahua, in the main plaza before the cathedral. Ask him the way to Casas Grandes."

Matukami then reached out and took not the pure nuggets but a handful of the mixed ores.

Zacarías tried to hide his relief but wanted to be fair.

"Here, take at least two of these," he said. "I know that they will buy you much food and cloth."

Matukami shook his head.

"If I were to walk into a store with even one of those, these mountains would be overrun with soldiers and goldseekers," he said, just a hint of amusement in his eyes. "They would think I had found it around here, and start turning over every rock in order to take it away. "I value my land and my privacy."

Zacarías nodded in understanding, then swept up his gold. Even with the little he had shared, he still felt its lacking, the lightening of its value, as though the sheer weight of the gold gave substance to his own reality.

After many fond farewells from the family, and his promise to return again, Zacarías followed Matukami's directions to the next landmark. After the better part of a day—although Zacarías practically had to carry the burro off the mountain like the legendary Sansón, a great brute of a man who carried his lame horse back to Saltillo—he was clear of the Lagunero home territory and back in open country. He was now in country which he had never before explored, the land of the Tarahumara, the indígenes famous for running long distances over the rough and unforgiving terrain, often, it was said, for the pure joy of it.

Hear my prayer, oh Lord.
I wait like a dove in the desert
coyotes all around
mine enemies have surrounded me
they have smelled my fear and claimed me for their own
they have sent up a call
they rejoice at my suffering.

Hear my prayer, oh Lord.
I have kept your law in the waste places
I have honored your holy Name
and kept the sabbath
I have not blasphemed or eaten of unclean things
I have prayed faithfully
and honored your word.

Smite down mine enemies, oh Lord
send down Thy wrath upon them
destroy the strong places and
exalt the humble
Thy name shall live forever.
I will live in the house of the Lord
forever.

9

Sueños y Dichos

He forced open the seldom-used front door to his home, the one facing the street. At the threshold were upturned flagstones and a hole perhaps three feet deep had been excavated. It was night. A strange dog, one not from the neighborhood, approached. It had an expressive face, almost like a man. It appeared to be a mastiff, a hunting dog, but with uncropped ears and a coat of brindled grey and brown. The dog came forward as though to enter the house. Julio pushed it away forcefully, again and again, placing his hand against the neck or muzzle. He even offered the dog his arm to bite, to show that he was not afraid of it, for this was, after all, a dream.

The dog was attracted by something, a smell, and eventually it approached the excavation from the right and breathed its air. The dog then slunk away, chastened, saddened, frightened, repelled. Julio then struggled to close the heavy door, but was unable to do so before a miasma, a dark fog of evil intent, rose from the hole and flowed over the threshold and into the house.

Julio awoke troubled and found that his wife was gone from their bed. It was already dawn. "Do you remember your dreams, querida?" he asked Mariana.

She sat beside the low stone fountain, feeding the birds, which rose in a cloud and roiled around her before settling again. She turned to Julio's approach. "I never dream," she said, and Julio realized that it must be true.

To be more precise, she always dreamed, because she was always aware of the signs and symbols around her, the omens and signifiers that are revealed to most of us only in a dream state. She grasped the meaning of the look that accompanied the word, smelled the rot beneath the perfume of a flower, saw the spider beneath the rock. Mariana saw in every wing beat, every iridescent color in a feather, the meaning of the world. Julio saw that she was a vessel filled with perfection, and if she could speak as well, she would be too perfect, would shatter the fabric of our existence, for she was of a higher order, a plane of existence more perfect than ours.

Julio feared that this knowledge of the meaning of the world would always escape him, that the harder he tried, the more elusive it would be, ever out of his grasp by one prayer, one rainbow, one illumination.

He felt, for a moment, on the verge of something great, as though an awesome truth was about to be revealed there, in his garden, the fountain gurgling and his wife surrounded by birds. He felt as though something like perfection was about to pierce the fabric of their existence, but the moment passed.

Mariana sat at the kitchen table, looking dreamily out of the grated window at the remnants of the garden. Ever since Zacarías had left, Julio had worked harder and harder at taming his hidden courtyard, so that now it was so barren and uninviting that not so much as a crow came to seek shelter near the gurgling fountain. Mariana had finally retreated to the kitchen where, after completing her chores for the day, she sat making lace and gazing calmly at the devastation left by Julio's shovel and pruning shears.

Julio wondered what she was thinking about. He had always imagined that she spent such times remembering her childhood encounter with the angels. But she had never really told anyone what she saw in the depths of her fever brought on by the attack of the vicious schoolchildren. Julio realized that he had spent his entire adult life imagining Mariana — that she could be anyone, could be thinking anything, and he would never know. Is this how we spend our lives? he thought. Imagining each other?

Every night, Julio struggled with unseen forces in his dreams. Hands, tentacles, vines grabbed at his hands and face, tried to rip the spectacles from his face. And when he touched his face, the spectacles were gone, he was blind, and he would cry out and start up in bed only to find his calm wife and his calm room and the quiet night of Saltillo all around.

"I have allowed our son to fall into great sin," said Julio to his wife one early morning. "First it was marrying outside of the faith. But it has gotten worse and worse. He has fallen into the *kelipot*, the realm of evil."

"It is not for you to take the blame," said Mariana. "He must find his own way."

"But what if he doesn't come back?" asked Julio, anguished.

"He will," said Mariana, "he will. If only because we are waiting for him. And we wait so long and so hard! Remember, he could return at any time, and probably when we are least expecting it. Three things come unawares," quoted Mariana. "the Messiah, a found article, and a scorpion."

Julio peered at her in the pre-dawn light. "You've been reading my texts!"

"Not at all," she answered. "It is a saying my father used often."

Julio sat for a moment. He could not shake his misgivings. "We have become like those over whom thou hast never ruled," said Julio in a tired voice, quoting Isaiah. "Like those who were not called by Thy name."

"He has not forgotten," said Mariana. "He will not forsake all that he holds dear."

Julio went back to contemplating his texts. He was searching for something but he was not sure what it was. The old ways were beginning to seem meaningless and he yearned for the fellowship of an open community, a place where he could take his questions and concerns and discuss them with learned rabbis. At times there had been such people in Saltillo who would convene a discrete service on Fridays or Saturdays; but for the present, there were none, only their own relatives struggling in the same darkness and hope as himself.

Only ten years had passed since a Jewish marriage had been allowed in Buenos Aires, the first allowed in the former Spanish Empire. Forty years had passed since non-Catholics were allowed to even be buried in cemeteries in Mexico, and only because of a treaty with England that promised to bring more foreigners to the country.

Juan de Dios Canedo had given a brilliant speech in the legislature sarcastically proposing alternatives to burial if such a measure was not passed. Canedo told his fellow legislators that he agreed with them in principle, but that large numbers of British heretics might be expected to enter the country as a result of the treaty. While here, many of them could be expected to leave this life for the doom that they so richly deserved, and the practical problem of disposing of their unwanted remains had to be faced.

Burning the bodies would consume valuable fuel; to eat them he was disinclined, and to export them would require an amendment to the trade regulations. He therefore advised his fellow senators to permit burial. The clause was approved.

Juan de Dios Canedo was brutally murdered on Holy Thursday of 1850. His murderer was never identified, but there was wide speculation that the murder was politically motivated. The marranos of Mexico continued to exercise caution and prayer, a combination that had become nearly second nature.

Looking for words and passages that pertained to the situation of the hidden Jew in the New World, Julio came across some verses that had been in his father's collection of secret writings. They had been composed shortly after the Inquisitorial trial, torture, and execution of their ancestor, Governor Luis de Carabajal, his nephew by the same name, and other family members, condemned in 1590 "for having preserved and believed in the dead law of Moses and performing its rites, celebrations of Passover, fasts, observing the Sabbath, and other ceremonies of the oral law; waiting for the return of the Messiah, who would give them riches and take them to glory, not believing that this was our Lord Jesus Christ and that his law is false and made of air."

As was common with such texts, they were anonymous, written and disseminated in secret:

primer cántico

Si con tanto cuidado cada día
cantásemos loores al señor,
como el tiene de darnos alegría
y en todas nuestras cosas su favor,
no fueran nuestros males tan continuos,
no durara tan grande adversidad,
de sus bienes todos nos haría dignos
y de poblar su santa ciudad,
en la que fueran largos nuestros años
exceptos de peligros y de daños,
confieso que por ser inobedientes
fuimos de nuestra patria desechados,
vivimos entre incircuncisas gentes
con hambres y con guerras afrentados,
todos con crueldades diferentes
fuimos de nuestra patria desechados;
volvamos al señor que el es piadoso,
que el hará nuestro espíritu gozoso.
cantemos su loor en este día
del señor escogido y regalado;
ensalcemos su recta y santa vía
pues sólo a nos la ha encomendado
de cuantas generaciones criado había
como la de israel, por mayor grado,
multiplicando sus generaciones
más que las estrellas en el cielo son;
no ha de ser en vano la esperanza
que no puede faltar lo prometido,
muy presto gozaremos de bonanza
si inclinamos a bien nuestro sentido,
porque aquel que en dios espera, todo alcanza

first canticle

If with such care every day
we sang praises to the Lord,
the way he gives us joy
and in all things his favor,
our woes would not be so continuous,
adversity not so hard,
from his benevolence we shall be rewarded
and will live in his holy city
where our years will be long
free of dangers and hurts,
I confess that for our disobedience
we were cast from our native land
we live among uncircumcised people
with outrageous lusts and conflicts
each by different cruelties
we were cast from our native land;
we return to god for he is merciful,
may he find our spirit rejoicing.
we sing his praise today
the Lord select and exalted
we praise his righteousness and holy way
for only to us has been entrusted
of many generations bred
like that of israel, the highest quality,
multiplying our generations
more than the stars in heaven;
the hope should not be in vain
the promise cannot falter,
soon we will enjoy the reward
if we steer our sentiments to the good,
for to those who wait for god, all will come

si del bien esperar no es movido;
el señor haga que siempre en él esperamos
y que toda su santa ley guardamos;
prometido ha el señor si nos tornamos
a la ley de su santa voluntad,
y si del corazón y alma asentamos
haber de ejecutar su voluntad.

Si con justicia por favor clamamos
estando en la mayor adversidad,
nos volverá a juntar en ese instante
de norte, sur, poniente y de levante,
qué más señas o muestras pretendemos
para reconocer la obligación
que de santificar tal día tenemos
con toda alma y todo corazón;
pues el señor nos veda que busquemos
en él mantenimiento y provisión;
gastémosle cantando los loores
del señor que nos da tantos favores.

segundo cántico

Hay razón de estar siempre loando
mi lengua al señor que la ha hecho,
y así himnos y salmos ensalzando
al que gobierna el escondido pecho.
si hay razón de estar siempre enseñando
los que no siguen término derecho,
ellos la saben bien, que lo han leído,
sus ojos muy mejor que lo han sentido.

be not moved from the good wait
the Lord wants us to wait always on him
and keep all of his holy law;
the Lord has promised that if we return
to the law of his will,
and in heart and soul we are determined
to execute his will.

And if we insist on justice
even in the greatest adversity,
we will reunite in that instant
from the north, south, west and east,
what more signs or signals do we seek
to recognize our obligation
some day we must recognize his holiness
with all our souls and hearts;
for the Lord will see that we seek
in him maintenance and care;
let us extoll the praises
of the Lord who gives us many favors.

second canticle

There is reason for my tongue
to always praise the Lord who made it,
and also raise up hymns and psalms
to him who rules Abraham's bosom.
There is reason to always teach
those who have left the true path,
they know it well, they have read it
their eyes know much better than they feel it.

tercer cántico

Sobre mi corazón tengo esmaltado
el nombre del señor, santo y bendito,
y tanto que me siento desmayado,
en sólo pensar en el se alegra mi espíritu;
acuérdame del tiempo en que enseñarme
fué para libertarme del Egipto,
y en ver que el que era entonces es ahora
espero por momentos mejor hora.

cuarto cántico

Sobre el más gracioso y alto otero
del Monte Rafadí, orando estaba
el mas santo profeta y el primero,
aquél por quien la Ley de Dios fué dada
y en cuanto el valeroso caballero
Josué, con el enmigo peleaba;
en aquel tiempo Josué vencía
cuando Moisés al cielo las manos erguía.

Third canticle

Over my heart is enamelled
the name of the Lord, holy and blessed,
and as much as I feel dismayed,
just in thinking of Him my spirit rejoices;
I remember the time in which you taught me
by freeing me from Egypt,
and see that he who was is now
I wait for a better time now.

Fourth canticle

On top of the most graceful and highest hill
of Mount Rephidim, he was praying
the holiest of prophets and the first,
the one to whom the law of God was given
and on which the brave warrior
Joshua fought with the enemy:
Joshua was victorious at the times
when Moses raised his hands to the heavens.

quinto cántico

En ____ estaban levantados
seis tribus de israel que respondían
con clara voz y gritos levantados
a los levitas que los bendecían;
y en eva estaban apartados
los otros seis que a veces consentían
en que fuese maldito el viviente
que a tal señor Dios fuese inobediente.

sexto cántico

Cuán suave cosa es, cuán deleitosa,
muy más que nadie sabe imaginar
seguir aquella via gloriosa
por donde Dios nos manda caminar;
toda la Ley de Dios es muy sabrosa,
y aquel que la osare blasfemar,
blasfemado será en aquella vida
a donde no hay tiempo cierto ni medida.

fifth canticle

In _____ they were lifted up
six tribes of israel who responded
with a clear voice and loud cries
to the levis who blessed them;
and to eve were apportioned
the other six who sometimes consented
to that which was evil in life
and who to the lord were disobedient.

sixth canticle

What a smooth way it is, how delightful
more than anyone can imagine
to follow the path of glory
where god commands us to walk;
all of god's law is savory,
and he who dares to blaspheme,
will be blasphemed in that life
which has no time or measure.

séptimo cántico

Pues mi señor te agradan nuevos cantos,
como hacer nuevas obras cada día,
allá en el ayuntamiento de tus santos,
alabaré tu nombre cada día;
acaba, poderoso, nuestros llantos,
júntanos ya en tu santa compañía
y no nos des según que merecemos
pues nuestra confianza en ti tenemos.

octavo cántico

En mi corazón tengo asentado
desde el principio de este nuevo año
de no dejarme más ser engañado,
del enemigo del buen estado humano;
antes con el favor de él, ensalzado,
omnipotente, santo y soberano,
espero proceder con tanto tiento
que en nada desatine el pensamiento.

noveno cántico

Mi flaco aliento esfuerza y fortalece,
mi ronco pecho aclara y da alegría,
mi entendimiento alumbra y esclarece,
toca mi alma, lengua y albedrío,
y el corazón también porque comience
con nueva fuerza y nuevo poderío,
a pedirte socorro y a llamarte
dios, para saber glorificarte.

seventh canticle

May my Lord be pleased with new songs
I will write new work every day
over there in the congregation of your saints
I will praise your name every day
finally, our heavy tears will cease,
we will gather at last in your holy company
and you will give us at last what we merit
we place our trust in you.

eighth canticle

In my heart I am convinced
since the beginning of the new year
that I should no longer be deceived
by the enemy of the well-being of humanity;
with the favor of Him, Exalted,
omnipotent, Holy and sovereign,
I hope to proceed with such a steady hand
that nothing will bewilder my thoughts.

ninth canticle

My feeble breath strengthen and fortify,
clear my hoarse chest and give joy,
illuminate and clarify my understanding,
touch my soul, tongue and will,
and my heart as well because I begin
with new strength and new power,
to lose sorrow and name you
God, in order to glorify you.

"I have seen that woman again," said Julio.

"Which?" asked Mariana.

"The one from another place, who looks like a gitana."

"In your study?"

"Yes, through my meditations. I was looking for Zacarías."

"Maybe she can help you," said Mariana.

"I don't know. I think she may be near him in some way, perhaps geographically. But I think that she is on a different plane, from a different *shemitah*."

"The future?"

"Perhaps. Sometimes I can see her walking around, or talking to people. But everything is strange and unfamiliar. Other times, I feel as though I am in the bubble and she is looking at me."

"Do you think she can see you, us?" said Mariana.

"It is possible. Perhaps there is a window between us, a window between worlds."

"Who is she?"

"I don't know her name. People call her Hermana, sister. But she seems familiar somehow. I only know one other thing about her. Under her bed is a metal trunk, a small one. And in it are important papers, very old. But she does not care much about them, or think them important. She is saving them for someone else, a young niece or nephew."

"She is not married? Does not have children of her own?" asked Mariana.

"She has no children. She may have been married, but she lives alone now. She seems to make her living by telling fortunes."

"She does not converse with the dead?" asked Mariana, alarmed.

"No. She tells the living about their own futures. I would say that she is a charlatan except that I can see her, and perhaps she can see me."

Mariana laid a cool hand on Julio's arm. "Be careful," she said.

Julio nodded absently, patting her hand, and rose to prepare for the day.

Mariana, too, had seen strange visions of late. She was loathe to tell Julio, but ever since his war on the garden, in which he had attacked and apparently conquered the luxuriant nature of its plant and animal life, Mariana had noticed a change in its environs.

In the way that fewer birds flocked to the garden, the frogs and lizards that had thrived on the small insects living out their many generations in the shade of Julio's opulent garden had gone to seek new shelter. The songs of peepers and crickets no longer filled the mild evenings. The cicadas of summer could be heard in the neighboring trees but not in Julio's courtyard.

Even Mariana, who seldom went out, had taken to late afternoon walks along the shaded streets in order to visit with her friends the birds. Melchorio sulked and began scrapping with the neighbor cats over the scarce wildlife.

Mariana had found this increasingly to her dislike and had been about to abandon her customary place by the side of the fountain altogether, until the day that she leaned over to retrieve a ball of embroidery thread and happened to glance into the waters of the fountain.

At first she thought they were tadpoles, hatching in the beneficent green shade of the lip of the fountain. She had often seen them out of the corner of her eye and had associated them with the peepers that held forth at the end of each season.

But as she focused on the tiny figures this particular day, she could see that they were people, acting out their tiny lives, oblivious to the giantess who loomed over them.

This greatly puzzled Mariana until she remembered Julio's rationale for curtailing the rampant natural growth of the garden: the garden could be treated as an analogue for Mexico, perhaps even for the world at large.

Mariana watched the little figures, tracing their journeys across the garden, under the rose bushes, along the grooves in the paving stones that formed a pattern of water from the overflow of the fountain. Eventually, she decided that it functioned as a sort of map, with the fountain representing itself at the middle: you are here.

Mariana searched and searched until she found a figure that might be her son. He was very far away, and the activities in which he appeared to engage—disappearing into antholes, riding his tiny horse for long distances, climbing up precipitous walls and dwelling in unusual places—seemed unhealthy to Mariana. She wondered if his poncho was still any good, if he ate well.

Julio noticed Mariana was taking an unusual interest in the fountain and in the grounds of the garden. "What do you see, querida?" he called to her one day as she regarded the flagstones beneath the delicate, fern-like leaves of a jacaranda.

She looked up as though startled, then looked back at the ground, as though waiting for a reaction from Julio. Julio saw only ants.

"I'm just looking for designs," she said, "as you do."

"For order? For resolution?" he asked.

"For beauty," answered Mariana, holding up her crochet work.

It was of a delicate green thread, and into it, in a shade of pale brown Mariana was working leaves that appeared to have died and fallen from the tree above. The design was so restful that Julio wanted to lay his head upon Mariana's lap and close his eyes. Yet it saddened him as well, for it incorporated the feeling of seasons passing, of youth never again to be revisited, of the temporality of all things.

"I'd better water," he said. "This fierce sun takes it out of everything."

Mariana looked slightly alarmed but then she relaxed. The figures she had been watching had moved on.

While Julio was gone fetching a bucket, Mariana went and looked again at her favorite sight in the mapamundi, the map of the world of Mexico in her garden. It was a miniature fountain, exactly like the real one in her own courtyard, only nestled behind the plants at the far north end of the garden.

Here was a forgotten place by the wall, a section never planted or developed in the long years of cultivation by her ancestors. Perhaps the original builders of the house had used the place to store their tools or stones as they worked. In any case, the ground was rugged and piled high with rocks and stones, cut by a single, deep crevice which ran with water during the rains. On the edge of this cut, snugged against a hill of reddish earth, sat the fountain. Mariana could not see the people who lived by it—somehow the light was always dim in this section of the garden—but she was sure that she had much in common with them, and that the fountain was included in the map for a good reason.

At Julio's approaching footsteps Mariana let go of the foliage that she held back, screening the far corner of the garden, and she turned to go inside the house.

10

Estela

The doctor was in but he did not understand why this man wanted to see him.

Señor Vargas had arrived at his office precisely at 8 A.M., and although Captain Carranza was used to working in his office early in the morning, he was unused to having people request meetings at that hour. He felt tired and a bit worn, and although meticulously dressed, he had neglected to shave.

Ever since his last clandestine visit with Estela two weeks earlier he had been undecided about what to do. In spite of himself, she seemed to be occupying more and more of his thoughts.

"Good morning," said Carranza as the man was ushered in. Carranza did not recognize the man, who was dressed in formal civilian clothes.

"Ernesto Vargas de Caraval, a su servicio."

"Likewise," replied Carranza. "How can I help you?"

"I've come on behalf of my client, la Señora Quintanilla Carabajal."

Carranza looked sharply at the man. This did not bode well.
"Oh? How is the Señora? Is she not well?"

"As far as I know, she is in good health. But that is not why I
came to see you today," replied Vargas. As the doctor had not
asked him to be seated, he remained standing.

"Did she send you?"

Vargas hesitated only a moment. "As the family counsel," he
said, "I feel it is my duty to look out for the welfare of my clients.
And it seems to me that you may be endangering that welfare."

"How so?" asked Carranza. Something about this man bothered him, and he wished him gone as soon as possible.

"You may not know sir," said Vargas, shifting his briefcase
from one hand to the other, "that the señora and her husband are
legally separated, at her request."

"No, I did not know that. Nor is it any of my business."

Vargas continued as though the doctor had not spoken. "This
is a delicate situation, for she has gained this separation on
grounds of financial recklessness on the part of her husband."

Carranza did not speak.

"However, the laws pertaining to a wife's behavior are equally
severe, and community judgment even more so."

"Why are you telling me this?" asked Carranza coldly.

"I only wish to warn you, doctor, that should you persist in
your attentions, you will endanger both the Señora's property and
her parental rights."

Carranza's blood began to rise. "In my brief acquaintance with
the lady, I assure you, she has been nothing short of exemplary in
her behavior," he said through stiff jaws. "And I sir, have been
completely professional in mine. I have no idea where you could
have gotten this notion of impropriety. Again I ask you, did the
Señora ask you to come here today?"

"Not exactly," said Vargas. "I come here in my capacity as her
legal counsel and friend.

"Let me be completely honest." Vargas looked Carranza directly in the eyes for the first time. "This is not the Capital, but the city of Saltillo. Behavior that may be acceptable in a more cosmopolitan setting can be a matter of grave concern in the provinces. Perception is ninety-nine percent of the law," Vargas continued. "And what people perceive in this case, Doctor, is potential, if not actual, infidelity.

"The Señora Carabajal is no mere —" and here Vargas' lips curled around the word—"camp-follower, if you will, but a lady of high standing in the community. Please sir, consider the lady's well-being and reputation, if not your own."

Carranza stared at him, disbelieving. "Is that a threat?"

"Merely a request. A suggestion, if you will," said Vargas. "In addition, there is the possibility of charges of the corruption of the morals of a child."

"What on earth are you talking about?"

Vargas smiled thinly. "I think you know, sir. If not, just ask your men."

Carranza shook his head, staring at him. "My behavior since coming to this city has been completely honorable," he said. "If you have anything to say concerning charges of any sort, I suggest that you say them to a judge in a court of law."

Again, Vargas smiled. "Let's hope, for your sake, that it doesn't come to that. I bid you good day."

Without waiting for a reply or a dismissal, Vargas turned on his heel and left.

Carranza sat at his desk, furious. He decided that the lawyer had been sent by her husband; still he had no idea what this business about the corruption of the morals of a child could be about. Estela was hardly a child. He realized that he ought not to see her again, but he had one very important thing to tell her, and it must be done in person.

Carranza decided to get some breakfast. He put on his coat

and hat and walked outside. There, one of his soldiers flashed him a radiant smile along with a snappy salute, which the Captain returned. Had everyone gone mad today? Carranza made his way to a small café, where he hoped he could be left in peace to contemplate his situation.

On what Captain Carranza intended to be his last visit to la Señora Carabajal he did not take the telltale palomino to stand impatiently in the dark street, nor did he wear his impeccably pressed uniform, as he had on earlier occasions. Rather, Carranza affected the dress of a civilian, covering all with a dark sarape of the design common to the area, and walked quietly and contemplatively through the narrow cobbled streets of Saltillo with the air of a friar attending matins.

Standing at the window he knew to be hers, he cleared his throat softly and was immediately rewarded with a glimpse of her face through the dark grill of wrought iron that guarded each window.

Estela flew to the barred door and opened it to admit Carranza, scarcely glancing at his face to ascertain that it was indeed him before burying herself against his chest. Her hair was down and she had been sleeping, for Carranza could see that her face was creased by the pillow; yet she had responded to his voice as though she had been waiting vigilantly that night, perhaps every night, for his appearance.

Carranza wrapped her with him in his cloak and they stepped softly down the passage to her bedroom, to which they had long since adjourned their nocturnal rendezvous so as not to wake the children.

"Querida," breathed the Captain into her hair, and Estela set upon him like a starving woman at a great banquet. They did not speak much after that.

When at last they paused for breath, Estela seemed to notice for the first time Carranza's unusual clothing. "Why have you come to me dressed as a townsman?" she asked. "Have you decided to give up the army and settle here for good?"

Carranza smiled sadly and pulled her near to him. "Sometimes I wish that I could," he said, "but it has been brought to my attention that you have other ties, and so, unfortunately, do I."

Estela sat up and looked into his eyes. She was sure at this point that Carranza was going to tell her that he was married, but he said nothing, only stroked her hair and back and gazed back at her.

"Go on," she said. "I have hidden nothing from you."

"I know, querida, I know," he assured her. "But it seems that our friendship has not remained a secret, as we should have realized it would not, and consequences may result if we continue like this."

Estela sat a moment in silence. "Who spoke to you?" she finally asked. "Was it my father?"

"No, it wasn't. It was someone more ... distant ... from the family."

"Who? Why are you being so indirect with me?"

"Because I do not wish to cause any hard feelings between you and the people around you. Besides, that is not important. There are other things you need to know. Things that are much more important."

"For instance?"

"We understand that we may soon receive orders to leave Saltillo."

"Why? Where would you go?"

"We do not know. Possibly north."

"To the border?"

"It's possible."

"But that's dangerous."

"I guess that's why we may go. The increasing trade with the United States continues to take people through the Apache and Yaqui territories. The roads are long and isolated and go through hard country, and they aren't safe unless there is a strong military presence. People don't trust the rurales, even though that's their job."

"Mere bandits," said Estela.

"Yes."

Estela sat quietly a little more. "You wouldn't return, would you?"

"I don't know. I have no way of knowing."

"But I can hear it in your voice."

Carranza held her and kissed her a long time. "There is something else you need to know," he said, "something more important than this, and that might change your feelings about me."

Estela looked up at him warily, wondering if she could shield her heart from one more hurt, one more desertion.

"You must take good care of yourself, and eat well. Let the children help more with the chores. And perhaps," Carranza hesitated, for he had never mentioned the man before, "you should send word to your husband to return."

Estela looked at him questioningly.

"You will have a new child in September." He watched as her face changed from puzzlement to amazement.

Estela grabbed her belly and stared at it. "You mean I'm ..."

He nodded.

"But I didn't think we ..."

He held up his hand.

"It is your husband's child. You were with child, it seems, when I first met you." He smiled gently, placing his hands on her arms. "It is not love that has made you so beautiful, though I hope that too," he added ruefully, "but your own body preparing for the joyful event."

Estela caught her breath, pressing the back of her hand to her mouth, then began to cry silently, a swirl of emotions.

Carranza held her in the quiet early morning hours before the dawn. He noted the details of the room, the tasteful furniture, the fringed silk scarf angled across the vanity, her perfumes and brushes placed upon it, their clothes scattered about the room like those of young lovers. He wondered if he would ever be here again with Estela, or ever have a home of his own that he could enter in broad daylight and be greeted as master, father, husband, beloved.

The wedding was held at daybreak at the side door of the church, in a small courtyard. It was not exactly what Estela had in mind, but she was happy to at least see a marriage out of the situation.

The young soldier, Jorge Telles, looked suitably dashing in his uniform, and seemed truly happy to be there. Captain Carranza, on the other hand, was somber and distracted. He couldn't help but think that his commanding officer had somehow heard the tangles of the situation and insisted that he be the official witness for the groom.

Victoria was near hysteria after nearly three weeks of accusations and denials, tears, revelations, and much use of go-betweens to make the civil and social arrangements needed to rectify their dilemma. Estela's father, Horacio, of course, had arranged much of it, grumbling at the extra fees he had to pay to speed up the paperwork.

The priest had agreed to waive the posting of the bans in exchange for a wedding held outside the sanctuary of the church, a form usually reserved for peasant couples with children whom they wished to legitimize.

Estela pulled a heavy knit shawl around herself against the morning chill and—catching Victoria's eye—she raised her own head and smiled regally to remind her daughter to do the same. "Te vez muy bella," she said in a serious tone.

Victoria's slight figure already showed the pregnancy. Although they had made a special dress for the occasion, it was roomy enough to accommodate her during the next few months of her confinement. The seamstress had rapidly spread the word. If we didn't have relatives, thought Estela, there would be no one left in Saltillo who would still be speaking to us.

At last the priest bustled outside, pulling on his vestments as he walked. A sleepy altar boy carried the holy water. Father Arzuba looked at Victoria, looked at Estela swathed in layers of wool and cotton, and a look between distress and panic passed briefly across his face.

The priest took each of the people to be married aside, heard hurried confessions, and performed the ceremony.

All of this time, which to Estela seemed an eternity, Carranza had his hatbrim pulled low over his eyes. At the moment the vows were exchanged, however, and Carranza handed a ring to the groom, his eyes met Estela's over the bride's head, and held them as the couple pledged their troth.

Estela had given a beautiful mantilla to Victoria for her wedding, made by the hand of her mother-in-law, Mariana. It was crocheted of the finest silk, and could be drawn through the mere circle of a ring. When the priest went to bless the bride and lift her veil, he drew back with a gasp, for her head seemed to swarm with pale butterflies. He wondered that he had not noticed them before.

Sensing his hesitation, Victoria lifted the veil herself and smiled at her new husband, who already knew the delicious secrets that lay behind it and bent eagerly to kiss her.

Father Arzuba wished the couple well, and Carranza passed him an envelope with a generous donation taken up by the young soldier's friends in the Army. The minute the priest had departed to say early Mass, Victoria abandoned all decorum and fell upon her husband's neck, weeping that she would miss him desperately. Her sister María and brother Gabriel looked at each other uncomfortably, for they knew that they would bear the brunt of this displaced emotion for the next few months.

Estela and Carranza pulled the young couple apart, Estela not daring to meet his eyes again. There was to be a small wedding feast at her father's house following the ceremony.

"I will see that the groom arrives at Don Horacio's house," Carranza said to her, "then I must go and make arrangements for our departure in the morning."

Estela watched him lead Jorge Telles away, clapping him on the back and making manly small talk. Leading her own weeping daughter away, she wondered if she would ever see Captain Carranza again.

11

The Photographer

To conceal in order to reveal. That was the essence of Corey's photography. By concealing all but the essential line of a subject, be it the shadow of a nopal, a person, or a jug of water, Corey forced the eye to fill in the detail, brought the viewer into play as a willing or unwilling collaborator with the photographer in order to reveal to the eye what it was seeing.

In the twins, Corey already had subjects which concealed all but the essentials of their humanity. By being neither male nor female, young nor old, the twins forced the people around them to conjecture everything, which is what made them enormously appealing. The human energy that was generated around and directed at them probably aided the diviners in their quest for water, Corey speculated.

She had to find a way to approach them, to make them see that she, too, conjured with concealment in order to unearth the essence of the images around her.

. . .

Calico. Corduroy. Wool. Flannel. Even velvet. A wealth of materials awaited the twins at the general store, where a shipment of supplies had been delivered from their father in Saltillo. The townspeople of Mayhem gathered around to feast their eyes on the riches.

Once a year, knowing that Manzana and Membrillo could not stand coarse homespun against their delicate skin, Horacio sent enough material to them to make a year's supply of clothing.

Manzana held up the rich green velvet, and a little girl stood on tiptoe to stroke it. Membrillo held a length of navy wool against his shoulder to see how it would look as a cape.

Corey stumbled into this scene of sartorial decadence and saw her opportunity. "Good afternoon," she said, tipping her hat.

The twins nodded a greeting.

"The landlady'd like some flour, please," said Corey, turning to the storekeeper. "And a bag of beans."

"How much flour?"

"I think she said," Corey frowned and touched her forehead, "fifty pounds?"

"How about twenty-five?" smiled the storekeeper, a middle-aged woman.

"Okay. I'll come back for more if she wants it."

Turning to the twins, who had gathered up their parcels, Corey said, "If you're staying in town tonight, you're welcome to stop over for dinner. Mrs. Moreno is a mighty fine cook."

The twins looked at each other questioningly, then one of them nodded. For whatever else they could do, neither of them had ever learned how to cook more than adequately.

Corey hurried back to the boarding house to tell Mrs. Moreno. In her hurry, she almost forgot the beans and flour.

The plank table was set for five. Corey prevailed on Mrs. Moreno to sit down and join them for dinner, for she sensed that the twins would be easier in another woman's presence. God knows what they thought of Corey.

Mrs. Moreno, who was from farther south, knew about the twins and their mentor, La Sirena, and asked after her.

"We fear that she is no longer alive," said Membrillo.

"Last time we saw her, she was headed west to visit with the Pima in Arizona. That was over a year ago," said Manzana.

"Ah, well," sighed Mrs. Moreno. "In that case, Dios la bendiga."

The dinner was delicious, carne asada with hot flour tortillas, Spanish rice with potatoes and carrots, and apple pie.

The two other boarders, a broken-down general from the Confederate army and a young itinerant preacher, seemed subdued in the dazzling presence of the twins. The preacher was trying not to stare but would steal intense glances at first one twin, then the other, trying to discern which was male and which female. Membrillo and Manzana, so used to this behavior that they considered it natural, were kind and exceedingly polite.

The general, who, if he was aware of the twin's reputation was more interested in the fact that they were from Old Mexico, finished his meal and went to his room, only to return with a bottle of whiskey, which he offered around.

Mrs. Moreno and the preacher declined and the preacher helped Mrs. Moreno clear the dishes; but the twins, to Corey's surprise, accepted. She did, too.

"Ah, those señoritas," said the general suddenly. "Had me a few high old times in Eagle Rock. They's some mighty fine young ladies there." Fixing his good eye on one of the twins, he said: "I'll bet you two cut a fine swath through them before coming out here."

"We were very young, sir, when we left our home," said Manzana.

"Still, I'll bet you broke a few hearts."

"Well, maybe. A few. Customs are different there," said Membrillo.

Corey, who still couldn't tell them apart, couldn't discern any irony in the last reply, which she thought was from Manzana.

They still seemed little more than sixteen or seventeen, while Corey was a world-weary twenty-four.

"Your father," said Corey, hastening to change the subject, "does he ever visit you up here? I heard you say that he buys and sells cotton goods."

"No, unfortunately," said Membrillo, "he is an old man now. He prefers the comfort of his home and does not travel this far north anymore."

"I see," said Corey. "I would like to travel into Mexico someday."

"It is very beautiful," said Manzana. "Monterrey and Saltillo are big cities, very old."

"You ought to photograph these two," said the general. "They's a handsome pair."

"I'd like to," said Corey. "If they'll let me."

"Oh, yes," said Mrs. Moreno, entering the room wiping her hands on a flour sack towel. "Mr. Findlay is a fine photographer, very artistic. They publish his work in Denver."

"Perhaps," said Manzana.

"It would be something to send that poor old daddy of yours," said the general.

"Yes," said Membrillo, "it would."

"Good then," said Corey, her eyes shining with drink and excitement. "Come by tomorrow afternoon, if you have time. I'll have the studio set up for it."

The twins left on an agreeable note, thanking Mrs. Moreno profusely for the fine dinner, and Corey went to bed, her head spinning.

By the next morning, she knew exactly how she wanted to do it. Corey dug into the bottom of her trunk and pulled out a dress.

The day started out bright and fiercely sunny but by eleven o'clock a few wisps of white had drifted across the face of the sun, and by half past two a herd of dark clouds rode low on the western horizon.

Corey rushed about rearranging benches and draperies, adjusting the height of her tripod, and generally behaving as though she were about to deliver a baby.

At three o'clock a cool wind began to blow and Corey shut the small window on the room she used as a studio. It was at the back of the rectory attached to the church and offered Corey a private and inexpensive location for her photographic work. Besides, it was handy for weddings and funerals to have her equipment situated so conveniently. In addition, Corey had ready access to vases, flowers and furnishings, the latter of which were always difficult to come by in a frontier town.

The clouds moved in and Corey squinted at the sky out the window, rubbing her chin and wondering how she was going to control the light on a day like this. She figured she would have to draw the drapes and use artificial light.

As the tower of clouds grew taller, Corey heard the clop-clopping of two horses coming down the main street. She watched as people stopped and heads turned in wonder before the twins came into her view.

Even Corey had to gasp when she saw them. Dressed in identical sky-blue capes, much lighter than the color of the present sky, the twins rode their prancing, preening horses as though in a parade. They wore white felt hats with gold braid, and matching charro outfits of pure white with gold buttons down the legs.

Corey ran outside to hold their horses for them as they dismounted, unable to take her eyes away from the dazzling vision of the two most perfect people she had ever seen.

"You look like, well, like angels," she finally blurted out.

The twins smiled and looked a bit rueful.

"Our father had these made for us on our fifteenth birthday," said Manzana, "but we haven't worn them very much."

"We thought it would be nice for him to have a picture of us in them," said Membrillo.

"That's very thoughtful of you," said Corey.

The twins removed their hats and, spurs jangling, followed Corey through the small courtyard to her studio at the back.

Just then the rain began to descend in torrents.

"The first rain of the season," said Membrillo. "Praise be to God."

"Yes," said Manzana. "Praise be to God."

"Indeed," said Corey.

She had not thought of the twins as being particularly religious, having never seen them at Mass, but maybe it was because they traveled so much.

The rain continued to fall, but as long as it was overcast, at least the light remained constant.

Corey posed the twins standing at either side of a wooden bench painted white to resemble plaster or stone, each with a foot on the bench and a hat held at the knee. She hung dark draperies behind them and even ventured to arrange Manzana's hair with a small comb Corey kept just for that purpose. She positioned a white, fluted pedestal in back to the left and placed an arrangement of blood-red roses upon it. The colors would not show, but Corey was so used to composing for contrast and texture that it was all the same to her. Every black and white composition had as much dimension to her as any full-color scene from real life.

Corey removed her jacket and, sleeves held in place with black garters, began to work methodically and carefully. The twins stood solemnly, taking direction from her like obedient students. Their visage was so dazzling that Corey feared they would burn holes directly through the glass plates.

Finally, when she judged that she had taken sufficient care to capture their image for their father, Corey cleared her throat and set forth her proposition. Her voice was beginning to take on a permanent gravel from pitching it artificially low for nearly two years. "I reckon that at least one of those will turn out as a portrait for your family. But I'd like to ask you for one more thing."

Membrillo and Manzana did not look surprised but stood alertly like two young dogs or horses waiting for a command. Corey found their calm, even their mere presence in her studio, unnerving. Nevertheless, her vision burned so clearly that she had to try to bring it to fruition. "If you don't think of me as being too presumptuous, I'd like to pose you in native costume."

The twins glanced at each other.

"That would be acceptable," said Membrillo, "but we have only what we've worn."

Corey held up one hand, nodding, as she walked over to a large trunk she kept in the studio. "But I've got a few things that I think would work." She opened the trunk and took out two straw hats, a colorful poncho, and some peasant whites. Then she lifted out a riot of color and ruffles that resolved itself into a short dress.

Without looking either sibling in the face, Corey held the clothes out to them on her arms. "There's a screen over there if you want to try them on."

"But we'll need ..."

"I've got everything. You just let me know and I'll hand it back to you."

Manzana and Membrillo, looking a bit confused, retreated behind the folding screen. Corey handed them a pair of white stockings, sandals, and small black boots. The rain continued in a steady downpour, turning the street outside into a muddy river.

When the twins emerged, Corey could not stifle a quick gasp. Dressed as boy and girl, the twins looked younger than ever, pre-teenagers, with innocent, sparkling eyes full of mischief. They appeared to be enjoying themselves. She wondered if they had, after all, dressed according to his or her true sex. If only to preserve her own nerve, Corey assumed that they had.

Corey combed back Manzana's hair and pinned on a long braid behind each ear. She produced hoop earrings and bracelets to finish off the outfit. By now sweating with nervousness, she drew down a backdrop that showed an idealized countryside, for these were certainly idealized country people, with their fair hair, smooth complexions, and exquisite hands and wrists.

The trousers and shirt hung loosely on Membrillo's slender frame, but the poncho covered all and pulled the outfit together. After experimenting with the more authentic peasant hat and its impossibly tall cone shape, they decided to stick with the ranch-style hat worn by cowboys, with its smaller brim and creased crown.

As Corey posed Manzana before the backdrop, thunder and lightning descended on the town so fiercely it rattled their teeth. Even with the drapes drawn, the lightning filled the room with a blinding radiance. Corey shut her eyes tightly but each time a moment too late, so that her vision was dazzled and it was difficult to judge how long to expose each plate.

Without being prompted, Manzana suddenly fell into the most feminine of poses, and Corey's jaw nearly dropped at her gracefulness. Tilting her head slightly over one shoulder, a hand at her waist, Manzana fixed the gaze of the camera with the smoldering eye of a budding coquette, a mixture of innocence and knowledge to come.

The storm passed and the sun emerged as suddenly as it had been obscured. Birds were soon singing with sweet abandon. Corey led Membrillo outdoors and sat him upon his horse. The costume was incongruous with the noble palomino, so Corey borrowed a pony that was stabled at the rectory, one on which she sometimes posed children. This seemed a better match than a burro, which struck her as a bit too quaint for this solemn man-boy.

The twins then returned indoors and changed their clothes. In the bright sunlight, they still looked regal but not as mystical as when they had first emerged from the impending storm.

"Thank you," said Corey. "I'm much obliged to you for indulging me."

"Not at all," said Membrillo. "We look forward to seeing how they turn out."

"Come back in a week and I'll have something for you."

"How much do we owe you? For the portrait for our father, I mean," asked Manzana.

"Oh, nothing," said Corey. "It was my honor to work with you."

The twins smiled at each other, then each in turn stepped up and kissed Corey full on the mouth. The kisses were sweet as clear running water and left Corey reeling.

Manzana and Membrillo mounted their horses, pulled their hatbrims low, and rode out of town, the red mud splashing high on the white hocks of their pale horses.

Corey stumbled back to her studio and fell into a drugged slumber, her head cushioned on her arm on the low white bench, the red roses bending over her solicitously. Stockings and jewelry were strewn about, the red sash from Membrillo's costume draped artlessly across the end of the bench.

It was in this disarray that Father Newman found Corey sometime later, Corey having left the door to the courtyard ajar. He was not at all amused.

Corey stammered an explanation for her disarray.

"Those two are unnatural," said the priest. "They are an offense to God's natural order, and I would like to see them and their likes eliminated from this part of Texas. They set a bad example, especially to the young women, who are starting to think it's acceptable to sit astride a horse."

Corey was sorely tempted to say something about men in dresses and women in trousers but retained enough sense to keep her mouth shut.

The priest stood a moment looking at Corey, who remained in an insolently relaxed position on the floor. He seemed to be noticing her for the first time.

"And as for you," he said, finally, "I think you'd better get your things out of here tonight. We can't have scenes like this around God's holy church. People will think I condone it."

Father Newman stayed in town that Sunday and preached a thunderous sermon on the Creation. By the end of it everyone knew the natural order of things, their place in it, and what they were expected to do to those who did not fit in.

Corey, who had neglected to heed Father Newman's warning about vacating her rented studio, was startled by Mrs. Moreno's hasty return from church.

"You better see to your things, Mr. Findlay," she said. "Father Newman sent a group of men to clear out your workplace. I guess he doesn't want you there anymore."

Corey jumped to her feet.

"I'll find the general and Mr. Smith to help you."

As the three pulled up to the church with Corey's wagon, Corey could hear the sound of breaking glass.

They rushed into the courtyard in time to watch another photographic plate come sailing out the open door. The priest was nowhere to be seen.

"There you are, Mr. Findlay," said one of the men, a notorious troublemaker. "The padre asked us to help you move your things. Said there was something not quite right about them."

"We're not looking for trouble," said Corey, "though we'll give it to you if you want it. Just let me fetch my equipment."

The general strode up to a second man about to throw a piece of furniture out and stayed his hand with a cane. He still had a fierce military bearing and for once Corey was happy to have him along. Mr. Smith was very pale but he did not run away.

The men retreated and Corey loaded her wagon with what could be salvaged. She dumped the chemicals and saved only the plates and cameras. Stepping out of the small room for the last time Corey felt a crunching under her boot. She stooped to lift one of the earrings Manzanilla had worn for the portrait and barely suppressed a small sigh.

Returning to the boarding house, Corey knew what Mrs. Moreno would say. "Now, Mr. Findlay, you know I've liked having you here, and I think your work is very artistic—"

"I'll go," said Corey. "You don't have to ask me. And I thank you for all of your hospitality."

Corey finished loading her wagon and set off north to the next town, her emotions bruised from the extremes to which they had been subjected over the last few hours. She decided that her sojourn in the wild west was over and it was time to return to what she knew, time to be one Corey again. Assuming she made it back to civilization, she would unbind her breasts and let her hair grow but would never, she knew, be the same again.

12

Casas Grandes

Zacarías followed his Indian guide up a steep winding trail from the village.

After awhile they reached the mouth of a box canyon and Zacarías realized that his horse would be unable to continue across the round, shifting rocks and boulders that clogged the entrance. Zacarías gave a coin to one of the boys who had tagged after them, shifted the saddlebags to his own shoulders, and asked him to take La Gata back to the village. The boy mounted the beautiful animal with pleasure, and although his bare feet dangled far above the stirrups, he turned the horse expertly and rode away.

Zacarías clambered up and up under his heavy load. Although the guide offered help, Zacarías felt that he must do it himself. If this was indeed Cíbola, the fabled lost city of gold, everything would be worth it.

They followed a narrow path that sometimes ran alongside a gurgling stream and—when the passage between the stone walls was too narrow—ran high above it.

At dusk they stood looking in a northwesterly direction up a narrow canyon. A forceful waterfall fell from the far end.

"There," said the guide, pointing up the cliff to the right, "Las casas de los ancianos."

The last light shown on the northeastern cliff face while most of the canyon already lay in shadow. Zacarías could see a series of stone rooms stacked together into one great structure, the likes of which he had never seen before. They seemed glued at impossible angles to the cliff side, until he realized that they must have been dug out of the living rock itself. Swallows darted about, snatching insects in the late afternoon sun.

Zacarías continued the climb and after some hours stood in a narrow clearing before the ancient city. He could see a series of narrow stone footholds leading down to the stream on his left. Zacarías' bootfalls echoed back at him from the finely wrought masonry as he approached the structures. He saw no one.

Crouching low to peer in at a keyhole-shaped doorway, Zacarías found himself looking down into a large, well-made room, a squared oval in shape. It looked clean and dry, and was set apart by a small distance from the rest of the city.

"I will sleep here."

The guide shifted uneasily. "There are spirits here."

"That's alright. I will soon be one myself if I don't get some rest," he answered.

Zacarías unrolled his bedroll and removed his boots. He placed his bed against the south wall of the long room and quickly fell into a hard sleep.

At dawn Zacarías felt rather than saw the first presence of light. He opened one eye to see a single beam hit a flat surface at the west end of the room. Rising from his bed, Zacarías went to the spot. Turning, he looked back to the east end of the room and there saw the high, narrow window through which the first ray entered over the rim of the canyon. He had heard or read about things such as this. Maybe the ancient Egyptian pharaohs had practiced such scientific arts.

The spot began to fade as the sun continued rising but Zacarías marked it on the wall with his knife.

Outside, he climbed down the narrow foot- and handholds to inspect the stream and waterfall. He found shiny nuggets, beautiful metallic baubles of green and blue, but they were only peacock ore, impure variations of metals other than the pure, yellow distillation of sunlight that he sought.

He made the great room his home. Every morning at dawn, the single beam of light appeared on the wall, and Zacarías marked it. The progression began to form a curved line.

Zacarías took pick and shovel and tried to scale the north end of the box canyon, east of the waterfall, but found the terrain too steep. He wondered if the shaping was natural or had somehow been engineered by the ancients. It seemed unnaturally symmetrical, but Zacarías could see no telltale marks of tools on the rugged cliff face. High above, he could see the tantalizing blue of porphyry conglomerate, a mineral formation common with gold and silver.

His next attempt at scaling the cliff earned Zacarías a broken ankle. Dragging himself out of the stream where he had fallen, he fashioned a crutch out of a couple of sticks and hobbled back to the ruins. The Indian brought him supplies the next day and bound his ankle securely for him.

The guide had brought two children with him this time, and Zacarías, bored with his own company, decided to tell them a story. He told them about his mother, Mariana, who although mute, could talk to the birds.

The next visit, more children came, and Zacarías again told them a story. He told about his father writing words on a plate in an ancient, secret language that would hasten the coming of the last days of the world, which would be ruled by the Messiah, the long-promised saviour of his people.

He knew that he shouldn't fill their heads with such nonsense, that it would probably scare them, but the stories were all that he knew outside of the rough life of a prospector. Zacarías did not want to think about his own wife and children, what they might be doing right now.

By the time his ankle had healed enough for Zacarías to resume his prospecting, the children were bringing their parents. Zacarías would search the cliffs and streambeds until early afternoon, while the light was good, then return to the ruins where he would find lunch prepared for him over an open fire. Families began to spend the night, and soon some of the ancient, abandoned rooms were swept out and children chased balls down the narrow passages between them. The cooking fires were moved indoors and smoke emerged from the smoke holes.

Zacarías had noticed odd walls here and there along the canyon that didn't seem to be connected to larger structures. He thought that perhaps they were reservoirs but couldn't see the need next to a stream. One day, however, two of the men began to restore one of these walls. Zacarías watched their progress with interest as they restacked the loose rocks and began to pile dirt behind them. Soon they had planted squash and greens, and Zacarías saw that the walls were terraces to create level ground in a perpendicular landscape.

By the time a year had passed, Zacarías had pecked a reclining figure eight into the ancient stone wall of the oval room. It was below this figure that he sat when he told his stories, facing east towards his enthralled audience.

Zacarías told the story of the four worlds that he had learned from his father. He struggled to tell the story in el llanero, the common language used for trade in northern Mexico, phrasing the complicated Hebrew ideas in his sparse Indian vocabulary. He did not know much Tarahumar. As he spoke, he heard muttered translations roll to the back of the room.

"When God decided that he no longer wished to be alone in the universe," he started, "God hid himself, gathered himself in, so that there would be room for His creations.

"He first created the world of *atzilut*, or Emanation. This was the world closest to God, to spirituality, and the one for which we all yearn. The next world was that of *beriah*, or Creation. The third world was that of *yetzirah*, or Formation. And finally, God created the world of *asiyah*, or Making.

"Each of these worlds emanates from God, and there is a ladder of ascent from the world farthest away, *asiyah*, to the closest, *atzilut*. We live in the world of *beriah*, ruled by the laws of the Torah of *beriah*. But someday, the Messiah will return, and the world will be placed in perfect balance, *tikkun*. On that day, everything will change, the divisions between all the worlds will be gone, and we will live in the world of *atzilut*. Then, the laws of the Torah of the *atzilut* will reign, because everything will be perfect."

"But I don't know what any of those laws mean in this land. They are very old, and from very far away. Now, we wait for the Messiah in secret, we say our prayers in secret, for the authorities would persecute us if they knew."

Zacarías sighed and sat back against the wall. He could just see his father in his dark study muttering over the laws and opinions that meant so much to him. It occurred to him that he should be more discreet, even out here in the wilderness.

"But those are just stories," he added. "Old stories."

The people nodded and exclaimed as Zacarías described each of the worlds. He had never seen the elders so animated by one of his stories.

"We too, believe in four worlds," said Jesusita, an older woman.

"We believe that God tried several other peoples before he made us.

"The creating spirit made us out of clay.

"The first people were baked in the sun too long. They became animals.

"The next people were not baked enough, and he sent them away.

"We are just brown enough, and we pleased God. So he gave us this world."

The others nodded with satisfaction.

"We came from the land where the Apaches now live, to the north, where we descended from the sky. God gave us gifts of corn and potatoes in our ears, so that we could run fast, multiply and prosper.

"That is why we are called the Raramuri, the runners."

Zacarías was pleased to hear that they were called something besides The People, or God's Chosen People, which almost every group he had ever met called themselves.

"Of course," added Jesusita, "everything is changing, now that you, our vecinos, our neighbors, are here. But we still have our sacred places, the caves and lakes where the creator spirit lives. These things, too, are secret. We must also pray in secret. But these things, the caves, the mountains, the sacred lakes, will never change.

"We will wait as long as we need to, and our children will wait, until the coming of the fourth world."

"You are the ones," said Zacarías, "who know and understand."

Running out of family stories, Zacarías began to tell stories from the Bible. First those of the Old Testament he had learned as a child from his secretive family, then those from the New Testament he had learned from the nuns at school. He wished he had paid more attention to the lives of the saints, since they always met such spectacular ends.

Zacarías passed his days in tranquillity. He had all but ceased to speak in Spanish, except when he could think of no equivalent in el llanero.

One day, wandering along the west side of the stream bed, a little boy at his heels, Zacarías saw a twinkling on the ground. He stooped and retrieved the stone. Gold. Real gold. He pocketed the nugget and glanced up the cliff. Rosy quartz peeked out of the granite here and there, a common companion to gold. Zacarías did not know what to feel. He returned to the settlement at noon and did not say anything of his find.

Zacarías visited the site of the gold nugget the next day, and the next, but found no more loose stones. He would have to scale the cliff to look for the source. His ankle ached and his fingers were stiff and scarred from his years of prospecting; he was no longer a young man. He did not relish the climb.

Zacarías returned to camp for the afternoon; then, taking advantage of an especially mild evening, went back after supper to search one last time. He needed supplies. Another nugget, a small one, might be traded for them. He couldn't depend on the good graces of these poor people forever.

A barking dog drew Zacarías' attention and he glanced up at Casas Grandes. The light caught the cliff houses just so, bathing them in red and gold light. The stones seemed to glow as though lit by fire from within.

Suddenly Zacarías realized what he was looking at. Cíbola. The city of gold. The city was made of gold, but not the kind a Spaniard would kill for. It was made of light, a city from another world, another time, a city built by a civilization that worshipped the life-giving power of the sun, the eternal ankh, eternity.

Zacarías was filled with a great sweetness, a great calm. It had been in front of him all the time. It did not matter if he ever made a fortune. Zacarías had found it here, in this city of the ancients. The gold was in the brown skin of the people, the stone, the quality of light upon the cliff face. He would return home and ask Estela for her forgiveness; he would make peace with his father.

Zacarías looked at his hands. They were the same broken

hands as always, the nails ragged and black. He looked at his tattered clothes, his scraped boots. All the same. Touching his face, Zacarías felt the same angular features, the same care-worn brow, yet he knew he was not the same man. He felt that the glow came from within him, that the magic of the cliffs had entered into his body, his very bones, and radiated outward from his hands and face. Zacarías stumbled back to Las Casas, nearly blinded by a light whose source he could not name.

At the camp dozens of people waited for his return. The smell of posoles cooking drifted from the campfires. To one side, a baby lay squalling on a blanket. Zacarías picked her up and held her. The baby immediately stopped crying and stared raptly at the sparkling stone Zacarías turned this way and that before her wondering eyes.

The word went out that Zacarías had the power to heal. The child, sick with fever before he lifted her up, was immediately cured. More people came to the encampment—the old, the sick, those who could be carried over the rough boulders and along the perilous trail to the ancient city.

Zacarías abandoned his gold seeking; there was too much work to be done. In the morning, he meditated for an hour at dawn in the oval room, then told stories to the curious who filed in and filled the high shelf and flat oval space in the holy room. After eating a few morsels he moved among the sick who were laid out on the sloped clearing in front of the dwellings, passing his hands above them, holding the golden nugget to a painfully swollen liver or a tumorous breast. His hair had grown long and his eyes, always those of a dreamer, now seemed to behold a world beyond this one.

Zacarías had slept in the oval room for almost a year before he began to hear the drum beats. The ancients were still here, as he had been told, but he had been too concerned with the petty concerns of his own life to hear them.

On the night of the summer solstice, the chanting and dancing and drumming went on for three days, during which time Zacarías was unable to sleep or eat. During the days, he sat outside and described his visions of men with antlers on their heads and bells on their ankles. The rattles seemed to pound constantly, and Zacarías began to develop terrible headaches. At night he sat at the east end of the kiva, a captive to his visions, unable to close his burning eyes against the sights and sounds that assaulted his senses.

Word of Zacarías' visions spread rapidly, and more and more people came to Casas Grandes from the surrounding countryside, from Cuidád Chihuahua, Juárez, and even from as far away as Pitíc and places in Texas and Arizona. The Conchos, the Jova, and the Pima Bajo Indians came; so did the Opata, Guazapar, and the Varohío, as well as the Temori and the Tepehuan.

Where there had been division, there was now harmony. The air was filled with sacred smoke.

Hearing of his visions of the ancient deer dancers, the men brought out their old rattles, concealed in caves in the mountains, and recreated masks and headwear in the tradition of their forefathers. Women brought herbs and healing songs passed down from mother to daughter. Ceremonies thought to have been lost were revived or recreated from the memories of the old ones, wrinkled men and women who smoked cigars constantly and without apology, and had seen many people born and dead.

Most of all, people brought their faith—in the old ways, the new ways, the Virgin Mary, Christ the King, Father Sun, Mother Moon, healing signs, heavenly bodies and potions. For faith without works is dead, but works were witnessed every day at Casas Grandes.

Matachin came with his family and cleared out a dwelling a little farther down the slope. He tried to make sure that Zacarías took time to eat and rest, for between his visions and healing the sick, Zacarías was all but consumed by his new life.

The main plaza in the ancient city was smoothed and leveled and a cross erected at one end, in the style of the Taharumar pueblos. An archway of green branches and flowers framed the keyhole-shaped doorway to the oval room where Zacarías lived. Outside of the door, a pita rope manufactured from the maguey plant was hung. Over time, knots began to appear in the rope. Zacarías watched one day as a new group of people arrived. The leader, setting down his staff of office, placed a kernel of corn against the rope, then tied a knot around it.

When a group of Apaches was sighted from the look-out hill south of the pueblo, people grew alarmed, but the notorious raiders dismounted and proceeded up the valley on foot; that in itself was a sight worth seeing. Walking into the pueblo at the end of the day, the leader looked about defiantly, then fell to his knees before an astonished Zacarías.

"Help us," he said. "My son is dying."

Zacarías did not know what he could do. Taking the man's young son in his arms, Zacarías prayed as he had never prayed before. He passed his hands over the boy's body, then waved the nugget over him, too. Zacarías feared that his own overreaching would cost all of these people their lives. For the first time, he felt himself a fraud.

Meanwhile, Matachin and one of the Taharumar healers approached with a decoction of Hikali, the powerful cactus that the Taharumaras view as the brother of the Sun and address as Uncle. The people danced all night, partaking of the hikali, as the healers drummed. The drug left Zacarías elated, then shivering with cold for the remainder of the night. The women in their clean white skirts danced forward and back in a mesmerizing pattern, while the men, wrapped in white blankets, danced a variation. Although Zacarías, fighting sleep at the edge of the circle, expected to die shortly after the boy, he felt that at least he had witnessed this scene before he did so.

He wondered what his father would think of such a pagan spectacle.

The Apache boy did not die but opened his eyes at daybreak. Zacarías knew that it was not his doing, at least not his alone, that had saved him. The Apaches were so grateful that they left several sackfuls of precious salt, but they did not linger. By midafternoon of the next day they had vanished into the wilderness of the north.

Although Zacarías did not like it, a trade began to grow in objects which he had touched, and he was concerned when a new cup was brought to him, or cloth held out for a blessing. He tried to touch only the people, reaching out his hands to their hands and heads, muttering blessings in three languages, like a chant, over and over.

The authorities in Chihuahua sensed that something was going on but ascribed it to the latest of the healing cults that sometimes swept the frontier, preying on the superstitious and the sufferings of the people, leaving them a few pesos poorer in the process.

When workers began leaving the mines to go to Casas Grandes, however, the authorities grew concerned. The new Presidente of the Republic, Porfírio Díaz, was depending on the mines of Chihuahua to fuel the vast railroad and building projects he had vowed to accomplish, finally bringing Mexico onto an equal footing with the rest of the modern world. Besides, if the government didn't get its gold, the local authorities did not receive their bite.

A few constabulary were sent out to look over the situation. They arrived at the pueblo at the base of the mountains and saw that the box canyon was inaccessible by horseback. After some lunch and more conversation, and judging that it was more dangerous to call in the rurales than to leave them out of it, they deemed it a job for the Army.

Colonel Armadio was not anxious to lead his Eleventh

Battalion up into the barrancas of Casas Grandes after some self-styled leader with apocalyptic visions. It reminded him uncomfortably of an earlier campaign in which he had served, on the other side of the Sierra Madre, against the Yaquis and Mayos.

In that campaign, the four companies under his command had been sent to Batopilas on the report of some unrest. Expecting a minor disruption having to do with the mines, which was not uncommon, Colonel Armadio found himself confronted with a full-fledged insurrection.

It was just after Easter and the Indians had spent weeks involved in their particular and peculiar celebrations of the Passion of Christ, culminating with the mock defense of the church on Easter Sunday against the forces of darkness, the forces of good and evil being portrayed by costumed members of the tribe.

Rather than dispersing to their homes and rancherías upon the successful vanquishing of Satan and his hordes, however, the Yaquis had been further agitated to defend their towns in the same way from the forces of the Republic that now threatened their way of life.

The Yaquis, joined by their brothers the Mayos, had refused to return to work at the mines and instead, armed with rifles and lances, were barring entry to both the mines and the towns as others tried to do business.

The Indians had been led by a Yaqui known as Batan, who thought himself God, the Virgin Mother and the Easter Lamb all rolled into one. The real trouble, Colonel Armadio had to admit to himself, was that people whipped up by these quasi-religious leaders were willing to fight to the death. And in order to defeat them, one had to fight the same way.

Now this new one called himself El Tecolote, the owl, and was rumored to be white. What was even worse, though, in Armadio's experience, was that there were rumors of gold at Casas Grandes. The Republic, his superior officer had informed him, was most anxious to see if this was the case, so that mine owners who would pay taxes could be given charge of the location. Where there was gold, Armadio had learned, there was blood.

Armadio had been posted to the north country for most of his twenty years in the military and there never seemed to be clean-cut answers to the problems. If ignored, these people either killed each other or the hacendados took it into their own hands and killed them. If the militia intervened, Indians and soldiers always died. Entire towns had been obliterated and resettled several times in just this way.

To complicate things, the Apaches swooped down from the north on a regular basis, killing Indians and whites alike in order to raid their communities.

Politicians in the Capitol failed to understand the difficulties of enforcing law and order in the northern territories. They thought that if the indigenous population could be reduced and replaced with white settlers, all would be well. Officially, there were no Indians; everyone was simply a Mexican citizen. In practice, however, the whites got deed to the land. Earlier campaigns in the Yucatán against the rebellion of the Talking Cross had taught the central government nothing.

The main problem, Armadio felt, was too much land and not enough people—not enough soldiers, not enough settlers, not even enough Indians, for if there were more, they would of necessity be tied to farming, hence to place, and would be more easily controlled. Time and again, Armadio had pursued renegades only to have them disappear into the deep canyons and high mountains of the Sierra Madre—guns, baggage, women, babies and all.

The present situation promised to be no better.

Armadio's own long-suffering wife, Euleteria, after moving to half a dozen cities in order to stay near him, had finally settled with their five children in the city of Hermosillo, a fair city with good water, and grew prize roses in her garden. She had come to see that a soldier's lot was hard and uncertain but at least a respectable way to make a living.

Armadio had come to love the clean, wide streets of Hermosillo, the jacaranda fronds brushing the tall white walls of the courtyards, and had even come to consider it the closest thing he would ever know to home. As a second son who stood to gain no inheritance, he had left his parents home in Morelia long ago, as sons have since time immemorial, to seek his own fortune. He had not returned since, and sometimes wondered at the hazy memories that occasionally bubbled to the surface of his mind.

At forty-two, Colonel Armadio was determined to die of old age in a woman's arms. He wasn't about to pursue this madman without finding out a little more about the situation.

Making his headquarters in a small town, the Colonel sent a reliable soldier to the pueblo that was the closest point accessible by horseback. There the soldier came upon a fine mare and brought it back along with the peasant who said he was taking care of it for a gentleman.

Colonel Armadio looked at the poor man, who was clearly scared, as he stood with eyes downcast before him. A little taller and lighter than the Yaquis, the man showed signs of the northern Indian blood that characterized the people on this side of the Sierras.

"Tell me about this gentleman," said Armadio. "Is he armed?"

"Yes, I mean, no. He had a rifle, but he left it with the horse. I still have it."

"You mean there is additional equipment that was left behind?" said Armadio. This was directed at the soldier.

"I was unaware of it, sir," said the soldier.

"Just a few things," said the Indian. "Things that he did not wish to carry on foot. The way to Casas Grandes is very steep and treacherous."

"Casas Grandes?"

"That's what the indígenes call it, sir," said the soldier. "It is an abandoned pueblo in the mountains."

Meanwhile, a group of soldiers had gathered around the beautiful horse in the courtyard. They examined its teeth and hooves, and finally one of the soldiers approached the house in which Armadio was interviewing the Indian.

"Colonel, sir, I recognize this horse," said the soldier. "It belongs to a baker in Músquiz."

"A baker?"

"Yes, sir. He worked for la Señora O'Connell. She owns bakeries, sir."

"And this horse belongs to the same man who is now at Casas Grandes?" This was directed at the Indian.

"Yes, sir," he answered without raising his eyes. "But I don't know if he is a baker. I only know that he is a very good man."

"And why is that?"

"He cured my daughter, sir. She suffered from fits. He cured her and she no longer has them."

"I see." Colonel Armadio thought for a moment. He had seen no evidence of the massing of arms or armed men in the area. It hardly seemed possible to foment an insurrection from a place that could not even be reached by horseback.

Still, there was no telling what these Indians could be up to. The Tarahumara tribe had never been conquered and still roamed these mountains at will. And although the more troublesome of the Yaqui had been deported to the Yucatán to work the hennequin plantations, there were still many left in the north region.

Traversing the mountains on foot into a possibly armed camp did not seem a pleasant prospect to Armadio just at the moment. "Where does this Señora live?"

"Señora O'Connell lives in Monclova," the soldier answered. "About three, four days' riding from here. She has a fine ranch there, though she prefers to stay in town."

"I think I would like to pay a visit to this Señora," said Armadio. "See what she has to say about this baker." In the meantime, thought Armadio, maybe all this will blow over, the Indians will return to work, and there will be no need for military intervention.

Colonel Armadio took two officers with him, including the regiment's doctor, and five soldiers. The time was late summer and each day was interrupted by a brief shower around mid-afternoon, affording a perfect time to break and have a midday meal. The high desert was in bloom and the grasses flowed away in every direction like a vast sea of pale champagne. The small entourage saw few people, isolated ranch hands and parties of candelarios, collecting wax from the wild plants.

Armadio welcomed the break from the regimen of daily camp life, constantly making small decisions and issuing orders, and welcomed the camaraderie of his fellow officers. Only Captain Carranza, a handsome man from Mexico City, seemed melancholy.

"Captain," said Armadio one night as they smoked by the fire, "you act like a man dying of love."

"It is possible," said Carranza, without looking away from the fire. "I think that I feared to break her heart, but that she may have broken mine instead."

"Ah," said Armadio. "One of the beauties of Saltillo?"

Carranza smiled but said nothing.

"Oh, I see," said Armadio. "A married woman. Discretion is the better part of —"

Here he was interrupted by laughter from the other officers, so he stopped.

Carranza merely smiled, refusing to rise to the bait, so Armadio let it drop.

"It doesn't matter," Armadio said. "I was merely making conversation to pass the time."

"I fear that Carranza covets another man's mare," said Trujillo, the third officer.

"Isn't that what we were talking about?" said Armadio.

"No, sir," said Trujillo, grinning, "I mean a real mare."

"Really?" said Armadio. "Whose?"

"The mysterious man from Casas Grandes, El Tecolote. Carranza declared it one of the finest mares he's ever seen. The soldiers were placing bets on who would get to keep it if the owner is not brought into custody."

"And what makes them think that's the way the Mexican Army does business?" said Armadio with a grin.

"A connoisseur of horseflesh, Doctor?" he said, turning back to Carranza.

Carranza shrugged. "In a manner of speaking. My father raised fine horses."

"We can tell by your mount," said the Colonel, referring to the tall palomino standing in the shadows with the other horses.

"Tell us, what's so great about El Tecolote's mare? And more important, why would he leave such a fine mare with a stranger to go up into the mountains on foot?"

Carranza stretched his legs and settled back.

"First of all, the mare, while not especially well cared for, is in excellent health and condition. She appears to be satisfied with eating weeds and grass, with a small supplement of grain. In spite of this, she is especially strong for a mare, owing, I suppose, to having carried a full burden over long distances of rough terrain. This will break down many good mounts but a few will thrive on it, working as well as pack horses as mounts. I'm sure she's not speedy, but for a working horse it doesn't really matter. She'll get him there, eventually.

"But what makes her best of all," said Carranza, warming to his subject, "especially for this part of the country, is that she's a true walker. You can see that she always has one foot on the ground when she moves. This makes for a smooth gait, easier to ride over long distances. This is the kind of horse the conquistadors used to explore all the way to California, horses bred specifically to ride, not pull carriages. Added to her wide chest girth, this means that she's even comfortable at high altitudes, because she can breathe in the thin air. She's really remarkable for her match to the terrain, to the spirit of the north country."

Armadio was impressed. "That's quite a paean to another man's horse, Carranza," he said. "And have you entered the sweepstakes for her ownership?"

"No sir. I have a fine horse." He looked in the direction of his mount. "Someday he will take me home again."

"To Mexico?"

"Yes sir."

"And a sweetheart?"

"If she'll still have me, sir."

"Oh ho, now we make some progress."

Carranza blushed, got up, and walked away.

"There goes a man," said the Colonel to no one in particular, "who has let a woman get the best of him."

Is there perhaps another god? Tell me.
Because I am the owner of the sky and the earth,
because, my children, maybe you can postpone the
judgment over you here in the world,
the last day of final judgment
when I will raise all those to whom I have given life
and you can raise those that you want to judge,
o creatures of the world.

13

The Talking Cross

The party arrived in Monclova at mid-afternoon, tired and dusty from their ride across the desert. Taking rooms at a local inn, Colonel Armadio sent word to the widow that he wished to have an audience with her.

Magdalena pondered the note in her hand as the boy who had brought it fidgeted. "Where did they say they had come from?" she asked.

"The west, across the desert."

"And why does he want to meet?"

"I'm not sure, Señora. Inquiries about some man who has worked for you. A baker?"

Magdalena thought some more, turning to catch a glimpse of her own fine figure in a looking glass. "Tell the Colonel," she said, meeting her own gaze, "That I would be honored if he and his men would be my guests for dinner tonight at ten."

"Very well, Señora."

Magdalena paused a moment more before hurrying out

through the kitchen to the yard behind. There she found the cook's boy plucking a chicken for dinner. "Never mind with that," said Magdalena. "Are you a good rider?"

The boy nodded. He was about eleven years old.

"Good enough to control my best horse?"

"Sí, Señora," he said, his eyes widening slightly.

Magdalena squatted down next to the boy, who sat on a tree stump. "I'm going to ask you to do something very special for me. It would be a great favor, and very dangerous."

"Anything, Señora."

"Listen very carefully. I need you to take Diablo and ride a long, long way. All the way to Casas Grandes in Chihuahua.

"I need you to tell only your mamá, but not why. Remember Señor Carabajal? Who used to carve whistles for you?"

The boy nodded.

"He is in great danger. You must go to him and tell him he must leave. Otherwise the soldiers will come and get him. I will give you some money. And maybe a little something more when you come back. Now go tell your mami and then take the horse out the back way."

The boy ran off to find his mother, who cried the rest of the day as she prepared a sumptuous feast of chicken and mole for Colonel Armadio and his men.

Magdalena greeted the men herself at the door, wearing her best green silk, pearls twined in her hair. The Colonel found himself breathless at her beauty and was momentarily speechless, having expected an old dowager who ruled the estate wrested from her dead husband's family with an iron fist.

Instead, he found himself pressing his lips to a smooth, if strong hand, and looking upon a woman who was if not the lightest, certainly among the fairest in the region. He expected Carranza to be equally charmed, but the Captain merely bowed politely as he removed his hat and cape, seemingly impervious to her beauty.

After a fine dinner, during which Armadio described their recent travels and asked Magdalena about the region surrounding Monclova, as he was more familiar with the regions north and west, the Colonel and his five men were shown into a drawing room as chic as any in Paris, and appointed with furnishings that could only have been imported directly from Europe.

"To what good fortune do I owe this visit?" asked Magdalena finally, once the men were drinking good port and brandy. She stood next to a Tiffany lamp that cast lights of many colors around the richly decorated room.

"Well," said Colonel Armadio, trying to keep his eyes focused on Magdalena's face. "We wish that the visit were merely social, as befits a good lady of your standing, but I'm afraid we are part of an official inquiry concerning a gentleman in the state of Chihuahua."

"Oh?" said Magdalena. "And how can I help you?"

"It seems that the man had spent some time in this area, and may have been employed by you at one point."

"It is possible. I employ many men both for my ranch and in constructing my business properties."

"Now," said the Colonel, clearing his throat. He couldn't understand why this woman excited him so much. "We don't know his name, which is one difficulty. He is known among the Indians by a false name, which would be in keeping with his other activities."

"Which are?" said Magdalena, turning her head slightly, as though listening politely.

Carranza wandered around the drawing room, a glass of port in one hand, idly examining the breakables when he came upon an odd arrangement of small rocks. He couldn't place it, but the tableau seemed familiar. Picking them up and turning them over, Carranza realized that he had seen just such a collection at Estela's house. A sudden realization came over him, and he looked over the Colonel's shoulder at Magdalena with a stricken air.

"It seems, Señora, that he is known as a teacher and healer among the indígenes, having acquired his knowledge by long association with them."

"That seems harmless enough," said Magdalena.

"It is in itself," said Armadio, "but he is much respected and revered, and as these things go, has acquired quite a following in the region. This, too, would be fine, since God knows the Indians need all the guidance they can get, but men are leaving the mines to take their families to see him. The mine owners are concerned, as you as a woman of enterprise would understand: businesses are left without labor, households without maids, and El Tecolote is not telling them to go back."

"El Tecolote?"

"His *nom de guerre*, a common practice for someone in his situation among the Indians."

"Is this man starting a war?"

Armadio hesitated. "We're not sure. It's my duty as a representative of the Republic to make sure that it doesn't go any farther."

Magdalena moved to pour more wine into the Colonel's glass. "I see," she said. "But if you can tell me nothing except this man's *nom de guerre*, with which I am not familiar, I don't see how I can be of any help to you."

"There was one more thing," said Armadio, sipping the smooth port. "He has a fine horse that one of the soldiers recognized. A chestnut mare with a strong chest. He says it belonged to one of your men, a baker in La Frontera."

Magdalena paused, then laughed.

"I'm sorry, Colonel," she said. "But I couldn't tell one horse from another."

Carranza saw how she did not look directly at Armadio, could see that she was lying, and considered his suspicions confirmed. Armadio, who was not looking at her face, did not seem to notice.

The Army officers took their leave late that evening, their appetite for good food, if not information, satisfied for the time being. Magdalena stood at the doorway to her townhouse, backlit in a becoming manner. Armadio lingered in a bow over her hand as his officers waited in the street for him, until Magdalena returned the pressure of his hand on hers. "You may stay a little longer, if you like," she murmured.

Armadio straightened and smiled slightly, then followed Magdalena back into the house, the street door shutting behind him.

"Now that's what I call dessert," sighed one of the men.

The officers stayed for several days in Monclova, Armadio hesitant to leave a comfortable situation in exchange for such a bleak prospect. The other men amused themselves in town through discreet drinking and courting, for while Armadio loved the ladies, he expected his men to comport themselves in a presentable manner.

Carranza wondered at the situation and was not entirely surprised when word came back that a young boy from Magdalena's stable had been intercepted at Casas Grandes, bringing a message from Señora O'Connell.

Mysteriously, Magdalena had had to leave town the previous day on business and wasn't expected back for some time.

Colonel Armadio did not know whether to feel blessed or bested by Magdalena's duplicitous ways. He had obtained the information he needed, in any case, so felt that all in all, his time had been well spent in Monclova.

The ride to Casas Grandes was less leisurely, as Carabajal was likely to receive word in any case from the Indians that the authorities were looking for him. Colonel Armadio hoped that by the time he arrived, Carabajal would have come willingly out of the mountain stronghold to meet with them; but the man did not materialize, and Armadio's troops were growing restless in the small village.

Armadio found the village near Casas Grandes, Galeana, to be a curiously festive place. He had expected a siege mentality, such as he had encountered in previous campaigns against the Indians, with the non-Indian townspeople wary and armed, and the Indians either invisible or inscrutable.

Instead, Armadio found an impromptu mercado at the center of the village, with cooking fires preparing roast pork and tortillas, old women selling herbal remedies, and men hawking charms and amulets. Roosters crowed with abandon, and games of chance were played in the alleys. If anything, there seemed to be more people in the village than before. Hardly the attitude if people expected trouble.

The officers strolled down the one road of the town, which was hardly more than a gravel bed running out of the nearby mountains. Carranza pointed at a curious object set out on a blanket and asked what it was.

"Un pintado santaficado de el tecolote," said the grizzled old man in the battered hat.

Carranza stooped to look more closely. It appeared to be a crude brush, the fibers cut from a longer piece of twine or rope and lashed at one end to form a handle. A dried red substance stained the tip.

"Why a sacred paintbrush?" he asked.

"El Tecolote will find a way to heaven for us, and mark the path with a brush. This one has been touched by his own hands. It comes from all the way across the desert."

Carranza realized that they stood in the midst of a saint's festival, only the saint being celebrated was still alive.

Armadio met that evening with the local officials, who demanded that El Tecolote be dislodged from his mountain fortress and the workers forced to return to the mines. An American owned company in particular threatened to pull out if their workforce was not restored.

The fact that the man's real name had been discovered did not seem to shed much light on the situation. He was a prospector from Saltillo who had spent much time among the indigenous population, but his motives for starting an insurrection were unclear.

Carranza was sure that it was all a mistake. From what Estela had told him, Carabajal had studiously avoided taking responsibility for anything all of his life, yet it took a certain tenacity of spirit to live off the land for extended periods of time; the Indians would certainly respect him for it. This didn't explain, however, the tales of healing and miracles which were told and retold at every street corner in the village.

Carranza couldn't quite bring himself to say what he knew about Carabajal, since it would entail revealing his relationship with Estela. Colonel Armadio also kept his own counsel; however, he saw no choice but to go in.

Mustering his men the next morning, Armadio marched up the gravelly road towards the mountains. The men, glad to see action again after so many days of indolence, were in good spirits. What they did not see was that as they left the view of the village, the merchants and herbalists, the gamblers and cooks were folding up their wares and leaving Casas Grandes in all haste.

After only about four miles, Armadio's troops found that the way became steeper and narrower, a sheer-walled canyon choked with rounded rocks and boulders that were difficult for the horses. Hawks circled high overhead against a blue sky.

Armadio decided to leave the company of cavalry behind while the rest of the men proceeded on foot. Carranza was left in charge of the cavalry. For reasons that he could not articulate, he found himself filled with a huge relief not to be continuing up the canyon.

"As you said," said Armadio to Carranza, "Carabajal must have loved his horse too much to make her walk this path to hell."

The men proceeded with caution, fearful of an ambush from above, as the terrain was so steep and uneven that they had to watch the placement of each boot in order not to go sliding and stumbling backwards. A rushing stream sometimes took most of the available space between the canyon walls, forcing the men to walk in the water or walk one foot before the other along a path that compelled the traveler to cling to the canyon wall.

After what seemed like many hours, the regiment rounded a bend and found themselves facing a scene from the ancient past. Smoke rose from a group of houses that appeared to be carved out of the living rock. Dogs and children darted between the stone walls, set without mortar, and women gathered laundry from the edge of the stream where it had lain on the rocks to dry. As the soldiers came into view, the people receded like a vision into the buildings, leaving the place looking as uninhabited as it must have been for hundreds, if not thousands, of years.

The Colonel gazed up the narrow valley at the cliff dwellings in the dying light. There was something about the scene that struck him, the way the sunlight fell on the stones or shimmered along the knife edges of the shadows. He blinked, turned away, and ordered the men on alert. In that time the light shifted, and when he looked again, whatever had caught his attention the first time was gone.

Zacarías had heard that there were soldiers in the village but it meant nothing to him. His days were filled with healing and prayers, his nights with visions of the Old Ones, and the mysterious carving on the wall, formed by the knife cut he inflicted each day at dawn, which had resolved into a loop with a point, pointing north.

Even when the soldiers came and stood in the rocky streambed while their leader talked gibberish, Zacarías was not alarmed. The language seemed vaguely familiar, like something he might have heard as a child. He wondered what had brought them to visit but was not moved to speak.

Not until a soldier lowered his rifle and the face of a woman next to Zacarías erupted in a bloody bloom did he understand. She slumped to the ground at his feet.

All at once, everything surrounding Zacarías burst into motion. People dove behind walls. Children shrieked in terror and Zacarías was pulled out of the plaza by a group of men as the soldiers fired into the crowd of people.

Much to Zacarías' surprise, the indígenes appeared to return fire. He had not realized that anyone at Casas Grandes was armed, although hunting parties regularly went out and returned with game for the community. People scrambled for higher ground above the ancient pueblo, and boulders were rolled down on the soldiers, who were unsure and disoriented without their horses.

As though he were no longer animate or conscious, Zacarías was passed from hand to hand and conveyed through narrow slots in the rock walls. He was shoved up a precipitous path where he stumbled and clawed his way up, many hands reaching and pushing. A bundle was shoved into his arms. Turning, he found himself high upon the cliff face looking down at a scene of carnage below. Soldiers knelt and fired while others fought hand to hand, bayonet to knife with the indígenes, both men and women. Zacarías watched a soldier bayonet a baby to the ground before a red wave of nausea obscured his sight.

It began to rain.

"Go!" someone urged him. "You must live! This is our struggle now."

Zacarías looked up the cliff face and could see the mere thread of a trail leading up. He began to climb. Bullets cut into the rock around him, above him, causing dust to fall into his already nearly blinded eyes.

He pushed his scarred fingers into the crevices and pulled himself up, up, past red and black layers of basalt, iron ore, bands of quartz, sheer granite, shining conglomerates of hard minerals, places that in a distant and former time he would have stopped to explore. In those bands of rock Zacarías saw the progress of his life—his quiet boyhood in Saltillo, playing in the sheltered garden, his mother's loving hands moving in the air before him; Estela, and their initial happiness; finding his first nugget of gold at the edge of a running stream; Magdalena seducing him over food and wine; entering La Esmeralda and descending into her depths; golden mornings at Casas Grandes.

The heavens opened up and poured down water. Mud washed over Zacarías' arms and into his sleeves.

Just as he thought he could climb no farther, that he must lose his grip and fall backwards to certain death, Zacarías heard a rasping voice from above.

"Take hold!" it said. "The burro will pull you up."

Zacarías sensed an animal presence before him, smelled dark donkey sweat and reached out his hand. It encountered a rough rope that turned out to be a burro's tail. The animal grunted and dug its hooves into the impossible terrain. Zacarías could hear a curious clanking noise, for the burro seemed to be covered in pans and tools and boxes of tin or silver. Its mistress danced ahead like a scarecrow, covered head to toe in black rags like a mad widow.

"Andale!" she cried, and the burro strained to pull its own and Zacarías weight up and over the edge of the box canyon. "Pull!"

The burro brayed and pulled, and Zacarías pulled with all his might, feeling that he might yank the donkey's tail out as he walked at almost a right angle up the cliff face. He tumbled over the crumbling edge and crawled forward before collapsing, covered in mud, and lay like a fish or a new-born baby gasping for breath upon the ground.

It was strangely quiet at the top of the cliff, the battle below muted by distance and the sound of rushing water as the stream gathered new force before plunging over the edge of the precipice into the besieged canyon below.

Zacarías noticed that he lay in a growing pond of water, and part of his brain admonished him to move or drown.

Sitting up, Zacarías saw that the streambed leading to the waterfall was clogged with fallen branches, and that the water was accumulating into a small lake at the edge of the cliff. Looking back over the lip of the canyon, he saw that most of the soldiers still stood or kneeled in the streambed, hiding behind boulders or standing back to back as they did battle.

Zacarías waded into the growing body of water and began tearing at the saplings and branches that blocked the waterfall. He beat at the blockage with his bare hands until he was able to pull some of it loose and drag some branches backwards out of the streambed. Suddenly the stream broke loose and rushed with renewed force over the edge, almost carrying Zacarías with it. He lurched to one side and grabbed a protruding root. Gathering momentum, the standing waters plunged over the edge, breaking the narrow spout of the waterfall and pushing a load of debris and rock into the box canyon below.

A torrential noise filled the valley, causing the combatants below to look up. Most of the Indians, understanding what had happened, scrambled up to safety as a wall of water, mud and branches swept towards them. The soldiers did not seem to perceive the source of the noise and stood looking about in fear and confusion. Zacarías stood and watched as the tiny figures were swept downstream by the torrent, like toy soldiers in a gutter.

After a while the flood subsided. Wiping his eyes, Zacarías looked around to find himself in a peaceful landscape, as though in a different world from the one below. The stream in which he stood was the culmination of several that meandered through an alpine meadow, much the kind that he favored for his gold explorations. Flowers unfamiliar to Zacarías bloomed on a low-growing bush and dark moss trailed into the streams, which swarmed with tadpoles. Farther west, pine forests dotted the landscape. A low line of black hills that appeared to be solid rock delineated the northwest horizon. Zacarías was on a sort of volcanic shelf. The soil was dark red streaked with black, contrasting sharply with the pale green grasses.

The woman and her clanking burro were nowhere to be seen, yet Zacarías could still smell the animal on his hands.

Zacarías fell to his knees and thanked God for his salvation. He called the place Cumbres de los Muertos, for many had died that he might reach these heights.

Picking up the bundle that he had somehow managed to retain, Zacarías saw that it contained a blanket, a knife, and a small amount of pinole, toasted ground corn good for travel. There was also a bud of hikuli, intended to protect the traveler from all harm. He tucked the hikuli into his belt and began to walk, wondering what lay before him. Zacarías was unsure about leaving the battle behind but sensed that the forces arrayed against each other there had little to do with him.

Below, the stream ran red not just with iron but with the blood of women, children, men, and soldiers. The stream ran red past the remainder of the battalion, which spooked the horses and caused them to whinny at the smell.

Captain Carranza dipped a finger in the suspicious tide and tasted it, confirming his worst fears. It ran red past the pueblo at the base of the mountains, which now appeared as empty as it had appeared full the night before. Not even a dog stood out in the rain.

In an open doorway, an old man sat down next to a bundle of sticks. He sharpened the longer ones first with a knife and then against the rough stone doorstep. He then took a length of crude twine and painstakingly began to form the sticks into wooden crucifixes, one by one.

Dear father
why hast thou forsaken me
now in my hour of greatest need?
The heavens are closed against me,
The sky a shut ear to my pleas
There is no shelter, no bread or oil
I lay my head upon a rock
Alone as the owl
upon the desert floor.

14

Return

Zacarías came to the house one afternoon, covered as usual with dust. Estela flung open the door as though expecting someone, although she did not know that he was coming. There was high color in her cheeks and she had put on weight since the last time Zacarías had seen her. In her arms was a baby.

Zacarías stared at the black-haired infant, its impenetrable gaze fixed, in turn, on him. He clutched a strand of Estela's hair that had sprung loose from her braid in his tiny fist.

"Hello," said Zacarías to the little boy. "Whose child is this?"

Estela's eyes widened. "Why, yours! Whose do you think he is?" She did not invite him over the threshold, and Zacarías did not enter.

Zacarías looked closely at the child. He did, indeed, have the curved nose and fine lips of his family. Still, the child's gaze was that of a stranger. For a moment, he wondered if he had fathered a child on Magdalena, and through some quirk Estela was raising it. Then he realized that the child was hers.

After a moment, his gaze still fixed on the child, Zacarías said, "You have been unfaithful to me."

Estela's face drained of color, then reddened. She pulled herself up to her full height and spat back at Zacarías: "I would never stoop to the things that you have done." Then she shut the door.

After a moment she reopened it.

"How can this be my son?" asked Zacarías.

"What do *you* have to show for yourself?"

Zacarías pulled his hand from his pocket to reveal a horned lizard. He had used the last of his gold to buy a ticket on the diligence back to Saltillo, riding in the open, while soldiers searched the streams and canyons. The lizard crouched flat against the fingers of his hand, the jagged contours of its head and neck like a piece of the landscape.

The baby shrieked and reached for the lizard, which shut its eyes and flattened its body even further.

Zacarías took the little boy into his arms, allowing the lizard to retreat up his sleeve. As soon as he did this, Zacarías knew the boy was his own — the dark widow's peak pointing to a curved nose, the dark slanted eyes with a slightly startled look, as though recently waked from a dream of perfection.

"We will call him Noé," he said, for Zacarías fervently hoped that the boy could save them from the impending flood that threatened to sweep them all down the spiraling stream of time.

Over dinner, as stiff as a visitor in his own house, Zacarías came to find out that his oldest daughter, Victoria, was married and due to deliver a child at any moment. Her husband was in the army and, along with the remainder of his regiment, was probably looking for Zacarías at that very instant. While the family seemed to understand that there had been a confrontation at Casas Grandes, Zacarías was not sure that they knew the extent and severity of the fighting. He did not bring up the possibility that Victoria's husband was already dead.

Zacarías felt that the house was golden, that these people, these near strangers, seemed to cast a glow of health and tranquillity around them, while he felt a mere ghost in their midst. Indeed, between bites of soup and bread, they surreptitiously regarded him as though he were a phantasm, an apparition come to visit them from a dark time they had all but left behind.

Estela could not help but notice how thin and haggard he had grown, how difficult it was for him to hold the spoon in his crooked fingers, and how he held his cup with both hands to drink. Zacarías' hair had begun to turn grey. Only his eyes remained young. If anything, they shone with a new luster, a brilliance that caught the candlelight and reflected it back to the rest of his family in a way that was both dazzling and unsettling.

Zacarías felt honored to be seated at his own table, eating and drinking like a king with real utensils and a fire burning in the grate, but he realized that he had become superfluous to this household; he had been gone so much that he was no longer needed.

Gabriel had left for college two months earlier, finally fulfilling his mother's dream. He had taken a train north to Michigan, in the United States, to study engineering. One letter had been received from him already, saying that he had arrived safely.

Zacarías slept that night in his wife's bed, the baby boy between them. He caressed her tenderly but they did not make love. Although Zacarías did not know about Dr. Carranza, he sensed that her affections had changed towards him and knew that for whatever reasons—and there were plenty to choose from—he no longer merited her affections.

Zacarías gazed lovingly at her still form as she slept heavily, her breathing deep next to the fits and starts of the infant turning in his childish dreams.

At dawn Estela was awakened by the sound of her baby crying.

It was an insistent cry that wouldn't stop as she groped blindly through the sheets to find him.

She opened her eyes to see that he wasn't there, that the cry came from outside, and she remembered that her husband had been with them. Rushing out of the room, Estela darted this way and that before realizing that the cries came from the courtyard. She nearly collided with Zacarías coming through the kitchen door, the red-faced infant squalling at the top of his lungs. Zacarías held a knife wrapped in a bloody cloth.

"What have you done to him?" screamed Estela, snatching the baby away. Only then did she see the blood on a cloth stuffed into the front of his diaper. She tore wildly at it until she uncovered the tiny, bloody penis.

"I have promised him to God," said Zacarías, "the way my father promised me. It is a covenant."

Estela began to shudder in great sobs of anger and confusion as she held her baby boy. "How could you!" she said as she turned away from Zacarías and put the baby to her breast, where he sucked urgently. "Is this what it means to be a Jew? To mutilate your own children?"

Zacarías looked at his own hands in anguish. "It is a sign that we are apart. That we will always be faithful to Him. The way the rainbow is His sign to us that He will never again destroy the world by flood."

After a moment Zacarías said, "A little brandy would help. I was just going to get it." He dipped a finger in the brandy, then in sugar. At first Estela would not relinquish the baby, but seeing Zacarías' quiet persistence, a sort of understanding beginning to dawn on her, she loosened the baby from her breast and allowed Zacarías to place his finger on the baby's lips. He mouthed the unfamiliar taste and then sucked, and his little body began to relax in Estela's arms.

For the first time Estela realized why Zacarías had looked different from Carranza. Having never seen any other unclothed adult male, she had thought the difference was a natural occurrence, like blue or brown eyes. Estela looked up at Zacarías and let him take the baby. Watching them together, she felt a surge of love. At the same time she knew she would never really understand this gentle man who seemed to generate violence all around him, and who had now marked their infant son as well.

By now the rest of the household was up. Josefina came into the kitchen and started water for coffee and atole. Victoria and María, after seeing that whatever had prompted the earlier crying and screaming had been resolved, went to their room and got dressed.

The family had gotten to the point where Geronimo and the Apaches had to be at the door before they were going to get truly excited.

Don Horacio came to the house early, Estela having sent word to him of Zacarías' arrival. Horacio was all business and little sympathy. He, too, however, seemed taken aback at Zacarías' appearance and his manner softened somewhat before he spoke. "Are any of these charges against you true?" he asked.

"Of course not. Why should I take any interest in bringing down the government?"

"Why should you take any interest in any of the things you do, with a wife and children and everything you could want here in Saltillo?"

Zacarías did not answer him for a moment, simply fixing him with that gaze that seemed to see the past and the future at the same time. "I am not asking your understanding, Don Horacio. I regret any misfortune I have brought on the family."

Don Horacio regarded him for a moment, sure of the sincerity but unsure of the reason, or lack of reason, therein. "In any event, you will need a good lawyer. Maybe that cousin of yours,

Señor Vargas, will agree to take the case. If you surrender, perhaps the charges will be lessened. Better to be apprehended here in front of witnesses than out in the wilderness where anything might happen, accidental or otherwise. I'm sure it will cost a great deal, but I'll see what I can do about borrowing the money."

Zacarías shook his head. "I have nothing to say in my defense because I have done nothing. And I won't have you go into debt for my misfortunes."

"Then what do you propose to do?" asked Horacio.

Zacarías shrugged. "Leave. I thought about it last night. No one saw me come into town. If I leave the same way, no one here can be held responsible for my reputation."

"That's what you think," said Horacio. "Already there has been some outcry against the Jews in town, saying that you, a Jew, were leading the insurrection. You might leave, but your relations have built a life here. Think of your mother and father. If your name is cleared, there might be some hope for the rest of them."

"Do you really think it would make a difference?" said Zacarías with surprising vehemence. "Hasn't there always been some excuse for going after the Jews?"

"Perhaps," said Don Horacio quietly. "At least let me warn them. There are men gathering in the plaza right now." Horacio reached for the door but was stopped by Zacarías' hand. It was the first time he had seen some strength, some power in his son-in-law's eyes. Horacio let his hand drop from the handle.

"I will tell them," said Zacarías. "I will tell them myself."

Zacarías stood and looked at his home, the patio full of the bright flowers of late summer, orange and yellow marigolds almost obscuring the water pump by the kitchen, his family, his wife and baby. He thought it would probably be for the last time. He touched the baby's soft, fat cheek with his finger.

Estela clasped her hand over his. Her eyes glistened. "Will I ever see you again?" she whispered.

"Perhaps in heaven," he answered.

They embraced, the baby between them, and Zacarías embraced his daughters as well.

"In that case," said Horacio quietly, "is there anything you need?" Zacarías thought a moment. "They kept my horse."

Mariana looked into the fountain and saw a rocky plain, and on the edge of it, tired and dirty and entirely without a thought for his physical state or well-being, her son, Zacarías.

Julio shivered. Ten days before he had looked into a plate made of copper only to see it turn a deep and bloody red. A wave of nausea had swept over him, causing him to set aside his work and avoid his study ever since.

"When will our son return?" he asked Mariana.

"Soon."

Cold, Julio returned to the house to dress and drink his morning coffee, which was already waiting for him on the bedroom table. A sharp blow to the high window startled Julio out of his revery. Stepping outside he found a swallow that had broken its neck. He picked up the soft, warm body and held it for a moment. Zacarías had returned. Julio, knowing that the cat would find it, set the still body back on the ground.

In the kitchen, Mariana was already preparing a meal for her only son, who would step through the garden gate momentarily.

Zacarías inhaled the doughy scent of fresh-baked flour tortillas as he ate. His mother had been in a hurry, she said, so she hadn't had time to make leavened bread.

"Why were you hurrying?" asked Zacarías, looking around the familiar kitchen, noting the birds in their cages on the wide ledge by the window, the fountain gurgling beyond.

"Because I knew that you were coming," she signed.

"Is this true?" asked Zacarías of his father. "Who else knows I'm here?"

Julio shrugged. "Ask your mother. She knows everything."

"No one else," she said, smiling. "But we were ready. We must always be ready for your return."

Zacarías smiled back at her and a great weariness immediately overcame him.

His parents sat and stared at him, hardly putting a morsel of food in their mouths, and Zacarías felt their expectations weighing upon him. It had been over a year since he had sat at this table.

"I dreamed of this place often," he said, "especially the fountain. That sound always used to put me to sleep as a child."

"We dreamed of you, too," said Julio. "I knew that you would come back. I tried to help you along, by taking as many obstacles out of your way as I could, by pruning the garden until there was no place your enemies could hide."

Zacarías frowned in uncomprehension and looked out of the window onto the garden. "Oh," he said after a bit. "But you see, papá, we are a part of it. That's what I learned out there."

Julio now frowned. "Our Father gave us sovereignty," he said. "Over the fish of the sea and the beasts of the field."

"But you see, papá," said Zacarías gently, "our relationship to nature is not that of the gardener to the garden but that of the rose to the garden, or the corn plant to the corn field. The question is not, when will the Messiah return, but when will the Gardener return."

"And the answer?"

Zacarías' face fell and he was silent. Then he said, "I've come only to warn you. They're looking for me and, and ..." His voice faltered.

His parents waited.

"They may bring harm upon you because of me. Because we're Jews."

Mariana nodded. "We're ready." She rose from the table and crossed to her pet birds. She began to release them one by one. The birds, finches and canaries, were reluctant to leave their loving mistress and clung to the bars until she gently shook them out. Twittering in confusion, they alighted on the nearby plants and the wide sill, calling out to one another like lost children.

"For what?" asked Zacarías. "To defend yourselves against a mob? To fight off the Mexican Army? They killed children in Casas Grandes. These people want blood."

Julio shook his head. "To live. To do what we have to do to ensure the survival of the next generation."

"What's that supposed to mean?" asked Zacarías.

Just then they heard horses coming up the steep road. Zacarías sprang from the table to look outside. Don Horacio was driving a small open carriage, a roan horse tied behind.

Mariana dragged a trunk from the corner and Zacarías realized that his parents were leaving their home.

"Where will you go?" he asked as his mother draped a shawl of her own making over her head. Her face was all but obscured by the black leaves of the calla lily.

"Mexico City. Friends there will protect us. Remember us," she said, and kissed her only son on the cheek.

"God's blessing be on you and your children," said Julio.

"And God go with you, also," said Zacarías.

Horacio and Zacarías carried the heavy trunk to the carriage while his mother climbed up. Horacio untied the roan and handed the reins to Zacarías. "Hurry," he said. "Some soldiers have just arrived. All that mob needs is somebody official to give them permission to wreak destruction."

"And Estela?"

"She's safe. Your family is with Blanca and Gustavo. The whole city will be at war if they go after them there."

"Where is Don Julio?" asked Horacio, looking anxiously around.

Julio stood for a last time in his study, a few precious books tucked under his arm. What to save? It was too dangerous to take anything at all, in case they were stopped on the way.

He opened a book called *El Paraíso en el Nuevo Mundo* and looked at a passage that he had studied many times. He saw for the first time, at an angle across the text, "encomberto," The Hidden One. He closed the book gently.

"Alabaré tu nombre cada día," Julio whispered. I will praise your name every day.

He set the books on the massive table and tipped a candle onto a nearby stack of papers. As the flames leapt up Julio closed the door and locked it, tucking the key absently into his vest as though he would return momentarily. He seemed to hear whispers from behind the door, voices that followed him as he made his way out and to the front of the house, where the horses stamped their hooves impatiently.

The soldiers pushed their way into the courtyard of the ancient house and tried to break down the doors and shutters. The fountain flowed on impassively, oblivious to this intrusion onto its solitude. Colonel Armadio directed water to be thrown on the fire, but the ancient dry timbers were burning well by then and there wasn't much that would have stopped them.

A huge shadow loomed in the corner of the courtyard, imitating the menacing shape of a man in the mad, dancing light of the flames. A soldier took a plank and smashed the enormous terracotta pot at its base, which rang like the bells of doomsday before shattering to bits. What was left was a giant jade plant standing erect, quivering indignantly, its roots having long ago penetrated the base of the pot and the flagstones beneath and sunk themselves deep into the red soil of Saltillo.

Flames leapt from every room of the ancient house as the soldiers ran back and forth, shielding their faces from the intense heat. Someone—perhaps one of the townspeople—directed them to the odd door that opened directly onto the patio, saying that they would find the evidence they sought inside. In spite of the fire within and the battering by the soldiers, the thick door held fast.

An alarm had been sounded at the sight of the fire, but the ancient water wagon and its horses were still laboring up the steep streets while the flames reached higher and higher.

As Julio's chemicals were consumed, brilliant explosions ripped through the charred timbers and phantasms of smoke flew up into the sky above the house. They could be seen for miles, and farmers, mothers, townspeople, and people in the countryside, even the animals, stopped to behold the sight.

Mariana and Julio, in their hurried flight towards San Luis Potosí, looked back and saw the brilliant colors filling the night sky. Julio, so shaken that he could barely control the horses, saw that Mariana regarded the display with a serenity that bordered on bliss. Then he realized what she saw.

"Is that what it was like?" asked Julio. "When you had your vision as a child, Mariana, is that what it looked like?"

Mariana raised her hands and dropped them in her lap. Then she opened her mouth and shut it, all the time fixing her husband with a look of puzzlement. Then she opened her mouth again.

"When I saw the angels," she said, speaking slowly, raspingly, speaking for the first time in fifty years, "it was not through my own eyes. It was as though my body opened and I saw them with my whole being, the essence of my being. I felt them there, felt their presence all around me. I was the fireworks, I was the angels." She thought for a moment. "Nothing after that ever seemed worth saying."

Julio put his arm around his wife, drawing strength from her calmness, and the two old people made their way south through the perilous night to the first refuge that would take them in.

Everyone who witnessed the starry apparitions claimed to see something different that night; no two accounts were alike, and everyone who saw it was changed a little by the experience, like children of the street who are allowed, for a moment, to enter a warm, well-lit room with comfortable appointments and rich foods on the table, before being ushered back out to the cold alleys of reality.

The dogs of the region barked so hard that night that they were mute for weeks afterwards.

Giving the house up as a total loss, and seeing that its occupants had fled, the people returned to their houses and the army regrouped in their old quarters. The fire, however, was considered evidence of their guilt, and if not by a court of law, the family was considered guilty of conspiracy to incite insurrection against the government, revolution, and conspiracy to destroy evidence.

Ernesto Vargas, dressed in his usual dark suit, requested permission to see the prisoner before the hearing. He looked even more melancholy than usual.

After having spent the past several days in the municipal jail, Horacio didn't look any better. His face unshaven, his shirt dirty and torn, Horacio's advancing age was clearly etched in his features.

"I've brought you a fresh shirt," said Vargas, "and shaving implements, if you want them."

"Of course I want them," said Horacio. "You think I want to look like a desperado in front of that judge?"

"I would prefer that you let me do the talking," said Vargas as Horacio shaved. "I am familiar with this judge's preferences and procedures."

"As you wish," said Horacio. "I've done all that I can for now."

"And it's a great deal," said Vargas quietly. "Let's say no more about it." He helped Horacio into the clean shirt and a tie and straightened the back of Horacio's rumpled jacket. "Better," he said. "More like the fine upstanding businessman that you are."

"If only anyone would let me tend to my business," said Horacio.

The guard unlocked the door to the cell and led them down the passageway to the front hall. Two drunks slept soundly in one cell and a wide-eyed Indian family huddled in another.

After some waiting, the two were escorted across the street by a guard and into the municipal courthouse.

Justice Robles was a small man with a large, hooked nose and beady eyes. All other cases had been suspended for two days while he dealt with incidences provoked by or against the Caraval family. Several cases of malicious mischief had been dismissed and one case of vandalism suspended. This was the only case that the military had asked to have transferred to a federal court.

The military counsel, Captain Martinez, looked nervous. He was a young man who constantly stroked his black hair and looked uncomfortable in his gaudy uniform.

Vargas stood almost preternaturally still as the judge reviewed the papers in front of him through half-glasses. Abruptly Robles raised his head and addressed the military counsel. "State your case, sir," he said.

The young Captain jerked to attention, then regained control of himself. "The Eleventh Battalion, in the name of the Republic, requests that the accused, Horacio Quintanilla Navarro, be transferred to Federal jurisdiction in order to be brought to trial on the charge of aiding and abetting suspected criminals, withholding evidence, and obstructing justice."

"Is the accused military or civilian?"

"Civilian, sir," stammered the counsel. "But accused of impeding military actions."

"Speak up, sir. And where did these impediments take place?"

"In the City and municipality of Saltillo, district of the Centre, in the free and sovereign state of Coahuila de Zaragoza," said the counsel.

"Hmm," said Robles. "It's unusual for the military to make such a request of a municipality concerning one of its own citizens."

Vargas, who had continued to stand unmoving, raised his chin slightly and caught the judge's eye.

"And what does the accused have to say about these charges?" asked Robles.

"My client has asked me to speak on his behalf," answered Vargas. "He is extremely fatigued by his unaccustomed incarceration and possible mistreatment at the hands of the military."

A bruise was visible on one side of Horacio's face.

Captain Martinez tried to object, but Vargas continued in his calm but loud voice. He knew that Robles was a little deaf and favored his left ear. "If it pleases the court, my client would like to be seated during the remainder of the hearing."

The judge nodded to the bailiff, who brought a wooden chair in which Horacio gratefully seated himself. His features immediately relaxed from severe dread to polite exhaustion.

"Speak, then," said Robles to Vargas.

"Your Honor," said Vargas, taking one step forward, "Don Horacio Quintanilla Gutierrez is a well-known, well-respected member of this community. He has supplied the region with necessary goods for over forty years, often at considerable risk to himself. He has contributed generously to the church and raised one of the most exemplary and gracious families in Saltillo, this in spite of the fact that his wife died tragically in childbirth and Don Horacio never acquired a second helpmate. His own granddaughter is married to a member of this very battalion that now stands accusing him, although the don has shown every indication of fealty and patriotic duty to the Republic.

"In spite of his generosity to the community, he has suffered grievously over the past few days. His property has been damaged, his children accused of unbelievable acts, and worst of all, his reputation has been impugned."

Horacio glanced up at Vargas, a shadow of worry crossing his face. He had not known about the property damage.

"And this latter, your Honor," said Vargas, "to a businessman, who depends on the trust and good disposition of his neighbors to make a living, is the most serious. With so much property loss, public misbehavior, and ill-will behind us, your Honor, and with the absence of the prime suspect who provoked all of this chaos— in spite of the best efforts of the military—I think it is fair to assume that, to quote General Santa Anna upon his resignation from office, la vindicta publica, the public vengeance, has been satisfied. And since Don Horacio is a man who has made his reputation in Saltillo, is an upstanding civilian who has been wrongly accused of crimes that in any case took place only within the boundaries of Saltillo, and who has already had the vengeance of the public, with or without cause, vented upon him, I would ask that the military request to transfer this case from municipal to federal jurisdiction be denied.

"Further, I would ask that all accusation against my client be dismissed. If he were guilty, would he, too, not have fled? According to the charges, he certainly had every opportunity. But no. Don Horacio chose to stay in his beloved home town. The Republic needs men like Horacio Quintanilla Gutierrez. We need men willing to support the community, raise up the Indians, fend off the heretical Norte Americanos and act as a proud representative of the mother country. What greater hedge against the lawlessness of the provinces, if indeed lawlessness is what the military defends us against, than a man such as Don Horacio?

Especially here, in the northern provinces, where an honest man willing to settle in a community, raise his children here, support the church and invest in properties is worth his weight in gold. Saltillo needs men like Don Horacio, our friend and neighbor, for if we cannot trust our merchants, our businessmen, our doctors, our priests, teachers, and civil authorities, then who can we trust? Who can we trust with the future of this nation, if not our own?

"Rather than further impugning his good name, give my client a chance to begin to redeem his reputation. That is assuming," Vargas added, an edge entering his voice, "that the public appetite for vengeance has been satisfied."

Horacio sat stolidly throughout this speech, erect in his chair, his eyes straight ahead but not cast down.

Judge Robles nodded slightly as he listened, while the military counsel stood slack-jawed in the face of Vargas' speech. He had been told that the request for transfer of jurisdiction would be merely a formality in order not to offend the locals.

"I see no reason to dispute the defendant's reasoning," said Robles to Captain Martinez.

"My superior officer would object vigorously," said Martinez in desperation. "This man has compromised the security of the Republic!"

"Where is your superior officer," asked Robles, "if he thought this case so important?"

"Colonel Armadio is wounded, sir, in the battle at Casas Grandes. And suffering from exhaustion."

"As is my client," added Vargas.

"As are we all of this incident," said the judge. "I agree with the defendant's counsel. No further good can accrue to the Republic by pursuing this case. This is a local issue concerning our own citizens, and none of the charges involving this particular defendant go beyond our jurisdiction. Furthermore, may I suggest to the military's counsel that the Army put its energies into pursuing the actual miscreants, rather than descending on the victims they have left behind.

"Request denied," said Robles with finality, "and unless the local constabulary wishes to press charges, and I see none present, all charges are dismissed."

Ernesto Vargas bowed formally before the judge while the young military counsel hastily gathered his papers and took his leave.

Horacio grinned delightedly and, still seated, shook his lawyer's hand, a man he had always disliked until that very moment.

An uneasy truce was established within the community as they bought their groceries, their medicinal salves, and dry goods, settled their minor legal claims and borrowed money, raised horses, birthed children, and got on with the business of living.

The rubble of the old house was too hot to approach for weeks afterwards, and the ruins were left undisturbed where they had fallen in around the edge of the ancient courtyard, the base of the fountain still bubbling away amidst the destruction. Eventually, tenacious plants began to creep out from beneath the toppled walls, and vines and flowers softened the site and helped the neighbors hasten their forgetting of the regrettable event.

A standing order was left to bring Zacarías in for questioning, but Colonel Armadio was directed not to pursue the case any further, since there were plenty of other disturbances to quell all along the vast frontier that marked the border with their troublesome and acquisitive neighbors to the north.

The Army had cleared Casas Grandes of all undesirable elements, the men had returned to the mines, the women to their domestic work, the farmers to their fields, the ranch hands to their cattle, and the mining officials and municipal governors were no longer deprived of the benefits of Indian labor.

Still, something had changed. The mining foreman found that

a worker might meet his gaze instead of keeping his eyes cast downwards; the maids washed the clothes and sang to the babies but often, the mistress of the house might not recognize the melody or even the language of the song. The people who had been at Casas Grandes and returned carried about them the air of a shared secret, a renewal of resolve—in what, no one could say for sure. Perhaps they felt that they had hastened the coming of the fourth world.

15

The Secret fountain

A fine grit filled the air, filled Zacarías' eyes, and even the eyes and ears of his borrowed horse. Zacarías, on foot, led the unfortunate animal through the sandstorm, seeking a rock, a tree, a depression in the ground, anything that could offer shelter. The sun was a blind eye above them, offering neither heat nor clarity. Zacarías trudged north, he hoped, but the compass he clutched swung wildly and he could barely open his eyes, wedged between hat and bandanna, to observe it.

Zacarías wished that he had not broken camp that morning but had remained where he was a few miles north of the Rio Grande. But he feared discovery by the Texas Rangers, known more for swift resolutions than justice, especially for Mexicans. If the Mexican Army had portrayed Zacarías as a desperate outlaw, the Rangers would have no qualms about shooting him on sight.

He was not sure exactly where he was headed, but followed a vague set of directions that led him into the teeth of the storm. He wondered if the wind always blew this hard in Texas.

After some hours, Zacarías came to higher ground and the wind abated a bit, as the landscape was broken up by rocky ridges and sandstone outcroppings. An occasional gust sent both Zacarías and the horse lurching and stumbling, but he felt that the worst of it had passed.

Zacarías was desperately tired, thirsty and hungry, but he dared not stop. Besides, he had no supplies, no shelter. His horse, unused to such harsh conditions, was also spent. He reached into his near-empty bag of pinole and pulled out the piece of hikule he had been given in his flight from Casas Grandes. It was supposed to protect the traveler who carried it, but Zacarías also knew that it possessed great powers to alter one's perceptions if ingested. It figured in some of the Tahuramara ceremonies and was used by shamans as an aid to diagnosis. It was also supposed to allay hunger and thirst.

Zacarías took a bite of the wrinkled cactus button. It was soft and dry, and out of sheer hunger he ate the whole thing.

At first, he felt nothing, and continued on his way.

After awhile, Zacarías' vision lightened and he felt a renewed energy, like that provided by a good breakfast with coffee and a pipe. He felt that it had in fact done him good, and Tío Hikuli was a welcome ally at this point. Two, perhaps three hours later, a voice began to speak in Zacarías' head and he realized that the voice was his own.

Zacarías had never felt anything like it, never experienced the simultaneous thrill and absolute terror that coursed through his veins.

Whatever the difference is, I cannot say.

Whatever the terror, I cannot say. Whatever there is to know, I cannot know it.

Fleeing the inevitable.

Who could have known what would happen? Who could have known what the prophets saw? Who interpreted the speech of the seven-headed beast, the vision in the flames? What was the voice that he heard? Had his father heard this same voice?

He could not say, he could not know. Mute, like his mother.

All he knew was that it drove him to the wilderness. Beyond the parted waters, beyond the burning bush. There was no place to hide from the eye of God. Was it God's eye he saw in the stream depths? Staring back at him from the dregs in the gold pan? Only the flashing metal soothed him, the smooth, heavy nuggets weighed in the palm. Only then did the clamor in his head stop, the voice in his head silence. And then, only for a short while.

The tongue held, the clapping hand. Deserts like rippling sheets of copper stretched out below the gray, roiling sky, like sheets of paper upon which the quill must move, lonely birds like harbingers of death as they wheel upon the thermals above. What was this place he returned to again and again in his dreams? Was it something his father could explain? Somewhere in his many books, the Prophets, the Zohar, the heretics? Was there an answer?

Oh God, let this cup pass from me, let it pass from these lips. I am not worthy, But perhaps my son....

The burden of being chosen. Could Joseph have been chosen and begged off? Moses tried. Jonah tried. Why did God make his son die? Why was Abraham willing to sacrifice Isaac? The knife, the little limbs trussed up like a goat, the throat bare and trembling. Did Isaac forgive him? The greatest inheritance. A table of stone. A stone in the mouth, like his tongue. Birth, death and resurrection passed off to the son, over and over again. God took everything from Job, then replaced it. But was it the same? Another wife? Children? How could it be? What is inheritance, really, but duty? Perhaps a curse. Estela. Estela. Estela. Forgive me.

La gitana, bending over her shining road, her gnarled fingers stretched out to the black marks upon it. If only she could write.

Is there an answer? Answer me!

· · ·

Zacarías came to a trail and began to follow it. He had been avoiding the main roads since leaving Saltillo, sticking to open country and heading almost due north, but this seemed little more than a footpath, and he felt that he had put sufficient distance between himself and his recent notoriety to use it. He saw no habitations in any direction as he crossed the bleak countryside, only an abandoned ruin of a farmhouse, the roof fallen in, the yard choked with weeds and rocks. The horse snorted as they passed and Zacarías himself felt no inclination to stop or make any further investigation of the place.

The trail ended at the lip of a rocky ridge, turning south to run along its edge. North, it became a mere rabbit track.

Zacarías could just make out a curious set of buildings to the northwest in the lee of the ridge. The gold in his breastpocket, the gold he used for healing, began to tingle. Zacarías clasped his hand over it as he surveyed the situation. He could see no way down the steep incline, which was nearly concave, except to follow the trail south and hope that it eventually led to a lower point on the ridge from which he could descend and approach the ranch from that direction.

The wind continued to slacken as Zacarías rode his horse along the spine of the ridge, leaning back to compensate for the grade. His journey had been exceptionally hot and dry since Zacarías had crossed the Rio Grande, and he was nearly out of water. He reached a point of descent, and was able to turn north and west again, licking his dry lips in anticipation of sanctuary at one of the magical haciendas he had heard described so often.

Zacarías approached the buildings in the dying light, but all seemed curiously still. Perhaps no one was at home. He was able to make out odd branches of metal that protruded from the roof and a terraced yard of neatly placed rocks that enclosed native plants. A fence of organ cactus ran along one edge of the property, and a welcoming stand of willows formed a small oasis.

He rode up to the main house, which appeared dark and un-inhabited, and his unease increased. The hikuli appeared to have run its course, but Zacarías still did not trust his senses. He rode slowly around the back in hopes of some refreshment, up the steep incline to where he could see a curious waterworks.

As Zacarías looked into a wide ditch that ran down the hill and past the house, where a wheel was set into the path of the water, he realized what was missing. He had expected from family accounts to hear the sound of running water, but the ditch was empty. Something was wrong.

Riding slowly up the length of the ditch, Zacarías became filled with dread. The gold in his pocket continued to tingle with quiet fury. He reached a well stacked round with native rock and began to hear a buzzing sound.

Dismounting, he dislodged some boards that covered the well and peered inside, only to be assaulted by a horrible stench. Covering his mouth and nose, Zacarías could see in the darkness the shapes of two bodies, broken and heaped like rag dolls at the bottom of the dry well.

Flies rose in an angry wave at his disturbance but he could see that the clothes were finely made, the matted and bloody hair had once been fair and wavy, the bodies seemed identical. The all but unrecognizable features had to belong to the brother and sister of his wife, Estela. A strangled groan rose from his throat as he realized that they had been murdered, and he could not help but think that his last refuge, his brother- and sister-in-law to whom he had been directed for safekeeping, had paid for his own of-fenses with their lives.

Zacarías staggered back and sat on the ground for some time, his hands slack and empty. His mind was blank, a gray fog. If someone had approached, Zacarías would have offered no resis-tance. He would have offered nothing at all, not even conscious-ness, although he was not unconscious.

When he regained his senses, it was quite dark. Rising slowly he lit a torch and went and looked again into the well, and again saw the bodies. He had not been mistaken. At length Zacarías found a shovel and began to dig two graves into the rocky mountainside. He worked through the night to give Membrillo and Manzana a decent burial, fearing at any moment to be apprehended and charged himself with this heinous crime. Fear had nearly run its course with him, and exhaustion, both physical and emotional, was now the predominant emotion of his life. He whispered a prayer over the crude grave, crossed himself in respect, and regretted only that he had never known their true names.

Zacarías became a phantom, a name carried by the wind, a set of letters that did not necessarily add up to a person. There were rumors of a man working in a bakery in Laredo, baking bread and tortillas just like a woman, but he turned out to be a displaced Italian.

People saw Zacarías all over Texas and Arizona, as far west as Nogales, but when the authorities arrived, he was always gone.

There were rumors of a printer in Las Cruces, a housepainter in Albuquerque, and a carpenter in Santa Fe who built a miraculous staircase in the convent of the Sisters of Loretto.

The only thing these rumors had in common was a cumulative trajectory: north. The rumors emanated in a gentle wave that seemed to push speculation towards the Rio Grande valley. But the people who lived there, like the high, open country, the chamisa bush and sage and white-tailed deer that fled at the scent of man, were silent on this matter. Zacarías disappeared as surely as if his beloved earth had opened up and swallowed him into its gem-studded depths.

After some time, Zacarías rode into a town high on the plains. It was cold, and he had his poncho well wrapped around him.

There was something familiar about the town, though he knew he had never been here, never ridden this far north. It had the same adobe buildings, the same forlorn cobblestones that threatened to turn the horse's hooves at every step as any other town along the Rio Grande. Maybe the same people built them all, he thought. Moving farther north every few years, farther from some threat, some enemy.

Riding slowly up the main street, Zacarías felt eyes on him from the darkened interiors, felt the chill wind cut through the wool of his poncho as though probing him for his identity. The sun was setting, and candles and lanterns began to appear in the cavernous windows. Many of the windows were draped and darkened from within, hiding the interior light from the street.

Zacarías turned a corner and found himself facing a wrought-iron gate. From within came the sound of a fountain, and Zacarías was drawn towards it until his horse stood parallel to the gate and Zacarías could gaze within.

There lay a sight that Zacarías could barely believe.

"Is this an hallucination?" he thought. "Am I so homesick that my vision has conjured up this gate, this garden?"

For the ancient wrought iron gate was a duplicate of the curious gate that opened into the courtyard of the home where Zacarías was born and had lived the first twenty years of his life. And there, surrounded by lush plantings and trees, now turning a mysterious dark green in the deepening twilight, squatted a massive stone fountain identical to the fountain in his mother's courtyard. It gave off a low, gurgling sound into the still night air, and Zacarías realized that it was this familiar sound that had attracted him.

After awhile, a man emerged from the house and came to stand at the gate. "May I help you, Señor?" the man asked.

"No," said Zacarías, "it's just ... the fountain. It is identical to that in my parents' courtyard, which is many miles from here."

"Oh?" said the man. "Where are you from?"

"I don't know, anymore," answered Zacarías. "I was born in Saltillo." He knew that he should move on but the horse stood rooted to the spot and he could not bring himself to urge it on. He hoped that the man would not ask his name.

"Come in," said the man, opening the gate. "It is late, and we are about to celebrate Shabbos."

Zacarías was startled at the word. He could not remember the last time he had heard it whispered, much less spoken aloud.

The man stood quietly, holding the gate open, and Zacarías realized the great risk the man had just taken.

"Thank you," said Zacarías, dismounting. "God bless you."

"And you," replied the man, taking the reins from Zacarías and leading the man and his horse inside.

There was a long silence, a period of mourning following Zacarías' last visit to Saltillo.

A drought took hold of the landscape in the north, then spread south, paralyzing crops and animals, felling cattle by the thousands, inducing epidemics of cholera and consumption and starvation.

People prayed for release, but none came. Some blamed la Señora O'Connell for having implicated a holy man, El Tecolote, and bringing a curse upon the land. After all, didn't that woman, who was so heartless and bitter that even the alacranes wouldn't sting her, didn't she sell off her dead husband's cattle before the drought? Didn't she profit from their despair by selling bread to people who could not grow their own corn?

The Señora herself was never seen, said to be enjoying her profits abroad, but in fact she was in the capital negotiating prices for wheat and corn flour in order to stay in business.

Entire towns were abandoned during this time, including Mayhem and Havoc—the churches left to crumble to dust, the saloon doors gaping wide like open jaws upon empty rooms. Dry lightning raged across the landscape as clouds passed overhead, refusing to drop their moisture, but selectively striking a tree or building or man or beast with fire from heaven. The beautiful homes built by Membrillo and Manzana burned to the ground, their interiors unseen to the end by the curious.

At the end of seven years, when the crickets no longer sang at night and the owls had abandoned their burrows in the heart of the desert, a few pieces of paper blew out of the northern regions like tumbleweeds upon the wind. People along the frontier stooped to pick them up, hoping for news or money, and tried to decipher their unusual message.

Although windblown, the pages still smelled faintly of ink. They appeared to be pieces of a larger work, a book perhaps, or a set of books. Yet each page contained a complete story, or a prayer, or a set of predictions or homilies, or an illustration. Each was different, yet each was distinctly the work of the same person.

A woman who lived alone at the western edge of this desert gathered up as many of the pages as she could find, thinking to use them to start fires in her cookstove, but thought better of it. Squinting at the curious text, she tried to make out the meaning; but she could not read words very well, only signs, so she put them in a trunk and saved them for a future time, for a face she had seen in the shimmering distance. Or was it in the past? It did not really matter.

I will wait for you in the high and lonely places.
I will keep thy secret name in my heart.
For seventy times seventy days,
I will sing your praises in reverence.
My sons will praise thee, oh Lord,
unto the hundredth generation.

Gabriel

I went away to college in the United States the summer of 1877, finally fulfilling my mother's dream for continuing my education. After a journey of many days by train, I found myself alone and far from home. I lodged in a boarding house, and the owners, Mr. and Mrs. Green, were very kind. My fellow students must have found me strange, with my poor command of English, and for the most part left me to my own devices.

In November, the first snow fell in Ann Arbor, the first I had ever seen.

One Sunday in late December, I was invited to a Baptist church by the Greens, and accompanied them to the morning service. The sermon: if someone would be like Me, then let him take up his cross and follow Me.

I dedicated my life to the Lord in the new year.

My father went north from Saltillo that spring, but it was unclear to me at the time that it was a permanent departure. News of the death of my aunt and uncle, who lived as water diviners in

Texas, also came at that time, but the news seemed distant and incomprehensible: like the death of angels.

I did not go home again until September of that year. I arrived at five in the morning of a glorious day and greeted my mother amidst tears and hugs. No one made any reference to me about religion.

I left that night an exile, rejected by my own mother because of Evangelism. As the train glided along, I could see, slipping away in the gathering shadows, the silhouettes of the mountains surrounding the city of my birth. I left with only my suitcase, leaving all behind that had ever meant anything to me.

My heart pierced by that rift, I was suddenly face to face with the world without resources or experience. I trembled for a moment, and I'll admit, a few tears coursed down my cheeks. A little later—for no discernable reason, since I was in a terrible predicament—there rose from the bottom of my soul a mysterious force. It was the Faith. At midnight I was alone in the train station at García, offering my soul to God. I prayed for divine guidance.

It was shortly after my last visit that my mother left for Mexico City, taking my young brother Noé with her. She never wrote or came back, and we can only hope that God helped and protected her.

I married my wife Rosa Canelos in Nogales, where I was sent by the Presbyterian Church to open a mission. The only daughter of an unfortunate Opata Indian woman, Rosa worked long hours as a housemaid to support herself and her ailing mother. She found time to attend our services on a regular basis, however. We were married on her fifteenth birthday, with her mother's blessing. Rosa's mother was present at Casas Grandes when my father was there, and seemed to trust me on this basis. She died shortly after the wedding.

Even now, years later, I am afraid the life I offer Rosa is not much easier than her life before our marriage. Without a word, she pulls on her old coat and black hat, picks up and packs our belongings, gathers the children, and moves to the next town with me, ready to serve the Lord as my helpmate.

Between missions, we stopped in Pitíc to visit my wife's aunt, Lucy Canelos. She is a very old woman who makes her living through divination, and dresses in garish costumes like a gypsy. She knows that I don't believe in such superstitions, but was gracious and kind nevertheless. Sister Lucy — as she prefers to be called — listened patiently as I shared God's word with her. She even allowed me to leave a Bible in the little house, which is turquoise and surrounded by walls and heaps of stones which she has collected over the years, building an enclosed garden and shrine in the back.

Sister Lucy showed me a valise full of papers which she had kept under her bed for many years. The pages were dirty and torn, much abused by the years, but she thought that they might be of interest to me, as they appeared to be religious in nature. She seemed expecially insistent that I take them. Although we were burdened with our household items, I agreed, as much out of respect as interest.

That evening, I began to look through the pages — I was always in need of inspiration for my sermons. Something about them gripped me immediately, and I read as much of the damaged manuscript as I could decipher amidst the distractions of the children. Hidden within this hodgepodge of proverbs, poetry, stories and prayers, songs, recipes and mathematical formulas, scientific experiments and metaphysical speculations, remedies and practical advice for the weary traveller, lay, to my amazement, a history of my own family.

Though it had been many years since I had seen him, there was no doubt in my mind that these errant pages were from the hand of my father. It was hard for me to imagine him with a pen in his hand, but his years of exile must have changed his disposition. From his writings, it was clear that he had undergone a deep and profound change—a revelation if you will—that had shaken him to the very foundation of his soul and brought him back to the traditions of his family.

The stories triggered a flood of memories of my own childhood, and I slept fitfully that night and for many nights after, troubled by dreams of a past that was no longer attainable to me.

I was playing with my sisters in the beautiful patio at the house of my grandparents in Saltillo. We were eating dates from a bowl on a table. Suddenly a bird swooped down with a red cap in its beak. We all chased it and tried to get the cap, but I was the one who got it. I placed the cap on my head, but it was too big for me.

Then it became night, and we could see all the constellations in the sky, each star burning like a little fire. One constellation seemed to grow brighter and brighter. My mother was calling us to come inside, but still we stayed in the garden, watching the constellation as it formed letters in the sky: $YT - \frac{v}{} = XLX$. We did not know what it meant, but as I tried to trace the letters with my finger, my soul filled with peace and reflected the splendor of the sky above me.

I prayed for guidance, and came to realize that I had no choice: it was imperative that I return to Saltillo. There were so many unanswered questions about my parents, my family, and now these pages had fallen into my hands like manna from heaven. I left Rosa and the children with her aunt in Pitíc and continued my journey alone.

The trip of twelve to fourteen hours took me across the beautiful fields of Parras, although the population presented a sad appearance owing to the ruin brought on by the drought. Some train cars served as the station, since the original was destroyed in a fire. There was hardly any fruit available.

There was some delay before reaching Saltillo; we passed

through Butcher's Gate between six and seven in the evening. It made my heart glad to see the mountains of my city again. Like a pilgrim, I drew closer to my ancestral home. The train continued along its course, making a long, roundabout loop until finally it stopped at the station, near Calvary.

Very early in the morning, I went to the home of my sister Victoria, in the new section of the city. After my mother's departure, my sisters and Victoria's husband were left with the old house, but sold it when María entered the convent. They received me with kindness. I was happy to find all of the family well.

A little later I saw my Aunt Blanca and Uncle Gustavo. I found them better than I had expected. We had a long conversation, seated in their comfortable home, with lots of iced tea and cookies at hand.

My great-uncle Horacio had suffered a stroke shortly after his incarceration, perhaps due to the mistreatment he received at the hands of the soldiers, and Gustavo had taken over the business. Horacio had since died, and Gustavo had persevered in spite of the all-consuming drought that had especially affected business to the north.

My aunt saw me looking at the framed photographs on the family altar, set amidst lace and candles. I was struck in particular by those of a young boy and girl in vestida typica—folk costumes of the era. "You look like them," she said. "The eyes."

I looked carefully at the radiant children in the photos. In spite of the long braids on the girl, it was obvious that they were twins. "Inasmuch as people resemble angels," I said, "perhaps I resemble them."

"Those are my brother and sister," she said. "Membrillo and Manzana."

"They were murdered by a mob of jealous townspeople," said Gustavo, "shortly after these portraits were taken. Probably over water rights, but the wells went dry at their death."

I told him that my father had blamed himself in his writings, but Gustavo doubted that there had been a connection.

"We often thought that your father might return," said Gustavo, "but although travellers sometimes spoke of him, he never came back."

"Zacarías was responsible for many things," said my Tía Blanca, "but not for their death. They were only loaned to us for a little while, for they were too perfect for this world."

My aunt pressed her trembling lips together, holding back tears, so I pressed them no further for news of the past.

In the afternoon I borrowed a horse and rode out to the old part of the city. I passed by the ancient plaza of San Francisco. The trees had grown and the benches were occupied by groups of young people of the new generation. It produced sad memories in me and made me consider the brevity of this life, but later I was cheered by the hope of that eternal life that is not subject to change or variations.

Up above were, successively, the houses of Don Juan Nuncio, that of the Mendez', and a few others on the rise above the arroyo. I reached the bridge and stood above the tumbling current. It made its way through heaps of almendrilla and was lost in the horizon.

Going up the steep road, I was grateful for the horse, loaned to me by my uncle, that took me across the treacherous cobblestones lining the way. I knew this path by heart, the way we remember the shape of a favorite toy or the words to a song.

As I reached the crest of the hill, the road curved gently to the right and I followed the path, now faint and overgrown, that led around the back of the house. Great cedars still shaded the way, as though impervious to the passage of time.

I entered through a gap that had once held a curious gate and dismounted.

A neglected bunch of calla lilies grew in a far corner, small-flowered and leafy. Near them, a fruit tree grew. Paving stones, now cracked and askew, still showed the outlines of the old house, and by pacing from the corner of the former kitchen, I could guess the location of my grandfather's secret study. It still bore an air of unease around it, and I found that I could not linger near it for too long.

As my boots crushed the straggling plants that twisted tenaciously across the cracked pavement, smells of my childhood rose up to me, mingling with my memories. I seemed to hear my grandmother's pet birds calling softly in the delirium of late afternoon.

Looking towards a far corner, where sunlight and shadow played against the crumbling garden wall, I could almost see them walking towards me, Mariana with a bunch of wildflowers clutched in one hand, Julio with dust on his shirt, tie askew. They were surrounded by children — my father Zacarías, my mother Estela, her sister Blanca and their beautiful brother and sister, Manzana and Membrillo — all of them children, and mixed together with them my own sisters and cousins.

They came towards me through the lengthening shadows. Their feet seemed to barely touch the dusty path, black shoes skimming the earth, as though they were all about to take flight like a flock of geese. They looked expectant, these children, their dark eyes turned up towards mine, as if to say, "We are here."

I understood that this was an hallucination of sorts, no doubt brought on by my strenuous journey and the heat of the afternoon. Nevertheless, I recognized the curly black hair and hawk noses of my family, the air of otherworldliness that marked and set us apart. They seemed not to fear the place, or at least, not to know it.

Behind them, as I watched closely, I could see my own children coming towards me — Ester, also clutching a bouquet of wildflowers, Pablo, Phoebe, Daniel who never made it out of infancy. All were dressed in white, and all had that look about them of having just awakened from a dream. I wept as I recalled my wife's face as she laid little Danny in his coffin.

The garden was filled with the heady scent of yerba buena. I could discern its dark green leaves along the damp threads running across the yard from their source. This was no hallucination. There before me lay the rubble of the ancient fountain, each stone toppled from the other. It had been crushed, as if by a great hand. Water oozed from the earth like blood from the severed stump of an arm or leg. I knelt and soaked my handkerchief in the dark water, slaking my thirst. Turning back to the dark corner of the garden, I could no longer see their shadows, but felt their presence and their blessing for what I was about to do.

Returning to the horse, I untied a shovel I had brought for this very reason. I rolled up my sleeves and tied the bandanna around my head. Then I returned to the fountain and began to dig.

The time had come to begin again.

Arise, shine; for your light has come,
and the glory of the Lord has risen upon you.
For behold, darkness will cover the earth,
and deep darkness the peoples;
But the Lord will rise upon you,
and His glory will appear upon you.
And nations will come to your light,
and kings to the brightness of your rising.

Isaiah 60:1-3